Other Books by Carolyn Brown

The Dove
The PMS Club
Trouble in Paradise
The Wager
That Way Again
The Ladies' Room
Lily's White Lace
The Ivy Tree
The Yard Rose
All the Way from Texas
A Falling Star
Love Is

The Angels & Outlaws Historical Romance Series:
From Wine to Water
Walkin' on Clouds
A Trick of the Light

The Black Swan Historical Romance Series:
From Thin Air
Pushin' Up Daisies
Come High Water

The Broken Roads Romance Series:
To Hope
To Dream
To Believe
To Trust
To Commit

The Drifters and Dreamers Romance Series:
Morning Glory
Sweet Tilly
Evening Star

A FOREVER THING

A Three Magic Words Romance

A FOREVER THING

•

Carolyn Brown

AVALON BOOKS
NEW YORK

Bro

To my daughter and son-in-law
Bobby & Ginny Rucker
Who are working on a forever thing!

Published by Avalon Books,
an imprint of Thomas Bouregy & Co., Inc.
New York, NY

Library of Congress Cataloging-in-Publication Data

Brown, Carolyn, 1948–
  A forever thing / Carolyn Brown.
      p. cm.
  ISBN 978-0-8034-7612-7 (hardcover : acid-free paper)
  I. Title.
  PS3552.R685275F67 2011
  813'.54—dc23

                                    2011025759

PRINTED IN THE UNITED STATES OF AMERICA
ON ACID-FREE PAPER
BY RR DONNELLEY, HARRISONBURG, VIRGINIA

Chapter One

Fancy Lynn Sawyer wasn't going a single mile over the speed limit. Not that she always drove strictly within the law, but that evening she was actually driving five miles below the limit—until that silly black cat darted out from the curb and headed straight for her front tire. She would never admit to being superstitious, but the first thought that ran through her mind was that the cat was a blasted bad omen.

She swerved to miss it and hit the curb, bounced back, overcorrected, and hit the curb again. By the time she had control of the car, the black cat had shot across the street to the courthouse lawn and climbed the nearest tree, and there were red, white, and blue lights flashing behind her. She dutifully pulled over and rolled down the window—and the aroma of almond extract hit her nose.

Ignoring the approaching cop, she grabbed the brown bag with the leaking bottle and had it in hand when she looked up into the mossy green eyes of the policeman. His expression was pure disgust as he stared at the small brown bag.

"I can explain," she said.

"License and registration, to begin with."

No smile; not even a hint of one in his eyes. The man was all business.

She carefully set the bag on the floor while she fumbled through her purse for her license and the glove compartment for the registration and insurance verification. There was barely an inch of extract left in the bottom of the bottle. Three dollars sucked into the carpet, and her car would smell like almonds for weeks.

"Fake ID if I ever saw one," he mumbled. "This says you're

1

thirty years old. Does it belong to an older aunt who looks like you?"

Fancy narrowed her blue eyes into slits and glared at the man. "I can explain this mess. A black cat ran out in front of me. I swerved. The bag has almond extract in it—for baking—and it must have fallen off the seat and broken when I stomped on the brake."

"Would you get out of the car, please?" He ignored her explanation. He'd heard better excuses from teenagers before, and never had he been snookered into believing a single one of them. He wasn't starting that night; not with the aroma of amaretto liqueur seeping through the window and the blue-eyed teenybopper wearing cutoff jean shorts and a tank top holding the evidence in plain sight.

Fancy Lynn opened the door, climbed out, yanked her jean hems down, then tugged the bright yellow tank top to cover her bra straps. A portion of her hair escaped its ponytail and stuck to her neck within seconds of her leaving the air-conditioned car. She'd forgotten just how hot Texas could be in August. One step outside of an air-conditioned car or house could flat suck all the breath out of a person before she could count to five.

He shoved an apparatus in front of her face. "Blow into this."

"I have not been drinking," she said from between clenched teeth.

"Blow."

She did.

He checked it and made her repeat the test.

"Well, I guess you were telling the truth, but I'm still taking you in for having an open bottle of alcohol inside the car. You can call your mommy and daddy to come get you. So hands behind your back."

Cuffs appeared out of nowhere. The snap was as loud as cracking thunder. Fancy was surprised that everyone in the little town of Albany, population less than two thousand, wasn't out on the front porches looking to the southwest to see if a tornado was on the way.

"Why are you doing this? I told you the truth."

"We'll see, young lady."

"I'm thirty years old, so stop treating me like a child," she protested.

"Let's go call your parents and find out how old you really are." He nodded toward the courthouse.

She giggled. Her mother wasn't ever going to believe this; neither were Sophie and Kate. In all her fourteen years of driving she'd never even had a speeding ticket, much less been handcuffed and dragged to jail. Leave it to a black cat to cross the street right in front of the Sheriff's Department and the Shackelford County Courthouse.

"You think this is funny?" he said.

"Yes, I do, but then, you are acting just like a short man, all cocky and jacked up on ego. Never met one yet who didn't think he had to throw his weight around to show he was just as important as a tall man," she said.

He led her across the lawn and into the sheriff's office, then put her into a jail cell and removed the cuffs. "We'll see who's 'cocky' after I make a phone call. What's your parents' number?"

She rattled off two numbers. "First one is the house. Second is Momma's cell. You'll want my stepdad's also. He's retired but still working for the Air Force at Tyndall Air Force Base in Florida. The office number is . . ." and she rattled off another number from memory. "I'd give you his cell phone, but he doesn't carry one, much to my mother's dismay."

He pulled out a cell phone and dialed the first number on the list. "This is Auxiliary Officer Theron Warren of the Albany, Texas, police department," he said. Then he listened to someone on the other end.

"No, ma'am, your mother is fine as far as I know. This concerns your underage daughter, who was driving with an open bottle of liquor in the car," he said. He listened some more. "Yes, ma'am, the whole car smells like amaretto liqueur. What is so funny, ma'am?"

Fancy giggled again, and he shot her a dirty look.

"I see. Then she really is thirty years old? Could you give me her date of birth?" He checked the driver's license and glared at

Fancy. How in hell did a woman get to be thirty and still look sixteen? Beauty-supply manufacturers would pay her big money to vow that she'd kept her looks by using their products.

"Thank you for your cooperation and assistance," Theron said.

"So?" Fancy flipped back her shoulder-length brown ponytail.

"You blew zero on the Breathalyzer, and I had another officer check that bottle in your car. It was almond extract for cooking, not liquor, and it was broken, not open," he said grudgingly. "I guess you're free to go. So you are thirty."

So his name was Theron Warren, and he thought he was only a step down from God. Well, today began Officer Theron Warren's voyage into reality. He was fairly good-looking, with those dark green eyes and thick brown hair feathered back from his face. He filled out the uniform really well too. But it all looked a bit surreal, as if he were a little boy playing cops and robbers instead of a grown man. From behind, he could be a high school sophomore in a school play. But when he turned around, his steely eyes and chiseled face with a five o'clock shadow told a different tale.

He opened the cell door and stood to one side. What kind of name was *Fancy* anyway? he wondered. Was her mother a by-product of the hippie days and high on pot when she had the kid? No decent woman would name a girl Fancy.

"I could have saved you a lot of trouble if you'd just listened to me. It's almond extract to make cookies with tomorrow, not amaretto," she said.

He unlocked the jail cell. "You are free to go, Miss Sawyer. What are you doing in this part of Texas anyway?" he asked.

"That, sir, isn't one bit of your business," she threw over her shoulder as she marched out the door. He didn't deserve answers about her personal life after he'd cuffed her and taken her to jail.

To her surprise, he walked with her all the way out to her car, which was still sitting beside the curb. Then, to her astonishment, he climbed right into his cruiser and followed her. Was he spying on her or simply at the end of his shift? She drove at exactly twenty-five miles an hour, far below the limit, and hoped it annoyed the devil out of him. When she pulled into her grandmother's driveway, he sailed by without even looking her way. Just a coincidence, then. He was on his own way home.

Two vehicles were already in the driveway. Sophie McSwain climbed out of the red club-cab Ford truck and Kate Miller from the white club-cab Chevrolet. Neither of her best friends, Fancy was happy to see, had changed all that much in the past five years.

Sophie was tall and had kinky, curly strawberry-blond hair she still tied up in a ponytail and tamed with mousse. But she now wore a sleeveless tank top and jeans with cowboy boots—a very different look from the time when she was the fashion queen among the three of them, always wearing designer suits and spike heels. Her eyes were smoky gray and framed with heavy, dark lashes, thanks to mascara, and her eyebrows were arched naturally and needed no plucking. A very faint sprinkling of freckles danced across her nose, and she did nothing to cover them.

Kate wore khaki shorts and an orange tank top and had her jet black hair pulled up in a clip with the ends going every which way. She had pecan-colored eyes, was slim built, and stood five foot six inches in her stocking feet. Her skin gave testimony to the fact that she was half Hispanic, and her lips suggested that Angelina Jolie could be a distant relative.

None of the three had aged much from twenty-five to thirty, and they acted like fifteen-year-old girls as they gathered in a group hug right next to Fancy's car and all talked at once.

"Good Lord, what is that smell?" Sophie asked.

Fancy held up the leaking bag. "I broke a whole bottle of almond extract. Stupid black cat ran out in front of me. I stomped on the brakes, broke the bottle, and wound up in jail, and that's why I'm late. Come on inside. We'll catch up, and then I'll tell you the whole story over our six-pack of root beer."

The house was a little white frame structure sitting on a small lot between two other houses that looked practically identical. Petunias and marigolds bloomed in the flower beds; the lawn was mowed and the porch swept; all was stereotypical of a small Texas town. The difference was the sign hanging above the garage that years before had been turned into a beauty shop. Most people driving down the street probably didn't even see the sign anymore on the now-closed-up shop that read HATTIE'S CUT AND CURL.

Fancy threw open the front door and led the way into a square living room with a kitchen directly ahead. A narrow hallway opened off the room to the left, where two bedrooms and a bathroom were located. When Fancy had arrived earlier that day, she'd put her things into her old bedroom and didn't even open the closed door to her grandmother's room.

Sophie stopped in the middle of the living room and did a three-hundred-and-sixty-degree turn. The sofa was the same: brown and yellow floral straight out of the sixties. The old Zenith floor-model television sat in the same corner. Crocheted doilies and lamps were on the end tables that flanked the sofa. The recliner looked new; at least maybe from the eighties.

"This is eerie. As if we're stepping back in time. I half expect to see Hattie come out of her bedroom and tell us we can't bring food into the living room," Sophie whispered.

"We'd better keep all food in the kitchen. I'm here to tell you that that woman will know if we don't, and she'll rise up out of that nursing-home bed and crawl here on her belly if she has to," Kate said.

"And beat us all with a peach-tree switch," Fancy said. "Come on. We'll keep it in the kitchen so she won't get any crumbs under her nails as she claws her way in."

"Don't tease. Hattie could put the fear of God into Lucifer himself," Sophie said.

The kitchen sported a red-topped chrome table with four red padded chairs around it, white cabinets, and a single sink. A rounded toaster sat on one corner of the counter, metal canisters on another. The stove and the rounded-front refrigerator were both vintage sixties. If Sophie opened the fridge, she figured she'd find Kool-Aid and egg salad inside.

Fancy set about pulling cold root beer in bottles from the refrigerator. "Have a seat, and tell me what's going on with you two. Imagine, real voices and real faces—no e-mails or phone calls," she said with excitement.

"I was listening to the oldies radio station on the way over here, and remember that song K. T. Oslin sang? '80s Ladies'?" Kate said.

"Yes, I do. Momma played it all the time when I was a kid. Sometimes I wondered if she wasn't reliving her past through that song," Fancy said. "I even have it as her ringtone now."

"It says that one of the girls was pretty, one was smart, and one was a borderline fool. Sounds more like us three than your momma and her pals," Kate said.

"Well, we sure know which one of us is the pretty one, don't we?" Sophie, the obvious "smart one," looked straight at Fancy Lynn. "Girl, you don't look a day over twenty."

Fancy's blue eyes twinkled. "The policeman who pulled me over thought I wasn't even sixteen. I'd better start buying all those miracle skin creams they advertise on television if I look as old as twenty."

"The policeman who was tailgating you when you drove up? Talk. We want to hear the whole story," Sophie said.

By the time Fancy finished recounting her experience, including Theron Warren's calling her momma, they were all laughing so hard that Kate had lost her breath and Sophie had the hiccups. She had no sooner finished telling the tale than the first bars of "80s Ladies" began playing in the vicinity of her purse.

"It's Momma."

She answered it and spent a couple of minutes telling her mother the short version of the jail story and then giving her an update on the house. "Thanks, Momma. I'll call the minute I know anything for sure."

She flipped the phone shut and turned around. "Now, where were we?"

"You are the one-was-pretty among us three. We were talking about that, remember?" Kate said.

"Oh, hush," Fancy said.

"What I want to know is, why the devil aren't you married yet? You're one of those little women that men drool over. One of those I-can-protect-you and you-make-me-feel-all-big-and-macho women. So how is it you're in the same boat with the smart one and the borderline fool?" Kate asked.

"Haven't found a man who can say the magic words and make me believe them." Fancy tipped up her root beer and gulped.

Sophie giggled. "And those words would be *I love you*?"

"That's part of it. But any fool with the ability to speak can say the words. I want to hear the words and know there's one of those forever things attached to them. Why aren't *you* married?" Fancy looked at Kate.

"Truth is—and I've faced it finally—I'm still not over Jethro Hart Ducaine. That sorry cowboy stole my heart when I was fifteen, and he's still got it. Part of the reason I came back to Texas was to get it back and get on with my life."

Sophie sputtered, "But . . . but that was fifteen years ago!"

"Yep, it was, but I gave him my whole heart, and no matter how hard I try, I'm still missing a good-sized chunk. That makes me the 'borderline fool' of the three of us. I always measure every man in every relationship against Hart Ducaine. A girl never forgets her first love."

"What 'magic words' will it take to make you get over him?" Fancy asked.

"Oh, I'd like the traditional words. But I want them said by a knight in shining . . ." The next word escaped her, and she waved a hand in the air, trying to remember it. Neither of her friends helped her out a bit. "By a knight in shining . . ." It still didn't come to her. "Well, dang it, he has to say the words from a big white horse and be my knight in shining whatever."

"Now it's your turn, Sophie. What'll it take for you to get married again?" Fancy asked softly.

"You never did tell us that whole story," Kate added. "You said you would only tell us when we were all together again. And why didn't you let us come to the funeral to comfort you?" she asked.

Sophie tried to smile, but it came out more like a grimace. "It's really a downer. Let's don't spoil our first evening together with that conversation. Besides, once you hear it, I won't be the 'smart one' anymore. *I'll* be the borderline fool."

"Might as well hear it and get it out of the way, then," Fancy said. "Besides, I just came from jail. Looks like I might be giving you competition for the 'fool' title. And that's not even mentioning giving up a job right next to the beach in Florida to come back to this gosh-forsaken piece of ground."

"Okay, but, honey, you'll never doubt who gets the dunce cap by the time I finish. Bring out the stool," Sophie said with a sigh. "Here goes. Matt was ruggedly pretty, and the TV cameras loved him. His voice was deep, and the microphone loved him as well. Trouble was, the women loved him too. And he loved 'em right back. But I found out all of that *after* I married him." Sophie stopped to take a drink.

"I hear bitter herbs coming forth from thy mouth," Kate teased.

Sophie laughed. "That you do. We were living in our nice big house in Tulsa. Matt had to fly to Fayetteville to lead a conference on staying married in today's crazy world. Nothing new. He was constantly flying somewhere. But while he was gone, I found a receipt for a very expensive piece of jewelry, and it wasn't my birthday or our anniversary. I called the jewelry shop and with a little fibbing found out that it had been engraved to Molly Devine with all his love. I called him and confronted him, and he just laughed it off. I hired a private detective and planned to call a divorce lawyer the next week. Then I got the message that his plane had crashed in the desert. The papers covered up the fact that not one but two women unconnected to the conference were on the plane with him."

"I'm so sorry," Fancy said.

"It gets worse. I had thirty days to vacate the house. The station brought in a new couple. The show must go on. Souls must be saved. Money must be made. So I came to live in Baird with Aunt Maud until I could get my head on straight again, which is what I'm trying to do," Sophie said.

Kate's eyes widened to the size of silver dollars. "The Aunt Maud you hated to spend a week with every summer?"

"That's the one. She's not such a bad old bird after all. I'm keeping the books for her and helping out wherever I can. The peace of the ranch is a little different when I'm a cynical thirty instead of a hormonal thirteen. Matt had a monstrous-sized life insurance policy with enough zeros to boggle the brain, so I've got plenty of time to do whatever I want."

"One of those double indemnity things when the person is in an airplane?" Kate asked.

"That's right. And I don't feel one bit guilty about a dime of it either."

"You shouldn't," Fancy said with angry determination.

"So, to answer what it would take for me to get married again?" Sophie said. "He'd have to prove to me there could be 'life after wife.' Because according to that private detective's report, there certainly wasn't a faithful life after wife, just lots of deception."

"Sounds like, ultimately, you're still the smart one, which means I hold on to *my* dunce cap," Kate said. "Which reminds me, I've been dying to tell you both, I decided to move back to Breckenridge permanently a couple of weeks ago."

Two whoops went up from the table, and Sophie and Fancy raised their bottles to clink with Kate's.

"Tell us about it," Fancy said.

"When Daddy died of cancer in the spring, Momma wanted to move back up here to be near her sister. I took a leave to come with her to get her settled in. My grandmother's house was still empty next door to Aunt Ilene, and we moved her into it. And now I've decided to stay, so I quit my job in New Iberia, Louisiana, and moved in with her. Y'all remember Momma Lita?"

They both nodded.

"But you'd just made detective," Fancy said. "That was a promotion you'd been after for quite some time."

"Yep, but Daddy's death, well, it hit me hard too. I needed a change, and a big one. So I made one. But now, of course, I'm wondering if it was the right thing to do," Kate said with a sigh.

"I can't believe we're all back in this area together," Fancy said.

"We are. I'm working at the Three Amigos with Momma and Aunt Ilene for now, and the Breckenridge police department is giving me some relief work. I got two shifts last week. Graveyard for the moment, but maybe it'll turn into something more."

Fancy shook her head. "Oh, Kate, you have so much more to offer than waiting tables. You are smarter than that."

"Nah. Sophie remains the 'smart one.' If I was so brilliant, I'd still be a detective in New Iberia and eating at the same restaurant Dave Robicheaux frequents." Kate's giggle had enough brittleness in it to worry Fancy. But what was done was done, and they'd all find a way to make the best of it.

"Dave Robicheaux? Do I know who that is?"

"Yes, *chère*. That character in those mystery novels by James Lee Burke. Dave Robicheaux has made New Iberia famous. I've even had people ask me if I knew him. Funny, ain't it?" Kate said in her best Louisiana twang.

"Okay, enough sad stuff. It's time to come up out of the doldrums. We're all three back in this area, and we'll make the very best of it," Fancy said.

"Yes, ma'am," Kate said in a deep southern drawl. "We are the girls of the nineties, and we sure won't let the girls of the fifties or the eighties outdo us. There won't be 'nothing these ladies won't do,' just like K. T. sang about."

"Hear, hear!" Sophie raised her bottle for another toast. "Now, who's heard anything about old Hart Ducaine? And how about Chris Miller?"

Fancy blushed scarlet at the mention of the latter.

Kate pointed a long, slender finger at her. "Hot-seat time."

"I haven't heard from or seen that boy in fifteen years. Not since that last night we were all together," Fancy said.

"Still in love with him like Kate is with Hart?" Sophie asked.

"No, I got over that long ago. When Momma caught us kissing on the playground and yanked me home practically by my hair, I thought my world had ended. She embarrassed the devil out of me and, I was sure, ruined my life for all eternity. It took a long time for me to admit it, but her having us leave here was the best thing she ever did for me."

"Well, at least *I* didn't get caught," Kate said.

"Aha, now the truth surfaces," Sophie said.

Kate nodded, but she didn't blush. "Thank goodness Momma and Daddy were so involved with our move that they didn't come checkin' on me like your momma did on you."

"So?" Fancy raised an eyebrow.

"So what?"

"Hart must've been a good kisser for you to carry a torch all these years," Fancy said.

"I just thought of something funny." Sophie changed the subject before the issue of who *she'd* kissed when she was fifteen came to light. "We 'girls of the nineties' look like we're all about to burn our candles at both ends."

Kate nodded. "You got it. Me with two jobs. Fancy with her new teaching position and takin' care of Hattie when she gets out of the nursing home. And Sophie with her new bookkeeping and ranchin' duties. Okay, back to Chris Miller. I hear he's living in Albany still. On about his third wife," Kate said.

"That's ancient history. What's present is this job I'm interviewing for tomorrow. You two will keep your fingers crossed for me and say a prayer, right?" Fancy asked.

"I'll do the finger-crossing. I'm not so sure I believe much in prayer anymore," Sophie said.

Kate nodded at Fancy. "You already got the job. That person from the school you talked to said you were the best applicant and that no one else had even applied. Tell me, how is Hattie?"

"Demanding as ever. I went to the nursing home to see her this morning. She says she's coming home in three weeks. She and the doctor made a deal," Fancy said.

"That woman really did scare me when we were kids," Kate said.

"Me too," Fancy said. "Only time she was happy was in the beauty shop. The rest of the time she was constantly telling Momma how she'd messed up everything."

"I remember," Sophie said. "I bet Gwen didn't even look back in the rearview mirror when y'all left for Florida."

Fancy slowly shook her head. "She cried all the way."

"You are kidding me," Kate said.

Fancy's head continued to go from left to right. "No, I'm telling the gospel truth. Want me to make a pot of coffee?"

Kate nodded.

Fancy stood up and filled the Mr. Coffee machine, then sat back down. "Momma felt like she was leaving unfinished work. That she'd worked so hard to make Granny Hattie love her, and she'd failed. She cried until we got to our new home, and then she dried her tears and never shed another one. Les was good to her and for her. They're happy, and I'm glad. She deserves it."

"She ever come back?" Sophie asked.

"Every other year, for two days. Arrived on Friday night. Left on Sunday morning. We flew into Dallas, rented a car, and stayed the weekend with Hattie. Nothing ever changed."

"Then why did you stay?" Kate asked. "Why not just hire a home-health aide?"

"I'm the only grandchild, and the least I can do for Momma is to take care of her mother for these next few months when she gets out of the home," Fancy said. "I can take it, and Momma would be looking at designer straitjackets if she had to do it. I'll be teaching during the day, so it'll just be the evenings. Besides, y'all are close by. You can be my support system if the going gets tough."

Her friends left at midnight, and Fancy took a quick shower and went straight to bed. The next morning at ten o'clock she had the formal interview for her new job, and then she'd sign a year's contract with the Nancy Smith Elementary school to teach first grade.

She reminded herself that it was only for a year and that she could endure her grandmother that long. Then a vision of that black cat darting out in front of her popped her eyes wide open, and a bad feeling wrapped itself around her heart. She had to tell herself a hundred times that everything would be okay before she could finally go to sleep.

Chapter Two

Fancy dressed in navy blue dress slacks, a white cotton sweater, and a simple gold necklace that matched her hoop earrings. She checked her reflection in the mirror on the back of the door and changed the earrings to gold-ball studs. She slipped her right foot into a white sandal and the left into a navy blue pump with a chunky heel.

After looking at herself sideways and head-on, she decided on the pumps. They definitely said first-grade teacher more than the sandals. The next thing was her hair. Leave it down or twist it up? She held it up and looked at her profile. She decided to leave it down so she wouldn't come across as trying too hard. She picked up the lightweight jacket that went with the slacks and slipped it on.

It was only two blocks to the school, so she walked, which turned out to be a big mistake, because even at a quarter to ten in the morning it was already ninety degrees, and navy blue soaked up the sun. A blast of cool air hit her when she opened the door to the school, and she sighed. She was five minutes early, so she found the nearest bathroom marked GIRLS, where she rolled off brown paper towels and dabbed at the sweat beading below her nose and across her forehead and reapplied a touch of makeup. That was the best she could do. Her face still had a faint red cast, but it was Texas, and it was August. Heat was a big part of the territory. She fluffed her hair and went to wait to be summoned to the lion's den.

Another woman was sitting in one of the two leather chairs on the far side of the room, so Fancy sat on the sofa. Dust had settled

14

around the lamps on the end tables, testifying to the fact that few people were in and around the school in the summer. The plants looked a little droopy, and the whole place smelled like fresh wax. Fancy felt right at home.

She tried not to stare at the stern-looking woman, but she did sneak peeks. The lady was about her mother's age, late forties perhaps. A little gray showed at the roots of her dyed black hair. She wore crisp khaki slacks, a yellow knit shirt, and white sandals, but sweat had gotten most of her makeup.

Fancy introduced herself after a couple of minutes of heavy silence. "Hello, I'm Fancy Sawyer."

"I know who you are. You're Hattie Sawyer's granddaughter. I knew your mother."

"And you are?"

"Wilma Cripton."

"I'm pleased to meet you, Wilma. Are you here for an interview also?"

"Yes, I am—a last-minute plan. I've got twenty years experience over in Breckenridge, but we're building a house closer to Albany. I could commute, but it would be nice to only be five miles away from my job. Heard about this job last night when my husband and I were out to dinner," Wilma said.

"Well, good luck," Fancy said.

"Luck won't have anything to do with it. Experience and an excellent reputation usually win out over beauty and youth," she said.

A woman opened the door of the principal's office and poked her head out. "Mrs. Cripton, would you please join us?"

Wilma smiled smugly at Fancy, who watched the two women disappear into the inner sanctum. Fancy crossed one leg over the other and waited. In her experience job interviews could take anywhere from five minutes to an hour. Her appointment was at ten o'clock, so it should have been her name called first. That stupid black cat was coming back to haunt her.

She thought about Mrs. Cripton. Was she applying to be a third-grade teacher? Sixth? Surely with that hatchet face and gruff demeanor, she didn't teach younger children. Fancy hoped it was sixth grade, because at that age boys were bullheaded and trying to break out of their babyishness, and girls cried about everything. Wilma Cripton might be just the ticket for that age group.

Fancy turned in her chair to look out the main door of the school. Around the corner to the south, the swings would be moving gently in the hot wind, kicking up dust devils across the playground. With very little imagination she could picture Chris Miller pushing her on a moonless night in the same swings when she was fifteen and he was nineteen, a high school dropout with about as much ambition as a lazy slug on a blistering summer day. But he was so good-looking, and he told her she was beautiful when he wrapped his big, strong arms around her and smothered her with breathless kisses.

Fancy's brow wrinkled as she remembered the rest of that particular night. Her mother had appeared from the end of the school and told Chris to stay away from her daughter and then took Fancy home.

She'd sat down on the porch and patted the step beside her. "Fancy Lynn, I've got something to say."

Fancy would never forget the sound of her mother's drawl as she'd told her the course of her life was about to be changed forever.

"I'm going to marry Les, and we're moving to Florida. He's stationed at a base close to Panama City Beach and has a house there where we will live. I'm sorry to spring such a surprise on you, but I didn't want to say anything until the plans were final. You know how your grandmother is, and she's going to throw a fit. I didn't want to have to listen to her, so I decided to not tell her until the day we're going."

Fancy could well remember the cold knot in the pit of her stomach that night. "I'm not going!" Fancy had cried. "I like Les, and he's good to you, but I won't give up my friends. I can live right here with Granny like I've always done and finish high school."

Gwen had set her mouth in that way that said she wasn't going to have any of that idea. "You are going with me. End of argument. I won't have you wind up like I did, and Chris Miller is nothing but trouble waiting to happen."

"I love Chris! He is *not* like my father," she'd said defiantly.

"He's going to join the army when I graduate, and we're going to travel and see the world."

Gwen patted her hand. "He might join the army, but you'll be left right here in this town with a baby to bring up all alone or with the help of your grandmother. I'm not even sure she'd help you. Besides, I wouldn't wish that on my worst enemy, much less the daughter I've loved since I first laid eyes on her. We're moving to Panama City Beach tomorrow morning."

Fancy remembered the hot, stinging tears flowing across her lips, the very ones that had just kissed Chris and promised him that she'd be on the playground the next night. "I won't go. You can't make me go. My friends are here."

"Your two best friends are leaving town too. You've been moping around here all week over that fact. Sophie and Kate are both moving away before the school year starts, and now so are you. You'll probably hate me for a while, but someday you'll find out just how right I am."

"But, Momma, I love Chris. I can't leave him."

"Fancy, if that boy loves you . . . if he truly loves you, then he'll be here when you graduate from high school. I'll even give you a wedding."

"He loves me! He'll be right here waiting for me, and you'll be *wrong*." She'd stomped off in a snit to the room she'd shared with her mother her whole life at the back of the white frame house.

"I hope so, if that's what you really want, baby," her mother had whispered to the hot night air, and the words had carried through the open window to Fancy's ears.

Shaking her head now, Fancy returned from the past to the present and smiled, even though her heart wasn't in it, when Wilma Cripton came out of the interview with a big grin on her face.

"Contract all signed," Wilma said.

"Congratulations," Fancy said, and she meant it. Wilma would probably make a wonderful sixth-grade teacher, and maybe when they worked together, they'd even find common ground for friendship.

"Miss Sawyer?" The lady in the office called her name at the same time Wilma pushed the front door open.

Fancy stood, straightening the legs of her pants and her back. At least with the pumps she was over five feet and didn't look so much like a little girl playing dress up. A vision of the policeman who'd attempted to arrest her flitted through her mind. He really had looked like an undersized high school kid in a play.

"Miss Sawyer, I am Lisa Waller, the school secretary. We've spoken on the phone." The woman led Fancy through an office and into a larger room. Several men and a woman sat in a row at the far side of a long table.

"This is Miss Sawyer," Lisa announced, and she left the same way she came in.

"Just Fancy, please. My students in Florida called me Miss Fancy."

"Then, Fancy, please have a seat," one of the men said, rising to greet her. "I am the superintendent, Mr. Gleason. Board members Rick Whitten, Thomas Howard, and Lora Ford."

Fancy nodded at each of them.

"And this is our elementary-school principal, Theron Warren."

The two of them glanced up at the same time. Her gaze looked into the same jade eyes of the police officer who had treated her like an errant kid and hauled her to jail; his nailed the bright blue eyes of the woman who'd driven like she was drunk.

The look in his defiant, cold, green eyes told the tale without saying a word. She might as well gather her pride around her and go home.

"It's nice to meet you all," she said without taking her eyes off Theron Warren. He might hold her future in his hands, but she'd be hanged from the nearest pecan tree with rusty baling wire before she'd grovel.

"We appreciate your coming all this way for an interview. I understand you had plans to help your grandmother here in town?" Mr. Gleason said.

Had? Fancy caught the past tense.

"Yes, sir, I do," she answered.

"That's very good of you, Miss Sawyer," he said flatly. "And while your background is impressive, and I'm sure you are a competent teacher, I'm afraid that the last candidate we met has the years of experience we're looking for. We have decided to hire her. I thank you for your time."

In that instant Fancy wished she'd flattened that black cat on the street without even checking in the rearview mirror to see if it was dead. "Thank you for your consideration. I'm sure Wilma Cripton will do a fine job for you. Could I fill out an application for substitute work?"

"I'm sorry. We have plenty of help in that area and aren't taking any more applications for this year," Mr. Gleason said.

"Then good day," Fancy said.

The two blocks home felt like six miles. She kicked off her shoes at the front door and stripped out of the hot clothes as she made her way down the hallway, cussing the whole time, figuring she could take out a healthy black cat and an egotistical short man with one bullet if she lined up the sight and her targets just right.

Now what was she going to do? It was too late to get a job in any of the surrounding towns; school would be starting in a few days. At least she didn't need the money. Her savings would easily support her for a while, since she wouldn't have to pay rent or utilities or make car payments.

She had no doubt she'd been rejected because of a misunderstanding over a bottle of almond extract—and all because the elementary-school principal had a part-time job as a policeman. Talk about bad luck!

She slipped into a pair of khaki shorts and a white tank top. If she wasn't a teacher, then she didn't have an image to maintain around town anyway. She put on a pair of rubber flip-flops, picked up her purse, and headed for the grocery store. When she was mad or stressed, she would eat anything in sight, and there was very little in the house and absolutely no potato chips or chocolate.

She drove to Brookshire's, careful to keep an eye out for any more suicidal cats. She mumbled as she loaded the cart with staples: bread, milk, two kinds of chips, ham, cheese, eight candy bars of various kinds, since she liked them all, a case of Dr. Pepper, and a box of tea bags. She tossed a box of Fruity Pebbles into the cart and argued with herself. She didn't need a job anyway. She'd done nothing but work since she was fifteen. School and a part-time job on the Florida strip mall at the gift store that her mother owned. Then college, and when she wasn't in class, she was at the gift store. After that it was teaching nine months out of the year and working with her mother the other three. A sabbatical would be good for her.

A whisper of a moan escaped her lips. A whole year of Hattie Sawyer's demanding and belittling would drive her to drink. That idea brought on a faint giggle. If it hadn't been for the almond extract that Theron Warren had thought was liquor, she would have a job. He would have hired her if she hadn't ruffled his feathers. She was sure of it.

Suddenly she felt someone staring at her and turned around very slowly, expecting it to be the short principal; she needed time to get a few snide words ready for him.

"Fancy Lynn Sawyer, is that really you?"

She jerked her head up to find the soft brown eyes that went with the image chiseled on her heart for fifteen years, and she waited for the flutters in her stomach to begin.

"What are you doing back in this part of the world?" he asked.

"Chris," she said softly.

She was amazed that after years of vivid dreams about what she'd say or do when she saw him again that her heart wasn't beating so hard that it could be heard all over the store.

"Well, what are you doing here?" His smile showed a missing eyetooth. He was thirty-four, and he looked sixty. Time had not been good to him. What had happened? He was supposed to be nineteen and the most gorgeous thing ever to set foot in Shackelford County, Texas.

"Just visiting Granny," she lied. "She's at the Bluebonnet Nursing Home for a few weeks, recovering from a broken hip."

"Oh," he said. "Thought maybe you'd moved back."

"Chris?" A very pregnant woman carrying a box of cereal tossed it gently into the basket in front of him.

"This is Fancy Lynn, an old friend of mine. And this is my wife, Tina," he introduced them.

Fancy noticed a tattoo of a heart with the name *Debbie* written under it on his biceps.

Chris followed her gaze to his arm. "Debbie was my first wife. Tina says it's not fair to have to look at it every day, but once you tattoo, you keep it forever. Only consolation is that Debbie has a heart with my name on it on her left ankle, so her husband has the same problem."

"Pleased to meet you." Tina nodded toward Fancy.

"Me too. Chris and I were friends before I left Texas more than fifteen years ago," Fancy explained.

"We need to get finished," Tina said to Chris. "Need to be home by three."

"Sure do. Well, we'll be seeing you around." He winked broadly at Fancy when his wife turned the cart around and disappeared toward the checkout counter. "Call me," he mouthed silently. "I'm in the phone book."

Fancy flopped down onto her bed in her old room, staring at the ceiling, as if answers to a hundred questions would come floating down from heaven and enter her brain by osmosis. Where were the pulsating emotions that usually vibrated all the way to her toenails every time she even thought of Chris' name? Where were the bells and whistles? Why didn't her heart do all the flutters? Even though he was missing a tooth and looked like he'd seen too much life too fast, he was still Chris, so why hadn't she reacted to him the way she'd thought she would? She'd been so sure at one time that he was the one man for her—the one who would wait for her until eternity if she just asked him.

She'd made dozens of excuses for him those long months after she moved to Florida and sulked around like the love-struck fifteen-year-old she was. He didn't like to write letters, and he didn't have the money for phone calls. He was in mourning for her and couldn't bear to write her name on an envelope. He didn't have a cell phone.

At Christmas, when she called Hattie to wish her happy holidays, she learned Chris had left Albany.

"Joined up in some branch of the service," Hattie had said. "Best place for him. They might make a man out of him, if they work real hard and don't give up too soon. Or if he don't get killed like that worthless boy your momma eloped with. If that happens, then Becky Barrington will be reliving your momma's life."

"What are you talking about, Granny?" Fancy had asked.

"Becky is in the family way and says she and Chris eloped the day he left. I knew that boy was bad news. I'm glad your momma moved away from here before he ruined your life like hers was ruined when she did the same thing with your daddy."

Fancy hadn't believed it, not back then, but fifteen years later she had matured from a teenager with stars in her eyes. However, part of her had secretly still waited for Chris to reappear and offer her that forever thing she'd told Sophie and Kate about. A big part of her had wanted to prove her mother and grandmother wrong, but now, after all the years gone by, she wrinkled her nose in disgust. Why had she let so many wonderful potential relationships slip through her hands because she was using some kind of illusive dream as a measure?

She felt like a complete fool, lying there on her back with her hands laced behind her head. She couldn't imagine calling Chris. He was married! She wrapped a rubber band around a ponytail at the nape of her neck, amazed at how much lighter her heart felt without the extra weight of Chris Miller embedded into it like some kind of life-threatening cancer.

She'd planned to visit Hattie for a while that afternoon. Maybe the old girl would be in a good mood. That would be hoping for a miracle, but then, Hattie had always been independent, and perhaps the broken hip and having to depend on others was what was making her even more caustic and demanding than Fancy remembered.

She braved the first blast of heat from her car when she opened the door and quickly started the engine so she could turn on the air conditioner. Ten minutes later she parked in front of the nursing home. She absolutely dreaded going inside and sat in the car for a few minutes before opening the door. Finally, she took one last breath of cold air and opened the door. From there it was only a few feet to the lobby, where Hattie waited, confined to a wheelchair and not liking one minute of it.

"Hi, Granny," Fancy said, and she kissed her on the forehead.

"You're going to muss my makeup."

"So what's going on today, Granny?" Fancy asked.

"I promised the doctor I'd stay here three weeks, and I will, but I want to go home, and I want you to get on back to Florida. I don't want you to live with me, and I don't want any help. Gwen made her bed when she ran off and left me, so I'm not going to ease her conscience by letting you come and help me out. If you want to live in Albany, find your own house, and get out of mine," Hattie said.

"Yes, ma'am." Fancy bristled. "I'm staying at your house right now. I didn't get the job at the school, so as soon as they let you come home and I get you settled in, if you don't want me there, I'll go on back to Florida. I expect the home-health services can help you."

"Yes, they can. I don't need you or Gwen. Don't you eat in my living room, and don't you overload the washer either. Run it on delicate so the motor don't wear out. If you use the stove, then I expect you to clean it up. I won't come home to a mess that you made," Hattie said.

"I'll see to it that everything is exactly as you left it, and if you like, I'll make arrangements to be out of the house before you even come home. Now, do you reckon we could have a little conversation like a grandmother and a granddaughter?"

"Why waste the time? You're leaving as soon as they let me go. Only reason you came back was to sponge off me for rent and groceries while you teach. What'd you do, get run off down there in Florida? Probably acting like that no-account good-for-nothing father of yours. Blood is blood. You got his blue eyes and mouth and God only knows what else. That's why they fired you in Florida, ain't it? You couldn't behave yourself."

"Granny, I left my job there because Momma and I thought it would be nice for you to have family to help you. I came to do that and to teach at the school here, but I didn't get the job."

"Good. Now you are free to go. So get on out of here and leave me alone."

"Okay. Maybe you'll be in a better mood tomorrow," Fancy said.

"Don't count on it."

On the way home Fancy stopped by the Dollar General Store to pick up cleaning supplies. She wheeled a cart to the back of the store and tossed in some kind of lemony-fresh cleaner. The hype on the label declared it was the best thing ever invented for hardwood floors. She added a box of laundry soap and a new mop. Far be it from her to leave a speck of dust or a trace of herself anywhere in the house when she left. She was whipping around the end of the aisle when she bumped into another cart.

She looked up to see Chris' wife, Tina.

"I'm so sorry," Fancy apologized honestly. "I wasn't watching what I was doing."

"That's okay. They need to put traffic lights in this place. Looks like you're going to be busy. I came for cleaning stuff too, and a couple of other things I forgot. I've got to clean the trailer—or buy some seeds and plant a garden in it, it's so dirty," she said with a soft southern accent.

"I can't let my grandmother come home to a single evil dust mote," Fancy said.

"Old folks have their ways set. My grandmother is the same way over in Alabama," Tina said with a smile. "Nice seeing you again."

They went their separate ways, with Fancy heading toward the checkout counter and Tina to the back of the store.

Fancy paid for her purchases and was putting them in the backseat of her car when that eerie, uneasy itch began to prickle her neck. It was the forewarning of someone being too close or something horrible about to happen. It crawled up her backbone and caused the hair on the back of her neck to stand straight. She banged her head on the door as she whipped around and bumped right into Chris Miller.

For heaven's sake, she thought instantly. *Years of nothing and then twice in one day.*

He slung an arm over the door and looked down at her. "Fancy Lynn?"

She didn't like the insolent look on his face, and he had a wife who might be coming out of the store at any moment who wouldn't like it much either.

"Hello again." She moved back several feet.

He smiled. "Hellllloooo to *you* again," he drawled. "You are just as beautiful as you were way back when."

"Thanks, Chris. So, when's your baby due?" she asked pointedly.

"Any day now. I meant to write you a letter, you know."

"But Becky kept you kind of busy after I left, I suppose."

He raised an eyebrow. "Jealous?"

She couldn't help but let out a laugh. "No. But thankful. Very. That was a long time ago."

"Chris?" Tina called from a few feet back.

He jumped like he'd been hit with a branding iron and whispered, "Call me. We've got a lot of catching up to do."

Fancy muttered, "Don't bet on it."

Fancy was seething by the time she parked back at the house. It was a good thing they weren't going to hire her at the school, because she didn't want to face Chris Miller every time she bought groceries or glass cleaner. She filled a bucket with warm water and cleaner, realizing finally that the yardstick with Chris Miller's name engraved on it—the one she'd depended on all these years when she measured any man in her life—was broken.

In the twinkling of an eye and in less time than it took to fill a mop bucket with water, Fancy Lynn Sawyer had let go of the past. If Chris believed she was going to call him or invite him to her grandmother's house, he'd better exercise the two or three brain cells left in his head and think again. She slammed the mop down into the water and attacked the kitchen floor.

"And to think I could be the one with a tat of his name on my ankle. Wonder if Debbie ever drops down on her knees and gives thanks he's out of her life. I can't wait to call Momma and tell her she was right and I was wrong. I might be hardheaded and a determined brat, but I was wrong about that two-bit jerk!"

Chapter Three

God hated Fancy.

It was the only explanation.

She stood in the doorway of the Sunday school class for six- to eight-year-old children and looked across the room straight into Theron Warren's green eyes. She'd only planned to go to Sunday school and church, sit in the young singles' classroom, attend morning services after that, and go home to an afternoon with Sophie and Kate. They'd decided to have a weekly gabfest, and Fancy was the middle point of the triangle. It was about twenty-five miles to Breckenridge off to the east and twenty-five down south to Baird, so they'd decided to meet in the middle for an afternoon together once a week.

The preacher had caught her as she was entering the church and informed her they needed help in the little kids' class, and, since she was a teacher, she'd do very well. He'd talked the whole way through the sanctuary, down the hallway to the classrooms, and quite literally shoved her into one.

"Theron, this is Fancy Sawyer, Hattie's granddaughter. Of course you already know her, since she's a teacher at your school. Tina Miller had the baby last night, so I'm moving her down to the nursery when she's able to come back to church. Fancy is going to help with this class, since she's familiar with this age group," he said; then he hurried off before Theron or Fancy could say a word.

"Trust me, it's a one-week job," she said.

"You quitting or am I?" he asked.

"Seniority wins. I'll quit."

Ten children rushed into the room, all dressed in their Sunday best, hair combed, smelling fresh instead of like the sweaty six-year-olds she was used to seeing first thing in the morning. This time of year they came off the playground with their hair plastered to their heads, red cheeks, and sweat already pouring off their faces, and it didn't get any better as the day progressed. It was nice to see the kids all sweet and clean.

They stopped when they saw Fancy and looked at Theron.

Theron answered the questions in their eyes. "Miss Tina had her baby last night. It's a girl, and I'm sure Jimmy is with her this morning. Miss Frances will be helping us today."

"That's Miss Fancy," she corrected him.

Theron raised an eyebrow. "It's not a nickname you adopted because you hated *Frances*?"

She gave him a drop-dead look and turned to face the children. "It's my real name. From what I see, it looks like we are studying Jonah this morning. Shall I read the story aloud before we color a picture of Jonah in the belly of the great fish?"

"I do the reading," Theron said coldly.

He pulled out a chair and sat down in the midst of the children, motioning for them to gather around. They made a circle on the floor and looked up at him. He ignored Fancy and started the Bible story about Jonah.

"Sit by me," a little girl whispered to Fancy.

Theron shot Fancy a look meant to fry her on the spot. Evidently she was supposed to slither out the door in shame and disgrace. Well, Theron Warren could think again. Fancy had done nothing wrong.

She plopped down on the floor beside the child, who immediately took Fancy's hand in hers and squeezed. The gesture would have brought tears to Fancy's eyes if Theron hadn't been sitting close enough that she could smell his aftershave and see herself in the well-polished shine of his cowboy boots. No way was she giving him the satisfaction of seeing even one dewdrop of a tear.

When Theron finished reading, he asked the children a few questions, then turned them loose at the long, low table to color a sheet of Jonah in the belly of the whale. The little girl who'd taken Fancy under her wing colored her fish purple, and Jonah wore a pink robe with a turquoise sash.

"I miss Jimmy. He's my friend," the little girl said as she picked up a yellow crayon to work on Jonah's hair.

"What's your name?" Fancy asked. "And who's Jimmy?"

"I'm Rachel. Jimmy is in my grade at school, and he comes to church on Sunday too. His momma is nice. I don't like his daddy," Rachel said.

"Why not?"

Rachel shrugged. "He yells at Jimmy, and he's got a pumpkin smile."

A pumpkin smile? Fancy wondered what Rachel was talking about.

"She's talking about Chris Miller. He has a missing tooth." Theron was so close to Fancy's elbow that she could feel the warmth of his body.

She froze.

"Know him?" he asked.

"Did at one time, but that was long ago," she said.

"Oh?" Theron raised an eyebrow. "Well, I guess I shouldn't be surprised." He waved a hand in the air. "Birds of a feather."

"Leopards don't change their spots," Fancy said. "Is that what you're saying?"

"But, Miss Fancy, this is a fish, not a leopard." Rachel giggled.

"Seniority just lost," Fancy said.

Theron cocked his head to one side. "What?"

"You can leave. I'm staying. I love this class."

"I don't think so," he said.

"Afraid that I'll teach them to make amaretto cocktails?"

"I'm not sure I should leave small children in your hands," he said.

She glared at him. "Why not? I might even teach them some reality instead of fantasy. Jonah wouldn't have had a little table with a candle in the middle while he was in the belly of that whale or fish or the Loch Ness monster. He'd have been struggling among seaweed and gunk, trying to hold his head up enough to keep breathing. He wouldn't have put his finger on his chin and figured out he'd angered God by not doing what he was supposed to do. He'd have been begging for a second chance."

Theron gritted his teeth. "You don't tell six-year-olds a gory tale like that. I'm not about to leave this class in your hands."

"Then we'll both stay, and I'll give them a little reality to keep them from getting a spiritual sugar high from all your Santa Claus stories," she said.

"You are evil," he growled.

"Takes one to know one," she shot right back.

"Are you fighting?" Rachel asked.

"No, we're having a big-people discussion," Theron assured her.

"That's what my mommy and daddy say when they're fighting," Rachel said.

"If you fight, Rev'end Paul won't let you play together," another little boy said in a slow Texas drawl. "'Member when me and Jimmy had that fight? Rev'end Paul told us that if we weren't good, we couldn't come into this room together. We'd have to sit with our mommies in the big people's room, and there ain't no coloring in there."

"Then we won't fight," Fancy said. "I wouldn't want to go where there was no coloring."

"Come over here and look at next week's lesson plan," Theron said, taking her by the arm and leading her to a far corner of the room.

"Why do I think this has nothing to do with Moses and the Ten Commandments?" she whispered.

"This is my classroom. I've had it three years, ever since I moved here from Shamrock, and you are not going to run me out of it," he declared.

She looked up at him. "You don't share and play nice with others, do you?"

It was strange for Theron to look down at a woman. Most of the women he'd been involved with had been anywhere from one to six inches taller than him.

"How long are you staying in Albany? I figured you'd be gone when we didn't hire you," he said.

"I'm not sure, but I'll be here every Sunday until I leave. Consider it your punishment for judging me."

"I'm not judgmental," he said.

"Yes, you are, and if you argue with me, you'll have to go sit with the mommies and daddies, and you won't get to color," she taunted.

"I really don't like you," he said.

"Well, darlin', I love you," she teased.

The tinkling sound of music floated from the intercom system, and the children put all their crayons into the basket, picked up their coloring sheets, and lined up at the door. When Theron nodded, Rachel opened it, and they were gone in a flurry of speed down the hall toward the sanctuary, where they'd show their parents their work.

"Good day, Miss Sawyer," Theron said stiffly.

"I'll see you next week," she said right back at him, wishing she could restart the whole morning. If she could, she never would have gotten out of bed, would have read a good, thick romance book all morning, and had a candy bar for breakfast.

She headed for the sanctuary, where she planned to sit in the back row, avoiding the second pew on the right, where Hattie had laid claim to a seat long before Fancy was even born. But when she headed down the aisle, Tandy Stephens reached up and grabbed her hand from a pew in the middle of the church.

"Sit with us old women and make us happy," she said.

"Miss Tandy?" Fancy eyed the woman. She hadn't changed all that much in fifteen years, but still, there was a possibility she'd gotten the wrong name among the whole row of elderly women sitting together.

Tandy patted the corner of the pew. "That's right, darlin'. Sit right here. We've got a proposition we want to put before you."

Fancy slid into the seat. "In church?"

"It's not a godly thing or a spiritual one, but we aren't going to ask you to sell your soul to the devil either. We're not out to save your soul from hell or pray you through the Pearly Gates. We just want a place to fix our hair again. I saw Hattie last week in the nursing home. She says it's just for a few weeks and then she'll be back, but we don't want to wait that long."

"I'm a teacher, not a beautician," Fancy said.

"And we know that, but back when you were just a kid, you used to wash our hair and get us ready for Hattie, remember? We miss the beauty shop. It was our hangout. The old men go to the Dairy Queen for coffee. We went to the shop. Open it back up for us."

"I don't have a license," Fancy argued.

"Don't need one. We'll put a quart jar on the table and give donations. You wash and roll. We can show you what to do past that. Monday at ten. Wednesday at one. Friday at three. Work for you?" Tandy asked.

"Please turn to page one-twelve, and we'll sing together," the music director said from the podium.

"Well?" Tandy asked.

"Why not? I'll see you at ten in the morning," Fancy said.

Tandy looked down the row at her cronies and nodded. They sang with smiles on their faces that morning.

Sophie and Kate arrived promptly at two o'clock that afternoon and went straight to the kitchen. Fancy had Oreos arranged on a plate and set a pitcher of sweet tea in the middle of the table.

Kate hugged Fancy before she sat down. "I can't believe that school didn't give you the job after they did everything but promise it to you on a silver platter. I'm sorry, honey."

"Me too," Sophie said.

Fancy giggled.

"Was not being hired somehow funny?" Sophie asked.

"No, but this morning was," she said, and she told the story of being shoved into Theron's Sunday school room and the bickering that had followed.

"Ooh, sounds ominous," Kate said.

"That black cat was definitely an omen. It's brought me nothing but bad luck from the time it darted out in front of me. My car still smells like almonds. I have to face that abominable man every

Sunday or let him win. And now I have to fix hair three days a week for donations."

"Fix hair? I thought you hated doing that when you were a kid. If I remember right, it was what put the idea of teaching into your head. You said you'd never grow up to cut and curl other women's hair," Sophie said.

"And you said if you ever got away from mesquite trees and Texas dust, you'd never come back to Baird to see your aunt again," Fancy pointed out.

"And I said I'd never be a waitress at the Amigos if I ever got away from Breckenridge," Kate joined right in. "Maybe we've all three got lessons to learn."

Fancy joined them at the table and poured herself a tall glass of iced tea. "Never thought of it like that. I've been up to my ears in a pity pool ever since I left church."

"You only get fifteen minutes to whine, remember?" Kate said.

"And then you get on with your life. Momma always said that, and I'm learning why," Fancy said. "Okay, my minutes are over, so tell me what's going on with you two."

"I got three shifts this week at the police station but made more in tips at the Amigos than I did from the police department," Kate said. That afternoon she wore baggy sweatpants that had been raggedly cut off just above her knees and a faded gray T-shirt.

"Aunt Maud's been feeling poorly," Sophie said. "I took her to the doctor in Abilene on Wednesday. He wanted to put her in the hospital for tests. She told him she didn't have time for a vacation. She's got hay to be baled and a cattle sale to plan. Said she'd think about it in the fall. Which reminds me, the sale is next week, and afterward we have this big party. Band. Dancing. A thank-you to all the rich cattlemen in this area as well as half of Texas, Oklahoma, and even one from Australia for buying cattle. Y'all are both coming," Sophie said. She slipped off her cowboy boots and propped her feet on the extra kitchen chair. Her jeans were faded and her chambray work shirt tied up at her waist.

"Lots of food?" Kate asked.

Sophie nodded.

"I'll be there."

"Dessert?" Fancy asked.

Sophie nodded again.

"Tell me the time and place."

"Next Friday night at seven o'clock. The sale is Thursday night and Friday morning. I'll expect you both at six. It's western. Boots, jeans, and lots of glitter."

Fancy moaned. "I don't have boots or glitter."

"Then go buy 'em. You've got all week," Sophie said. "Hey, let's go shopping in Abilene on Wednesday."

"Can't. I now fix hair on Monday, Wednesday, and Friday."

"Then Tuesday. I've got to be at the sale on Thursday."

"I'm going too. I might not have enough glitter to impress that Aussie, and I do love that accent," Kate said.

"That's settled, then. Now, what else happened this week? Anything wonderful or terrible?" Sophie asked.

"I saw Chris Miller," Fancy said.

"And?" Sophie asked.

"And Momma was right. I called her and told her so."

"Is he still handsome?" Kate asked.

"He looks sixty, and I don't know how many times he's been married. First there was Becky, then Debbie, and the wife now is Tina. She seems nice enough, but she has to look at a tattoo on his arm of Debbie's name. Can you imagine snuggling up with him and seeing another woman's name? And he hit on me. He's got a pregnant wife, a six-year-old son, and he thought I'd call him just because he told me to."

"Be thankful for what we were saved from," Kate said.

"Not me. I didn't get saved like you two," Sophie said.

"Check the clock. She's got fifteen minutes to whine, and then she has to shut up." Fancy laughed.

The cookies were gone and the tea pitcher nearly empty at five when they had to go home. Kate wanted to a sneak in a nap before a graveyard shift at the police station. Sophie had to take Aunt Maud to Sunday-night services at her church. Fancy had to visit Hattie.

They paraded out of the house together. Sophie drove away in her red truck. Kate took off to the east in her white one, and Fancy got into her little Camaro and headed south toward the nursing home. She gave thanks for her friends as she drove. At least they'd made her laugh, and she needed something positive to sustain her when she walked into the nursing home.

Hattie looked up when Fancy rapped on her door. Her expression changed from indifference to disgust immediately. "Why are you still here? I told you to go home."

Fancy drew up a chair beside her grandmother's bed. "Granny, why do you talk like that? I'm your only grandchild. Why do you hate me?" She asked questions that had been worrying her for most of her life but that she had been too afraid to put into words.

Hattie glared at her for several minutes. "I'm eighty-seven years old."

"That doesn't give you the right to be hateful," Fancy said.

Hattie's stare softened a little but not much. "I've got every right to be any way I want to be."

"And what gives you that right?"

"You want to know? You really want to know?" she asked, leaning forward, her eyes glistening with fury. "I hate your mother. She ruined my life, twice, and I can be hateful if I want to be."

She was a wizened little woman with thick gray hair she wore short and combed back in waves, a style of the fifties. Her brown eyes held absolutely no warmth, her face was a bed of wrinkles, and her hands were dry from more than fifty years of hot water, hair dye, and permanents.

"Why would you hate Momma? She's been nothing but good to you. She just wants you to love her like a daughter. A mother should love her child." Fancy figured if she was in trouble for a penny, she might as well be in real trouble for a dollar.

Hattie shot her a look that told her where she thought Fancy oughtta go, then clamped her mouth shut. After a few seconds she sighed. "Might as well get it over with, I suppose. Hid it all these years, but like the Good Book says, evil will surface."

"Momma is not evil," Fancy protested.

"Yes, she is, and so are you. Draw that chair up closer, because I'm only going to tell this once, Fancy Lynn. I hated that name when you were born and don't like it any better today. She should have given you a real name, not a play one, but then, she was only sixteen."

Fancy waited. "Why was that such a horrible thing?"

"Be quiet. I'm going to talk, and you're going to listen. If you say one word, I'll stop talking. If I stop for a breath, you wait. Is that understood?"

Fancy nodded.

"I was seventeen when I married your grandpa. He was twenty-six, and folks thought we weren't a good match. But I loved him, and he loved me. At first I expected to have kids, but when I didn't, I was relieved. We settled down together, and we were happy, just the two of us, and I was glad there wasn't no kids. When I was forty, I decided I wanted to fix hair. I'd done it on the side for a few years, giving my friends home permanents and cutting their hair. Orville had some money saved up, and he let me get the schooling and license to put in a shop."

Fancy sucked in air to say something.

Hattie shook her head. "Not a word, or I'll quit, and you'll never know the story. At first I reckoned I was going through the menopause and had the flu at the same time. I went to the doctor, and he told me I was going to have a baby. There I was, past forty years old and expecting a baby I didn't want. Orville wouldn't let me give it away. I begged him to let me go away for six months and give the baby up. Say I was in a sanitarium for the tuberculosis or some other disease. He wouldn't hear of it. Said we'd muddle through it."

Fancy pinched her own leg. Yes, she was awake, and this wasn't a nightmare. Hattie had just said that she didn't want to have Gwen. How could a mother not want her child?

"I was the laughingstock of the whole town. Married at seventeen and took more than twenty years for me to have a baby. I named her Gwen after my sister. I was eight when Gwen was born, and when she died two days later, Momma cried. I hoped if I named your mother Gwen, she would die in the hospital when she was two days old, and I promised God I'd cry a bunch of tears if she would. She didn't die, but Orville did when she was six months old, and I was angry with her for living and him for leaving me to raise her by myself."

Fancy wanted to leave the room and run from the information overload.

"She wasn't a bad child, so that was a help. But I just never could love her like I was supposed to. I guess I wasn't born with motherin' instincts, or maybe I got tired of babies, since I'd been the oldest of six kids. I made sure she had what she needed, took her to church to teach her right from wrong. But I failed at that too."

Fancy cocked her head to one side.

Hattie went on. "She thought she was in love. What does a kid know at fifteen? Not a blessed thing. I forbade her to see that bad boy and thought it was over. Then there she was, married, expecting a baby, and he was dead. Another kid for me to have to raise when I didn't even want her. So there I was, shamed again."

Fancy felt as if time stood still.

"So Gwen finished her schooling with courses at home and then went to work at the bank when you was two years old. That meant I had to put up with you underfoot in the shop. Every time I looked at you, with those big blue eyes, I saw your father. The rest you know. Gwen met Les when he came into the bank for something or other to do with his great-uncle's money. A few months later she run off with him and took you with her. It was the happiest day of my life. And that's why I want you out of my house and gone when I come home. I didn't want your mother, and I don't want you around me either."

"But she was just a baby who didn't ask to be born," Fancy whispered.

"And I didn't ask to have her," Hattie retorted.

"You couldn't just love her because she was a part of you?"

Hattie shook her head. "I just plain didn't want a baby. Now go away. Tell Miss Tandy and the ladies I'll be back, and we'll set up our appointments like always. They like to come to the shop and gossip. I reckon I like to listen to them, and doing their hair keeps my hands from getting stiff."

"Yes, ma'am." Fancy was amazed she even had a voice. Every other part of her body was numb.

"Don't just sit there."

Fancy stood slowly and bent down to kiss her grandmother on the forehead.

Hattie wiped it away.

"Good-bye, Granny," she said.

Hattie turned her face to the wall and shut her eyes.

Fancy didn't know how she got home or how long she'd lain on the top of the twin bed in the room she and her mother had shared all those years. She blinked into the present when the digital clock on the nightstand separating the twin beds clicked over at eleven minutes past eleven.

That had always been an inside joke between her and Gwen. If either one saw the clock at precisely eleven-eleven, when all four ones were lined up, then they got to make a wish.

Fancy wondered what she'd wish for. That she fill her grandmother's life with love and happiness?

She slung her legs over the side of the bed and went to the kitchen, where she popped open a can of cold soda pop and carried it to the living room. Fancy figured she would abide by her grandmother's wishes and be gone by the time Hattie came home. She could always work at the gift shop until the next school year and get a few days a week at the school as a substitute teacher.

The phone rang, and she jumped. "Lord, don't let it be Momma. I can't tell her."

Her eleven-eleven wish was granted.

"Hey, girl, you still awake?" Kate asked.

"Yes, I am. You at work?"

"No, the person I was replacing decided to work, so I had a four-hour nap, and now I'm wide awake. I've got a panful of hot tamales left over from the café. Want me to bring them over?"

"I can make a pitcher of iced tea. I'll be so glad to see you. It's been a horrible day."

"Chris?" Kate asked.

"Worse than that. I'll leave the porch light on. Don't even bother knocking. Just come on in."

Kate found Fancy with a glass of tea in front of her at the kitchen table. She set the tamales in the middle of the table, got out two forks, and fixed herself a glass of tea before she sat down. From the look on her friend's face it had really been a stinker of a day.

"Okay, shoot," she said.

"You're not going to believe it. I'm not sure I do, and I was there listening to it," Fancy said.

"Hattie?" Kate asked.

Fancy nodded.

"Do we need to call Sophie?"

"Probably, but it's so late, and we'll see her in a couple of days," Fancy said.

"Then start talking."

Fancy laid it all out, verbatim, as best she could.

Kate whispered hoarsely, "She said it just like that? She hates you and your mother because she didn't want a kid when she was forty?"

"That's the way she put it. Do I tell Momma?"

"Lord, no!"

"It might bring her peace of mind."

"If you ever do tell her, do it in person." Kate still couldn't believe the story.

"You're right. I'm glad you got booted out of the job tonight. I didn't realize what a load would be lifted in just telling someone. Thanks, Kate."

"That's what friends are for. Get a fork and get busy before these tamales get stone cold."

Fancy dug in. "Hungry as I am right now, I could eat them with icicles on 'em."

"Are we going to tell Sophie?"

"Oh, yeah. We don't keep secrets from one another."

Chapter Four

They arrived in force at exactly ten o'clock on Monday morning. Tandy led the pack through the side door into the beauty shop. A tall, stately woman, she walked with confidence, blue-gray hair scarcely in need of a wash and set, green eyes twinkling as she donned one of the dozen snap-front dusters Hattie kept on hangers in the closet with her other supplies.

"What do we do first?" Fancy asked.

"I remembered and wrote it down. Myrle washes Tandy's hair, and you'll set it and put her under the dryer. I wash Myrle while you are rolling Tandy's hair so she'll be ready for the next roll-up. Then Viv washes my hair, and I'll be ready for the curlers. It's all right here," Leander said.

"So you take turns washing, and Granny does the rolling?" Fancy said.

"That and combing out," Leander said.

"I'm not so sure I can do you all justice on the comb-out," Fancy said.

Myrle was busy removing pins from her upswept hairdo. She was eighty years old, and her hair had always been dyed red, even back when Fancy was helping Hattie out in the beauty shop. "Don't worry. We'll help with that too." She grabbed a brush and went about getting all the tangles out of her hair. "It's good to be where we belong on Monday morning. An old woman ought to have a decent Monday when she couldn't find a single old man to dance with over the weekend."

"Ah, Myrle, if you did find one who was willing, he probably wouldn't be able," Tandy teased.

"Honey, if I find one who's willing, I'll dance the leather off his boots."

"Good grief, Myrle, you are too old to be going to honky-tonks and dancing like a teenager," said Mary, a Hispanic lady with salt-and-pepper hair and twenty extra pounds on her short frame who crossed herself and rolled her eyes.

"Old is for those who are half-dead. If I can talk one of those silver-haired dudes into two-steppin' with me, I'll buy him a big breakfast when the honky-tonk shuts down," Myrle said. "And don't you be praying for my soul. I'll get to heaven on my own merits."

Pansy giggled. She was a rancher, grew rodeo-stock cattle, and wore her dyed jet black hair in chin-length layers. Her eyes were crystal blue and her jeans tight.

Myrle pointed a finger at Pansy. "Why don't you go dancing with me?"

"Why should she? All them young men living in her bunkhouse. She can get any one of them to twirl her around the bunkhouse floor," Tandy said.

Pansy shook her head at the good-natured teasing. "Not a one of them young guys could keep up with any of us on the dance floor."

"Y'all need to talk about something other than honky-tonks around Miss Fancy," Viv said. Like Myrle, she had long hair she wore twisted up the back, but hers was gray. Standing at five feet three inches, she was probably fifty pounds overweight and had two chins and bat wings under her arms.

"I doubt it. Fancy is thirty years old. She's not a naïve kid anymore," Myrle said. "And I wouldn't be surprised if she's danced a few line dances in her life."

Fancy picked up the roller tray and started on Tandy's hair. "You ladies talk about whatever you want to. It won't bother me a bit."

"Thank you," Leander said. Of the six, she was the smallest, not much taller than Fancy, and the youngest, with brown hair in a wash-and-dry style that required little or no curling.

"I remember Tandy, Myrle, Viv, Mary, and Pansy. I don't remember you." Fancy looked at Leander.

"I'm Leander Wilson, and I was only here a couple of times before your momma moved away. I'm her age, and Tandy is my aunt.

She talked me into coming with her one day fifteen years ago. This place and these crazy women are addictive. I think the only reason they keep me around is because someday the law is going to take their driver's licenses, and I'll still be young enough to bring them to the beauty shop."

"So you're the only one with a husband?" Fancy asked.

"Had one. Got rid of him ten years ago. Haven't found a replacement yet, but then, I haven't been looking real hard. Got a daughter who's twenty-five and a grandson who takes up a lot of my time," Leander said.

"Don't listen to her, Fancy. She's got a boyfriend who takes up a lot of her time too. Policeman down in Abilene. Ten years younger than her, and if she ever tosses him out, I'm having a face-lift and a tummy tuck and setting traps for him," Myrle said.

"Did you go to school with my mother?" Fancy asked Leander.

"No, I went to school down in Baird. Wound up in Albany after I married."

Fancy put Tandy under the dryer and started rolling Myrle's long red hair. "How long until you need a dye job?"

"Two weeks. Every four weeks those gray roots start showing. Hattie's been keeping it red for me for more than forty years now. Back when she first put in the shop I lived down the street two houses. Them were the days, weren't they, girls?"

Tandy kept one ear out of the dryer so she could listen. "Depends. What was it? '62?"

"Yeah, about the time you started buying up everything in the county and turning it into rental property," Viv said.

"Been right profitable. Raised five kids on rental houses, so I can't complain," Tandy said loudly over the sound of the dryer.

"About the time my mother was born?" Fancy asked.

"That's it. Crazy times, those were," Pansy said. "Sometime during that year we were all pregnant or giving birth. Even Hattie. She didn't seem too happy about it. Been married all those years and no children, and then—boom—right out of the clear blue she thinks she's in menopause, only it was pregnancy. I always had the feeling she was embarrassed to be having a baby at her age, but then, she was a private person, so I mighta been wrong."

Fancy kept rolling hair and nodded.

"We were all younger, except for the dancin' queen over there." Mary nodded toward Myrle.

"Hey, I'm only eighty. Hattie is eighty-seven. I'm still younger than she is," Myrle argued.

At noon Tandy called the Dairy Queen and placed orders for lunch. Her hair was finished, so she drove her ten-year-old black Cadillac to town to bring back the burgers and malts. By two o'clock they were all beautified and fed, and the jar on the table was full. After they left, Fancy counted the money. One hundred and twenty dollars for doing practically nothing but listening to six women bicker, tell tales about the past, and tease one another about the future. Not bad for her first Monday of unemployment. She put the cash into an envelope and tucked it inside the money drawer for her grandmother. She had no idea how much Hattie still depended on the beauty shop to pay her bills.

After the ladies left, Fancy worried Hattie's news like a dog with a bone. She'd bury it for a while, then go dig it up and stare at it a while longer, then swear she was burying it forever. Finally at six that evening she decided to make another trip to the nursing home to assure Hattie that Gwen and Fancy both loved her even if she had trouble loving them.

She found a handwritten note on Hattie's door that read NO VISITORS, and she went straight to the nurse's desk.

"What is going on in Granny's room?" she asked.

"I'm sorry, but we have to abide by the patient's wishes. Especially Hattie's, since she checked herself into our facility and is able to check herself out when she is ready. If it hadn't been for the promise she made to the doctor, I don't think she'd be here today, but he gave her a three-week deadline, and she agreed. However, after you left yesterday, she called us and said to put the note on the door," the nurse said.

Fancy stared at the woman until she was a blur.

"Will there be anything else?"

"No visitors at all?" Fancy asked.

"Well . . ." The nurse blushed. "The rule was, only the ones on her list."

"And they would be?"

"I'm sure it's patient privacy," Theron Warren said at her elbow.

She jerked her head around to find him not a foot from her. Couldn't she go anywhere without running into him, or was he stalking her?

"Yes, sir, it is just that. She's entitled to see only the people she wishes. You and your mother, Gwen, are not on the list," the nurse told her.

"Why is that?" Theron asked.

"That is *visitor's* privacy," Fancy shot at him.

"Is Hattie in her right mind?" Theron asked the nurse.

"Oh, yes, sir, she is that. Doc said he'd never seen an eighty-seven-year-old woman with a mind like Hattie Sawyer's. No way would anyone ever get anywhere having her declared incompetent."

"I'd never do that," Fancy whispered.

"Guess she's got her reasons," Theron said.

Fancy gave him what she hoped was her very best drop-dead-on-the-spot look and turned to leave.

"Am I on the list?" Theron asked. "I'd like to see the old girl. She attends the same church I do. She and Uncle Joe were the oldest ones in the church until they both ended up here."

"Yes, sir, you can go right on in and visit with her. I'm sure she'll be glad to see you."

Fancy didn't look back. She didn't even wipe the tears streaming down her face until she got to the car, and then she used up two Dairy Queen paper napkins. Finally she sucked it up and checked the damage in the visor mirror. Her eyes were swollen and puffy, her mascara smeared, her lipstick blotchy.

She came near to jumping through the top of the car when someone knocked on the window, and she jerked her head around to see Chris Miller's face only inches away.

"What do you want?" she asked.

He mouthed words and made hand gestures. "Roll down the window."

She pushed the button.

"What's the matter, doll? That old woman hurt your feelings? I never did like her. Hadn't been for her, we'd have been together all these years, but she and your mother got it into their heads I wasn't good enough for you. I wasn't, but I've cleaned up my act," he said.

"Chris, you are married. You've got a son and a new baby. Go home," she said.

He reached inside the car and ran a finger down her jawbone. "I never stopped loving you, Fancy Lynn."

She pushed his hand away. "I mean it, Chris. Stop stalking me."

"Stalking you? Honey, your ego is too big. I'm not stalking you. I'm giving you one last chance. Tina is about to leave me. She just stuck around until that kid was born. You want another go-round?"

"No," she said as she hit the button to roll up the window and started the engine.

There was still plenty of light when she got home, if Hattie's house could be called that, so she hauled the lawnmower out of the storage shed and worked up a sweat cutting the grass. That job finished, she took out the Weed Eater and fired it up to manicure the lawn. When she was done, she set about weeding the flower beds.

Hattie would at least come home to a nice yard. She'd have to start paying to keep it up from now on, though, and that would plague her. Knowing her grandmother, Fancy wouldn't be surprised if she had a truckload of gravel brought in and the front yard covered in it so she wouldn't have to pay a local kid to mow.

She had dirt under her fingernails and a smear of it across her face, and her hair hung in sweaty clumps, but she felt better since she'd worked out her frustrations. She got an icy cold can of Coke from the refrigerator and was sitting on the porch when a pickup truck slowed down and stopped in front of the house.

Theron Warren climbed out of it, shook the legs of his dress jeans down over the tops of dark brown suede Roper shoes—cowboy tennis shoes, some folks called them—and squared his shoulders before walking up the sidewalk to the porch.

"Miss Sawyer," he said at the edge of the porch.

"Mr. Warren."

"I tried, but she said no," he said.

"What are you talking about?" Fancy didn't care that Theron was seeing her in a state of pure, 100 percent filthy mess. But she did wonder if he'd lost his mind since she saw him in the nursing home.

"Your grandmother. She's a salty old girl, and I've always admired her for it. I can't imagine why she's being so stubborn about you visiting, so I asked her. She told me it wasn't any of my business, and from now on I'm on her no-visitors list."

"Welcome to the club. It appears to be growing daily," Fancy said.

"What on earth did you do?"

"I was born, plain and simple. Leave it at that and forget it."

"I've got another reason I want to talk to you. I owe you an apology."

Fancy raised one eyebrow. "Reckon you'd better sit down for that. It might take all your strength."

"I imagine it will. I don't like to apologize."

"Want a Coke so you don't pass plumb out?"

"I'd love one," he said.

She set her can on the top step, went inside, and brought an icy cold soda out to him. He took a long swig while she sat back down, keeping at least three feet between them.

"Good and cold. Hits the spot on a hot August day. Thank you."

She checked the sky to see if the clouds were about to part and the rapture appear. Theron Warren had smiled at her!

"I'm sorry about the job. I wanted to hire you. Already had the papers ready for you to sign," he said.

"Sure, and that's why you called Wilma Cripton to come in for an interview," she said.

"She is a sister-in-law to one of the school board members, an aunt to another, and her husband works for a third. She wanted the job at the last minute. I thought I could change their minds, but I couldn't."

"You went to bat for me?" Fancy was amazed but wasn't sure she believed him.

"Hey, I'm fair. You proved you weren't drinking and you were of age."

Fancy looked over at him. "Why wouldn't they even consider me for the sub work?"

"We honestly do have all the substitute teachers we need."

"Then apology accepted."

He grinned again. "Just like that? No stinging barbs?"

"No, you deserve to be forgiven, since you tried to get Granny to see me. I appreciate it."

"Be glad you weren't at school. If today is any indication of the rest of the year, I may hand in my resignation and go to straight ranchin'."

Fancy smiled back. "The first days are always tough. It'll smooth out. It always does."

"Jimmy Miller got into a fight with another little boy on the playground. Tina had to come in for a conference. She says she's taking the kids and moving back in with her parents. God only knows how in the world she ever got hooked up with Chris anyway. He's bad news deluxe."

So it was true. Chris really was going to be single. Fancy almost moaned at the idea of his being around every corner and free from his wife and kids. Hattie was right. Fancy should gas up her car, pack up her belongings, and head to Florida. But she'd promised Sophie she'd be at the cattle-sale party on Friday night, and the beauty-shop ladies were supposed to be there two more days that week. Otherwise she might have started packing without even taking a shower.

"So who it is you go to visit in the nursing home?" She changed the subject.

"Uncle Joe. He's got Alzheimer's and doesn't know where he is most of the time, but every now and then he'll recognize me. He's the reason I'm in Albany. Never had any children of his own, so when he got sick, he called me and made me a deal on his ranch down south of town. I'm hoping to teach long enough to get it completely paid for before I quit, but another day like this one and I'll learn to live on beans and rice."

"What you got on your ranch? Horses?"

"Half a dozen. Mainly longhorn cattle. Grow my own hay. Few Angus for beef. Couple of hogs and some chickens."

"Cats?"

He smiled. "Two in the house. Six or seven in the barn. You like cats?"

She warmed to him. Anyone who had cats couldn't be all bad. "Love them. All but black ones who run out in front of my car. Momma is allergic to them, and Granny would never allow any kind of animal around here. I've always planned on adopting one when I get my own place."

He frowned. "You still live with your momma?"

"Yes, I do. Not exactly with her but pretty close. She and my stepdad have this wonderful beach home with a guest house off to the side. I pay rent, and we both have our privacy."

"Couldn't have a cat there?"

She shook her head. "Momma is in and out too much, and I'm in and out of the big house, so I'd be tracking in cat dander. Just can't happen."

He turned the Coke up and finished the last swallow. "Thanks for the cold one. I've got stock to feed, so I'll be on my way. Sorry about Hattie."

"Thanks for sticking your neck out for me, and for the explanation about the job. See you Sunday."

"I suppose. There's an opening in the nursery. You want it?"

"No, I do not. You trying to run me off?"

"Probably. I don't really need any help."

Fancy didn't want him to go but couldn't think of any reason to invite him to stay. "I'm not leaving just because you had a case of conscience over the way you acted. I'll be there bright and early. I've already got a project in mind."

"See, there you go, trying to take over. I can smell overbearing a mile away."

"That would be the kettle calling the pot black, now, wouldn't it?" She giggled.

He tried to come up with a retort, but nothing came to mind, so he left with a wave. She sat on the porch and tried to make sense of the craziest week she'd ever spent in her life.

Theron wondered as he drove to the ranch why Hattie Sawyer didn't want to see her granddaughter. Could it be the fact that Fancy had been hauled into the local police station and didn't get the teaching job? He'd feel terrible if he were somehow the cause of the breach. Hattie was a dyed-in-the-wool, old-time Christian teetotaler, but only a handful of people, if that, even knew about the half hour Fancy had spent in the jail cell. He hadn't said a word to anyone. Never would. It was just a misunderstanding, as far as he was concerned. Surely even Hattie wouldn't fault Fancy for that.

He still hadn't figured out a darn thing by the time he got home, so he changed from his dress clothes into overalls and started the chores. The cattle were still grazing, so they were fine. He fed the chickens and hogs and started back into the house when his cell phone rang. He fished it from the bib pocket of his overalls and sat down on the back porch step to talk.

"Hello, sis, what's happening in Shamrock?" he asked.

"I'll never get used to this caller ID stuff," Melissa, his older sister, said.

"Technology—ain't it great?" he said.

"Maria was at the drugstore today," Melissa said bluntly.

"It's a big state and a free world. I suppose if she wants to walk down the streets of Shamrock, she can do it," he said.

"She was making noises about you waiting to buy property until she was out of the picture and that she's going to make you pay."

"Maria was a six-month mistake. How and what can she do about my ranch? I borrowed the money to buy it. Granted, Uncle Joe sold it to me for a fraction of its worth, since I'm his kin, but it's no skin off her pretty little face," Theron said.

He shivered in spite of the blistering breeze blowing across the porch. Maria had been trouble from the day after their wedding. She thought she had married his family's money and was so disappointed when she found out what a Texas schoolteacher brought home, she literally whimpered.

"I know that. You know that. But she's been in town a week now, and every day she finds someone else to listen to her. Just thought you ought to know in case she decides to come down south," Melissa said.

"Thanks for the update. It's been three years since the divorce.

I wonder what she's really up to. Haven't heard a word in all this time, and now she surfaces."

"Who knows about Maria? I told you in the beginning . . ."

"I know. I know. But I didn't listen, so don't tell me again now."

She laughed and changed the subject. "Momma and Daddy are fine. Julie hasn't had the baby yet. It's hot up here. We need rain awful. Terrence is playing his first football game Friday night. I think that covers everything else."

"I'm glad that boy took after his father instead of his uncle," Theron said.

"The way you quarterbacked for the team was legendary, and you know it. *Little* don't mean *lazy*. It just means you had to work harder to get the job done. So don't be giving me any of that humility junk."

"Yes, ma'am."

"Theron . . ." Melissa said, concern in her voice.

"Yeah?"

"Watch your back."

"Always do, and thanks. I'll be home for Thanksgiving."

"I'm counting on it."

"Tell them all I love 'em."

"Will do. Bye now."

He sat for a while before he went inside. The back of the house faced west, so he could watch the famous Texas sunsets. Bright orange, brilliant scarlet, and an array of shades of pink followed the sun as it sank below the horizon.

He'd been twenty-seven when Maria came into his life. She was twenty-five and recently widowed after a seven-year marriage to a construction worker. He'd met her at a teacher-appreciation dinner given by the local banks. Maria was a new teller and very, very beautiful with her long black hair, big dark-chocolate eyes, and skin just slightly browned by her heritage.

Looking back now, years later, he guessed he'd been afraid that the best of life was passing him by. His friends were all married or at least involved in a lasting relationship headed toward the altar. He was looking thirty in the eye and wanting stability. Maria had seemed to offer it to him.

But their marriage had been a nightmare. Six months to the day after the wedding and at least one major argument a day, always over why she couldn't have a new car or a home like Melissa's or a bigger diamond, she left a note on the kitchen table and disappeared. She'd been there at breakfast. At supper she was gone. The apartment had been stripped. She had been kind enough to leave him the sofa bed and his clothing. But everything else, including the ratty shower curtain, was gone.

Theron had felt nothing but relief.

It didn't matter that she was in Shamrock. It wouldn't matter if she showed up on his doorstep in one hour. Theron was through with Maria and had declared himself a bachelor from there on out. Women were nothing but trouble, and he had no intention of ever having any kind of relationship with any of them.

Chapter Five

Well, if it ain't Fancy Lynn Sawyer," a high-pitched voice said from the other side of the rack of jeans.

Fancy tiptoed to look across at the tall lady. She should know the woman, and in a minute the name would appear, but at that moment nothing came to mind. The voice sounded familiar. Names flashed across Fancy's memory like data on a computer, but nothing matched this face with a name.

The woman stepped around the end of the rack and closer to Fancy Lynn. "I'm not surprised that you don't remember me. I was a year ahead of you in school. I'm—was—Becky Barrington, the one who picked up the pieces when you left Chris behind."

Fancy nodded slowly, trying to force words from her brain through her mouth. She opened her lips, but nothing came out. Becky had her chin jutted out and her eyes fixed in a glare. She took another step. "Tongue-tied, are you? You should be, because there ain't words to tell how bad you broke his heart."

Sophie came to the rescue from an aisle nearby. "Hi, Becky. How are you?"

"Couldn't be better, thank you. I might have known you three would be together."

Kate poked her head around a shirt rack. "Old friendships never die."

Becky looked to her left. "Hello, Kate. I knew you were here somewhere. Saw you when we walked in the door."

Becky was at least five foot eight and so slim that Fancy wondered how she found jeans small enough to fit her. Her hair was cut in shoulder-length layers, and the roots said she wasn't really a

51

blond. She'd toned down her makeup since high school but still managed to use enough eye shadow and mascara to keep the industry from declaring bankruptcy.

"I'm sorry. I didn't recognize you at first, but now I remember you," Fancy said. "I understand you have a daughter."

"Carrie, come on over here and meet who could've been your momma if she'd stuck around town," Becky said in a brittle voice.

A shorter version of Becky strolled over from the boot section. Blond hair pulled up into a ponytail and twisted around a clamp, leaving the ends poking out everywhere. Tight-fitting jeans. Round-toed pink boots that matched a pink tank top with a picture of a cowgirl on the front.

"Who?" she asked.

Fancy felt the blush crawling up her neck and flushing her cheeks.

"I'm just teasin', honey. This is the girl your daddy was dating before I landed him. This is Fancy Sawyer. That is Sophie McSwain, and the one by the shirts is Kate Miller."

"Pleased to meet y'all," Carrie said. "We'd best find that pair of jeans for Daddy and get on home, Momma. You know how he gets if Buck wakes up and starts cryin'."

"We're back together now, in case you're wondering," Becky said. "Chris always comes back to me. After his second wife, he did. Now, after this one, he's right back to me again. This time he's promised he won't even look at another woman again. So, Fancy Lynn, if you've come to town with thoughts of lighting an old flame, then you'd better think again. Just thought I'd clear that up right here at the beginning."

"Fancy came to take care of her grandmother, and, believe me, she's not interested in Chris. We all hope you are very happy," Sophie said quickly.

"You too? Do you hope me and Chris are happy?" Becky looked right at Fancy.

Fancy nodded. "I sincerely hope you and Chris are very happy and stay together long enough to celebrate your fiftieth wedding anniversary."

"I appreciate that. Well, Carrie, grab that pair of jeans for your daddy, and let's get on home. He does get cranky if we leave him with Buck too long."

Evidently Kate had a quizzical look on her face, because Becky giggled. "Buck is our son, mine and Chris'. Born before he married the last woman. Buck is a year old. That six-year-old ain't Chris' son except on the adoption papers. I'll be glad to have Chris full-time. Boy needs a father. See y'all around town." Becky followed her daughter outside.

"Can you believe that?" Sophie said when they'd cleared the store.

"Only thing that keeps running through my mind is that I owe my momma my life," Fancy said.

"Ain't it the truth?" Kate nodded. "Now tell me, does this shirt have enough bling to catch an Aussie?"

"You really think an Aussie could be your knight in shining whatever?" Fancy giggled.

After all that had happened the past two days, it lifted her spirits to laugh. She wondered what on earth she would have done if Sophie and Kate hadn't moved back to the area and she'd had to face her problems with no support group.

"*Armor.* My knight in shining *armor,*" Kate said.

"That's not what you told us when we were talking about our magic words. You said knight in shining whatever. And I thought he was Hart Ducaine," Sophie teased.

"No, his armor is tarnished. It will never shine again," Kate intoned dramatically.

Fancy picked up a pair of low-slung western jeans and a sleeveless white shirt with pearl snaps and beaded fringe and headed for the checkout counter. "He might find some silver polish and do a fine job of fixing it up all shiny and pretty."

Kate followed her, carrying a turquoise shirt with fake diamonds scattered across the chest. "Honey, there ain't enough silver polish in the world for that."

Sophie carried new boots to the counter. "You really think Becky is stupid enough to think Chris will stay with her?"

"Maybe there's a whole carload of stupid coming to Albany on the same train as that silver polish," Fancy teased as she pulled out several bills to pay for her purchases.

"Let it go. I don't want to hear anything more about Jethro Hart Ducaine," Kate growled.

"The beast is hungry. We'd better feed it," Sophie said.

Fancy's face held a quizzical expression.

Sophie shrugged. "Don't you remember how mean Kate gets when she's hungry? Let's go over to the Texas Roadhouse and have some barbecue for lunch. If we hurry, we can beat the lunch crowd."

"I'm not standing in line an hour," Kate said.

"If there's a waiting line, we'll go to McDonald's or buy a pound of bologna at the grocery store. Believe me, we won't stand in line for an hour. We couldn't stand that much mean," Sophie said.

Luck was with them. The lunch rush had barely begun, and there was a table for four available immediately. They threw their purses into the extra chair, and all three reached for a handful of peanuts from the galvanized miniature milk can.

"Thank God for peanuts," Kate said.

"Amen," Sophie said.

The waiter arrived, and they ordered ribs, fries, and iced tea.

"This would be a good place to bring a date," Kate declared.

"I agree, if I ever decide to date again," Sophie said.

"Why?" Fancy asked.

"Why would I date again, or why would this be a good place to bring him?" Sophie asked.

"Both," Fancy replied.

The waiter set iced tea in front of all three women and told them their order would arrive soon. Then he hurried off to another table.

Kate answered for Sophie. "Because you need to forget that idiot you were married to, and the best way to put him out of your mind is with someone new. Someone who is trustworthy. This is the place to bring him because he could make a mess, and you wouldn't have to clean it up."

"Was your ex a slob?" Fancy asked.

"Nah. My husband was so neat, it was scary. He even insisted that his socks be folded and arranged in the drawers by color," Sophie said.

"You're jokin'. My stepdad, Les, is a career military man, and he's not that picky," Fancy said.

"Who's picky?" Theron Warren stopped at their table.

Fancy almost choked on a peanut. "What are you doing in Abilene on a school day?"

"Principals' meeting here. Got an hour off for lunch. Who's picky?" he asked again.

Kate scanned him, from cowboy boots to feathered-back hair. "Who's askin'?"

"I'm sorry. This is Theron Warren, principal at the elementary school in Albany," Fancy said.

Sophie's eyes bugged out.

Kate smiled brightly. "Hello, we've heard so much about you. Too bad it wasn't all good."

Theron arched his eyebrows.

"And these are my friends, Sophie McSwain and Kate Miller, who's the outspoken one," Fancy said.

"If she's any more outspoken than you, I'm glad I'm not sitting at your table. It was nice to meet you ladies," he said politely before he kept walking toward the men's room.

"So that is the big, bad principal. I thought he'd be bald and paunchy," Kate whispered.

Sophie fanned her face with one hand. "Or at least old. Principals didn't look like that when we were in elementary school. You see the way he filled out those jeans?"

"Enough to make you think there's 'life after wife'?" Fancy tried to divert the attention toward Sophie and away from her.

"Almost," Sophie said.

"*Almost* only counts in horseshoes and hand grenades," Fancy told her.

"And you two would look so cute together. Bet you're the only woman in the world he wouldn't have to look up to," Kate said.

Fancy held up a hand in mock self-defense. "Enough already. I told you years ago, I want a Greek god with blond hair and blue

eyes, and I'm not settling for anything less than six feet four inches."
She could have kissed the waiter for bringing their plates at that moment.

"What in the world would you do with that much man? You'd barely reach his belly button, girl. Kissing him would be a nightmare," Kate said. "Now, with the green-eyed, yummy, more compact Theron Warren, you'd—"

"Enough," Fancy said.

"You think you've had enough, with Becky Barrington and Theron Warren all in one day?" Sophie grinned.

"Double enough. I'd looked forward to a simple day of shopping. It couldn't get any worse than this," Fancy said.

"Be careful, darlin'. You'll call down the wrath of God upon us," Kate whispered.

"And how's that?"

"You say it can't get any worse, but it could," Sophie said.

"Okay, then, I'll rephrase it. I *hope* it doesn't get any worse. All I need is for Chris to walk through the doors too," Fancy said.

"And bring little Buck with him? What a name, but then, Chris is his father, so what can I say?" Kate said.

Fancy shuddered. "What a mess!"

"Yes, and a big old mess at that. Now, with Theron Warren . . . ," Kate began again, giggling.

"His first name sounds Greek, doesn't it?" Sophie added. "Maybe *he* could be—"

"Changing the subject now!" Fancy gave them fair warning. "Who all is going to be at this party Friday night?"

"Every rancher in north central Texas and lots from all across the state. Some from up in Oklahoma. The Aussie that Kate is going to flirt with and whoever else is interested in buying some good Texas longhorn stock," Sophie said.

"I'm not going to flirt with him. I'm going to let him flirt with me," Kate said.

"See? Her attitude is getting better now that she has some food in her and the prospect of a party to go to," Sophie said.

"If the food at your party is as good as the Aussie cowboy is hunky, it might sweeten my attitude for a whole month. Y'all about finished? I told Momma I'd be home to help with the supper rush tonight." Kate pulled out a credit card and laid it on the check folder the waiter had left behind.

Sophie tossed it back at her. "My treat this time."

Fancy tucked several bills into the folder and held it up for the waiter. "No, it's mine. Nothing could be worse than this morning. You two got me through it. I owe you both."

They'd barely settled into Kate's truck when Fancy's phone played the first few bars of "80s Ladies."

"Hello, Momma, guess where I am? In Abilene with the girls, and have I ever got a story to tell you . . . What? . . . When? . . . I'm on my way. What do I need to do?"

She listened for a minute and flipped the phone shut. "Momma and Les are at the airport. They'll be here in a few hours. Granny died this morning."

Her voice was hollow in her own ears.

Tears didn't flow.

Grief didn't overwhelm her.

She waited for any kind of emotion. Nothing happened.

"I'm so sorry. What can we do?" Sophie asked.

Kate started the truck and backed out. "I'll call the café and tell them I won't be in today. We'll stay with you until Gwen and Les get here."

"I should cry. Why can't I cry?" Fancy asked.

"Because you are numb. It's a shock," Sophie answered.

"They think it was a massive heart attack. They went in to wake her up for breakfast, and she was dead," Fancy said.

"What a wonderful way to go. No struggling for breath. Just go to sleep and wake up in eternity," Kate said.

"It wasn't like that for your dad, was it?" Fancy asked gently.

"No. I wish he would have just gone to sleep. Those last two days I prayed for God to just take him and not let him suffer anymore."

They rode in silence back to Albany. The house seemed smaller, darker, and emptier when they walked inside out of the hot August heat.

"Where is she now?" Sophie asked.

"Momma said they'd taken her to the funeral home."

"Funeral in three days?" Kate asked.

Fancy shook her head. "She made her own arrangements a few years ago. We didn't know. Momma said there won't be a funeral. She'll explain when she gets here."

Sophie put on water to boil for a pitcher of sweet tea. "I'm not surprised. If Hattie didn't even want to see you or your mother, then she wouldn't want you to be a part of a funeral either. Maybe it's best. Everyone will chalk it up to her being such a strange woman, and in a few days it will be over. What will you do now?"

"I don't know. Maybe just go on home to Florida. Maybe Momma will ride back with me so I don't have to go alone."

"Come stay a few weeks on the ranch with me," Sophie said.

"And then a few weeks with me in Breckenridge," Kate offered.

"Thank you both. I just can't believe she's dead," Fancy said.

They all jumped when the doorbell rang. Fancy wondered how her mother had gotten there so quickly as she crossed the living room and opened the door.

"I heard Hattie died. I brought sandwich makings. What can I do?" Tandy asked.

Fancy stood to one side, and Tandy marched straight to the kitchen. She set two brown grocery bags on the counter and commenced unloading them. Paper plates, a large roll of paper towels, and a box of plastic cutlery came out of one bag. A shaved ham big enough to feed half the county, two loaves of bread, lettuce, tomatoes, mayonnaise, and mustard were unloaded from the second bag.

"Are any of you hungry?" Tandy asked.

"We just ate at the Texas Roadhouse. We were just leaving when we got the call from Fancy's mother," Kate said.

"Then I'll put all this in the refrigerator," Tandy said. "It'll keep you from having to cook until after the funeral."

"Yoo-hoo, I'm coming in," Leander called from the living room. "I'd have been here sooner, but I burned the first pan of brownies and had to start all over. I'm so sorry, Fancy Lynn. What can I do? When's the funeral?"

"There's not going to be a funeral. Momma said that Granny made some kind of arrangements years ago, and she told the nursing home about them when she went there. No funeral. No memorial. Nothing," Fancy said.

"That's the biggest crock I've ever heard. It's selfish, and it's crazy. This is the South. This is Texas. We cry when people die. We have funerals, and we will have one for Hattie Sawyer. She's dead, and she can't do a thing about it," Tandy said.

"Now, Tandy, if she left instructions, we'll have to abide by her wishes," Leander said.

"Whose wishes?" Pansy carried a casserole into the kitchen and set it on the stove. She wore faded jeans and a sleeveless shirt. Her arms were brown and freckled from too many hours in the sun. "I'm so, so sorry, darlin', about Hattie. Now tell me what I can do to help."

Tandy propped her hands on her hips. "Hattie left instructions that there wasn't to be a funeral."

"That's just plain not right," Pansy said.

"That's what I said."

"But if that's what she wants . . . ," Leander started.

Pansy propped her hands on *her* hips. "She's dead. She don't know what she wants. A funeral is for the living, not the dead. It's for closure for Fancy and Gwen and her church family. Oh, we're havin' a funeral all right."

Kate grinned. "She'll claw her way up out of the grave and haunt you all. I've always been afraid of that woman. If she told me no funeral, I wouldn't have a funeral."

"Knock-knock!" Mary's voice preceded her from the living room. "Is everyone in the kitchen?"

"That's right. You're not going to believe what Hattie did," Pansy said.

Mary carried in a foil tray of Mexican casserole that smelled wonderful. "She died."

Tandy delivered the news. "She left orders to not have a funeral."

"Jesus, Mary, and Joseph!" Mary exclaimed.

"Who's blessing the house?" Viv brought in a pecan pie.

"And why are they blessing the house?" Myrle asked. She carried a sack filled with bottles of soda.

"Hattie said no funeral," Mary said.

Everyone shook their heads.

"Hattie is dead. We'll do whatever we please with her," Myrle said.

"But it was her wish," Kate said.

"Sometimes you don't get what you wish for," Tandy told the girls.

The doorbell rang. Viv went to answer it and returned with the minister—and Theron Warren, who proved to be a deacon of the church as well as the elementary-school principal and part-time policeman.

"We came as fast as we heard," the preacher said. "I'm so sorry for your loss, Fancy Lynn. The church will hold the funeral, of course, and the dinner after will be held there too. Thursday would be good for us, but if you need more time, Friday is fine."

"We'll miss Hattie. Is there anything you'd like me to do?" Theron asked.

Fancy shook her head. "Momma said Granny didn't want a funeral or a memorial or anything. I think she left orders to be cremated."

The preacher frowned. "But she was a lifetime member of our church. Her friends will be expecting a funeral."

Viv nodded.

"However, if it was her wish, it should be followed," Theron said reasonably.

Fancy felt unaccountably irritated by his intrusion, however well-intended. He didn't have a say in the matter. He just went to Hattie's church.

"Momma will decide what to do when she gets here. Thank you both for coming by, and we'll be in touch," Fancy said in a way that she hoped was polite enough to dismiss them.

"I don't agree with this. Put it down somewhere that I think it stinks," Myrle said.

"You are in good hands, Fancy Lynn, so we'll go on. You let us know what you'd like to do when your mother arrives," the preacher said. "Maybe we could have a moment of prayer before we go."

Everyone's head dropped, and their eyes shut.

Fancy listened to the prayer. Evidently the woman the preacher knew was a very different woman than the one she and her mother knew. It was strange how so many different people in the same room could have such varied opinions on one wizened old lady.

"Amen," he finally said.

A moment of awkwardness followed. Finally Tandy picked up a glass and filled it with tea. "Anyone else want something to drink?" she asked.

"No, thank you," the preacher said.

Theron looked at Fancy. "You'll be going home to Florida now, I suppose?"

Again, his matter-of-fact question riled her. "Not until after Sunday, for sure. I'll be there, so don't give my job to anyone else."

"Wouldn't dream of it," he said in spite of his inner turmoil. He gritted his teeth. Drat the woman anyway. They rubbed each other the wrong way—that was for sure. Still, she'd just lost her grandmother, and her eyes weren't even swollen. Had she no respect at all? "Could I have a word with you outside, please?"

She nodded ever so slightly and followed him out to the front porch, leaving behind eight women and a preacher still arguing about whether or not to have a funeral.

Theron took a defensive stance: shoulders thrown back, jaw set, frown, eyes drawn down, arms folded across his chest. "Now, what is your problem with me? I came to offer condolences for your grandmother, and you treat me like dirt. What did I do wrong?"

Fancy thought about his questions for a moment before answering. "I owe you an apology for being rude. I'm just angry. You knew my grandmother better than I did, and that doesn't seem fair right now."

"I'm sorry," he said softly. He thought for a moment. "Hattie was a strange little bird, but you and your mother were her only living relatives. I don't remember ever seeing you around town. Why didn't you visit more often?"

"That isn't one bit of your business. I'll see you on Sunday." She left him standing on the porch and opened the door at the same time the preacher did. It was rude again, yes, but he'd hit a very sore spot, and he'd never understand their reasons.

"Just call if you need anything or when you figure out what you are going to do," Reverend Paul said.

"Thank you," Fancy murmured, and she went back inside the house.

"What was that all about?" Tandy asked.

"That man is an insufferable . . . ," she stammered, trying to find the right word.

"Theron?" Viv asked.

"Why, he's a prince of a man. I never noticed until I saw the two of you sparring out on the porch just how cute you'd look together," Tandy said.

Kate giggled.

Sophie smiled.

Fancy rolled her eyes.

Chapter Six

Fancy told her mother and stepdad the story of the last conversation she'd had with her grandmother.

Gwen listened with her head cocked to one side.

Les watched Gwen.

"From day one, it wasn't what I did, then, was it? Nothing I could have ever done would have made it different. She just didn't want me and was too proud to give me away," Gwen said.

Fancy nodded her head.

Les reached across the table and covered Gwen's small fingers with one big bear paw of a hand. Gwen was tiny and fragile-looking with big green eyes, light brown hair, and a round face that didn't show her forty-plus years. Folks had mistaken her for Fancy's sister on more than one occasion.

Gwen nodded. "I'm a strong woman. I forgive her. But I don't want to stay here any longer than I have to. I talked to her lawyer by phone on the way from the airport. We are to sell the house and give the money to the church. I'm never coming back to Albany, Texas. It's asking a lot, but will you stay and see this through for me, Fancy?"

Fancy waited for the weeping to begin. "Momma, are you all right?" she finally asked.

"I wish I'd known this sooner. I'd have saved thousands of dollars in therapy fees trying to figure out what I did to make her dislike me so much," Gwen responded.

"Therapy?" Fancy gasped.

"My one secret from you. Les insisted on it when we were first married. Even the therapist couldn't really figure it out, just tried

63

to help me accept it better. I may call her when I get home," Gwen said.

"Ready to go to bed and get some sleep?" Les asked.

For the first time Fancy realized that Les and Gwen would have to sleep in Hattie's bedroom. She'd have to open the door to that room, and that idea scared her even worse than delivering the news about Gwen's unwanted birth. Thank goodness Les was a big man, hitting the six-foot mark and as muscular as the day he finished his military basic training. His hair was prematurely gray, giving him an authoritative appearance. His steely gray eyes said he'd tolerate no nonsense. If anyone could keep Hattie's ghost at bay or prevent her from clawing her way back from the dead, it would be Les. He would protect them from whatever lay behind that door.

"It still seems strange not to have some kind of funeral for her beauty-shop friends and the members of her church," Gwen said.

"If she didn't want any semblance of a funeral or memorial, then you two should abide by her wishes," Les said. "I'm going to take a shower and read a spell before I fall asleep. It's been a long day, and you two need some girl time to hash this out. I'm here for you, darling, remember that. Through it all, you've got my support and my heart," Les said to Gwen as he made his way to the living room, opened his suitcase, and took out a pair of knit lounging pants and a T-shirt.

"Bathroom?" he asked.

"First door on the right," Gwen said.

"Guess we'd better get it over with. The sheets won't change themselves, and it would probably be best if we go in before we turn Les loose in that room," Fancy said.

Gwen nodded. They felt like they were opening the door to forbidden territory when they carried clean sheets into Hattie's bedroom. They'd never been allowed to open the door. Gwen said she remembered the room slightly from glimpses she'd had when she was a child and her mother inadvertently left the door ajar. Still, it was odd standing inside the strange room and realizing Hattie was truly gone.

"It's eerie, isn't it?" Fancy whispered.

Les appeared right behind them. He finished towel-drying his close-cropped hair and threw the towel over his shoulder. "It's just a room. Why are you acting like you've never seen it before?" he asked Fancy.

"I haven't," Fancy said. Her eyes took in the four-poster bed and the dresser with a picture of what had to be Hattie and Orville on their wedding day. Orville had his arm around her shoulders. She wore a lacy dress, a corsage, and a smile.

Fancy and Gwen removed the chenille bedspread and sheets.

"Why not?" Les asked.

"Because we weren't allowed in here. It was Momma's room," Gwen whispered.

"What if you had a nightmare or were sick?" Les frowned.

Gwen shook her head. "I sucked up a nightmare. If I was sick, I knocked on the door, and she came out."

"Then she came to your room and slept with you?" Les asked.

"No, then she gave me medicine and told me to go back to bed," Gwen said.

"Not so many happy memories, huh?" Les asked.

"Not until Fancy Lynn was born. Then I wasn't lonely anymore," Gwen said.

"Granny was pretty scary when I was little. I was glad to have Momma's skirt-tails to hide behind and was really glad when she came home from work every day," Fancy added.

Fancy tugged the corners of the fitted sheet over the mattress edge. "So, are you going to be all right with no funeral, Momma? No closure? Just knowing that she's gone and we don't have to come back here to visit?"

"I don't know. I feel guilty because I'm not mourning. She was my mother, for heaven's sake. I should be devastated. When my friend Linda's mother died, we both cried for days. We drank gallons of coffee and wept until our eyes were swollen. Now it's my mother, and all I feel is relief. I cannot sleep in this room. It's too . . ."

"I'll get dressed, and we'll go to a motel," Les said.

"I want to go home," Gwen whispered. One minute she was in complete control; the next, she was a bag of weeping bones that would have sunk to the floor if Les hadn't held her in his big strong arms.

Les looked across the room. "Fancy?"

"I can handle it. Take her home. Catch the next red-eye out of Dallas or stay at the airport hotel. Send her back to therapy. She really does need it this time," Fancy said.

"I can't leave you in this mess all alone," Gwen sobbed.

Fancy joined them in a three-way hug. "I've got Sophie and Kate. And the beauty-shop ladies come three times a week. Then on Sunday I fight with that abominable Theron Warren. I can take care of this, Momma. Let Les take you home and take care of you. I'll be home in time for Christmas, and this will all be behind us."

"Hold her while I get dressed," Les said.

Fancy led her mother out of the bedroom and into their old room across the hallway. She patted a twin bed, and Gwen sat down.

"I'm so sorry," Gwen said.

"Don't be. I can take care of it. I had you, remember? You were a fantastic mother, even if I was mad at you for tearing me away from Chris Miller. Even then you were the smart one. Thank you again for that. I can't imagine having Hattie for a mother. Having her as a grandmother was tough enough."

Gwen nodded and shivered. "Good feelings don't live in that room."

"We'll shut the door. I'll clean it all out later," Fancy said.

Later, she thought, she'd ask her mother if she'd like to have the picture of Hattie and Orville. She led Gwen to the living room, where Les was already dressed and had the suitcases sitting beside the door.

"You sure about this, Gwen?" he asked. "No regrets later?"

"More sure than I've been in years about anything," she said. She gave Fancy a long hug and blew her a kiss as they drove away.

Alone in the house, Fancy considered giving Sophie or Kate a call, but it was well past midnight, and they'd been sweet enough to stay with her until Gwen and Les arrived. Neither of them should have to drive twenty-five miles back to Albany just because she didn't feel like being alone in the house with Hattie's ghost. But she'd give half her bank account and all of the ham in the refrigerator to have someone to talk to right then.

The gentle night breeze might have been pleasant if the temperature wasn't hovering in the high nineties. Not unusual for central Texas in late August but not conducive for sitting outside. Still, it beat sitting in the house after opening the door to Hattie's room. Fancy poured a glass of iced tea and carried it to the porch. She leaned back against a porch post and put one bare foot on the top step.

A hoot owl sounded in the distance. Crickets and tree frogs sang in spite of the sweltering heat. A tomcat howled a couple of yards down, and that set a dozen dogs to barking. A pickup slowed down but didn't stop, at least not the first time around. The second time around the block it pulled into the driveway. Fancy looked up, half expecting to see Sophie coming back to town to take care of her. But it was Theron Warren who climbed out of the truck. He wore overalls and flip-flops, a shirt with ragged armholes where he'd cut the sleeves away and not finished the seams, and his tousled hair had hay stuck in it.

"You all right?" he asked.

"What are you doing here?" she countered.

"Got the feeding done and hay in the barn. Too hot to sleep. Uncle Joe put a little air conditioner in his bedroom, so it's cool, but I felt trapped and confined with the door shut, so I went for a drive. Saw you sitting here all alone."

"Want some tea?"

"Love some. I'll get it. Don't get up."

"Ice is in the freezer. Tea is on the counter. Glasses to the right of the sink."

Seeing Sophie or Kate get out of the truck would have been better, but she wouldn't turn down anyone to talk to right then.

He brought a quart jar of iced tea back to the porch and propped his back against a post on the other side of the steps. "So when is your mother arriving?"

"Where'd you get that jar?" she asked.

"Back behind the glasses. I like them better. They hold more."

"Momma already came and left," she said.

She could feel Theron's frown even though it was barely visible in the moonlight.

"Don't judge, Mr. Warren. It'll get you in trouble every time," she said icily.

"I just asked a question," he said.

"There'll be no funeral and no memorial, so why should she stay in this place?"

"Can't answer that. You'll accuse me of judging," he said.

"You have a history of doing that, so why shouldn't I expect it of you?"

"Fancy Lynn Sawyer, I did not tell the school board a thing about that night you were in jail for a few minutes. I could not have swayed their vote if I'd tried. On the basis of your resume I recommended you for the job," he said, then took a long gulp of tea. "As far as I was concerned, it was a simple interview and contract signing. When I got to school that day, they'd already made up their minds to hire the other lady. It was bad timing, that's all. So don't put words into my mouth or attitudes into my heart that are not there. And I'd looked at so many applicants that your name, weird as it is, didn't even ring a bell when I pulled you over for drunk driving."

If he'd had it to do over again, he wouldn't have even made that second trip around the block just now. He would have kept on going and left her to her own mourning, whatever and however it was. Every time he got near the woman, sparks seemed to fly.

"Okay," she said slowly, drawing the word out to at least three syllables. "Granny was a strange bird. We chalked it up to her having a baby when she was already too set in her ways. But the last time I went to see her at Bluebonnet, just before she put the ban on me or Momma visiting her, she admitted that she didn't want my mother at birth and never had a maternal instinct toward her. Maybe it was because she was past forty and set in her ways, or maybe it was because my grandfather wouldn't let her give the child away and then died six months after Momma was born. I just don't know how she could have a baby and not love it."

"Like I said, she was strange. A good person but strange," Theron said. "Who knows what went on in her lifetime to cause such a lack of feelings for her own child? Now we'll never know."

Fancy went on to tell him about the closed bedroom door they'd opened. "And that's why I'm on the porch. I can't go back in there right now. We left her bedroom door open, and it's scary," she finished.

"I didn't think anything would scare you." Theron chuckled.

"That room does," she said.

"Didn't you ever want to go in there when you were little? Just out of curiosity?"

"You ever see those scary movies about Freddy when you were young? Or those crazy *Halloween* movies?"

He nodded.

"Those were nothing compared to what I felt was behind that door. I asked about it once when I was really young, like maybe five or six. Momma said she'd never been in that room either, so I knew it had to be horrible."

"And was it?" Theron asked.

"It's just a room, but . . ."

"How 'bout we both go into the house together, and I'll shut the door for you? Would that help?"

She sighed. "Yes, it would." She was a grown woman, so why was she so afraid to go into the house alone? Hattie was dead, on her way to the crematorium by now; her life was over, her pain gone. Fancy's feelings didn't make a bit of sense.

Theron held the door open for her, and once inside the living room, she pointed down the hall. He found two doors open. One into a room with twin beds, the other with a full-sized bed and a Hattie aura about it. He shut the door to that room and studied the other room for a moment. Fancy was a neat freak, for sure. Not one thing was out of place in her room.

"Is it done?" She raised her voice slightly.

"It is. Not a single claw came out to grab me. Not even a whisper of a cloudy presence to brush across my face," he said as he walked back up the hallway and into the living room.

"Thank you." Now that the deed was done, she felt awkward in his presence and didn't know what to do with her hands or whether to sit or stand. "More tea? Would you like to sit in the kitchen? I could turn on the air conditioner to cool the place down."

"It's late. I've got school tomorrow," he said.

"Okay."

"Are you afraid to be alone in this house?" he asked.

"No, I've lived here the better part of a month alone. I'm not afraid," she said.

"I was married once for about six months," he blurted out.

She stared at him blankly.

For a moment Theron didn't know why she looked so stunned. She'd once mentioned his being short; did she think short men were destined to be bachelors forever? Then he realized how crazy his comment had sounded. It was totally out of context and had nothing to do with Hattie Sawyer's passing or her house.

"It lasted six months, and she left me because I wasn't as rich as she thought I was." It was as if his mouth and his brain were disconnected. He kept saying things that were none of Fancy's business.

She blinked fast. Surely she was hearing wrong. Why would he make those two comments out of the hot summer night?

"I guess I'm sharing this with you because of what you told me about Hattie's not loving your mother. No one in town really even knows about my ex-wife, Maria." Every sentence made the atmosphere even more awkward.

"I see," she mumbled.

"There were no children—she wasn't around long enough, luckily. I'm going to be a bachelor from now on—until my dying day. And now I'm going home before I say anything else that I have no intention of sharing or that you are interested in hearing."

"Good night, then. And thank you for shutting the door," Fancy said.

"I'll see you in church on Sunday, then?" he said.

"Yes, you will, and I'm not going to the nursery either," she countered.

"You're testing my patience," he said.

"Maybe so, but you're testing mine just as badly."

He left, and she went straight to the bathroom, where she stood under a cool shower for a long time. She turned on the air-conditioning unit in the window of the bedroom and stretched out on her bed. Numbness set in a few minutes before her cell phone rang. The digital clock she'd brought with her from Florida said it was 1:59.

"Hello, Momma. Are you at the airport?" she asked.

"Yes, we are. There's not a flight until morning, so we got a room. Are you all right? I shouldn't have left you in that house alone. Did you call Sophie or Kate?" Gwen sounded breathless and miserable.

"No, but the guy who teaches Sunday school with me was out driving around and stopped by for a glass of tea. He shut Granny's door for me," Fancy said.

"Marry that man. If he's brave enough to do that, he can protect you forever," Gwen said.

"He's a self-avowed bachelor now until his dying breath." Fancy giggled. It was good to hear her mother's voice.

"Then you're okay?" Gwen asked.

"I'm fine. Please tell me you are too," Fancy said.

"I'm horrible, but I'll be fine once this all settles," Gwen said.

"Momma, why would a man blurt out of thin air that he'd been married for six months and that he would never marry again? Theron Warren, the man I told you about, the one who teaches Sunday school with me, did that tonight."

"That the same man who tried to arrest you for drunk driving? The same one who wants you out of his Sunday school class? The same one who didn't hire you at the school?" Gwen asked.

"The very one."

"He's drawn to you, girl."

"Theron? I don't think so. It was just so strange. Maybe some strange, eerie thing happened when he looked into Granny's room and made him say things he had no intention of saying out loud," Fancy said.

"Looking in there did the same thing to you, didn't it?"

"I'll have Tandy clean out that room," Fancy mused aloud.

"Or burn the house to the ground. She wanted to be cremated. We could do the same with the house."

"But then where would the ladies go for hair-fixin' days? I reckon we'd better sell it to a beauty operator they all like."

"Good luck. Go to sleep. Isn't tomorrow a workday?"

Fancy groaned. She'd forgotten that the ladies would arrive midmorning.

"Thank you, Fancy," Gwen said.

"I love you, Momma."

Fancy shut her eyes but was wide awake at six o'clock. She turned off the air conditioner in the bedroom and turned on the one in the living room. She put on a pot of coffee and poured a cup before it was finished dripping and carried it to the front porch. Was it truly just twenty-four hours ago that she and the girls were in Abilene shopping?

She wore a pair of red boxer shorts with white hearts on them that Gwen had given her the previous Valentine's Day and a purple nightshirt with a big yellow smiley face on the front. Her hair hung in sweaty strands around a face that didn't have a drop of makeup applied to it.

It was going to be another hot day. Already the thermometer on the porch read eighty-five degrees, and the sun was barely over the horizon. She made a mental note to go directly to the beauty shop and get the air conditioner going so the ladies wouldn't swelter.

She turned when she heard the crunch of tires on gravel. Theron got out of his truck looking totally different than he had the night before. He wore dark, western-cut dress slacks, a pale green shirt, and a black and green paisley tie. His hair was combed back perfectly and didn't have a bit of hay stuck in it.

"Good morning. I was on my way to school. You got another cup of that?" He scanned her from toe to heart-covered boxers, up across the smiley face, to the face with no makeup and the hair that looked like she'd combed it with a hay rake. There was certainly nothing there to appeal to any man, so why was his heart tossing in an extra beat and his mouth dry?

"In the pot. Help yourself," she said.

"I hoped you'd be up and out here," he said when he returned.

"And why is that?"

"I didn't like the way we left things last night. I felt pretty silly saying what I did."

"Well, I wasn't about to propose to you," she said.

Theron actually blushed scarlet. "I didn't think you were."

"It was just the moment. Everything was a little weird last night. Forget it. I won't tell," she said.

"Then we're back to normal?"

"As in, you are obnoxious and unbearable?"

He smiled. "As in, you've evidently been lookin' in the mirror and describing the person you see there rather than me."

"You going to give me that Sunday school class?"

"You going to go to the nursery?"

"I'm not budging," she said.

"Then I guess we're back to normal. Thanks for the coffee. Mind if I leave the cup on the porch?"

"Suit yourself."

He set the empty mug on the porch and left without saying another word.

Fancy almost felt like she'd won an argument but had to admit that it was more like a tie. She went inside and turned on the air conditioner in the shop, ate cold chicken casserole out of the pan for breakfast, and took a long, warm shower. The whole time she wondered what Maria Warren—if that was still her name—looked like. Was she Latina? Or maybe Italian? Could she cook? Was she tall and beautiful?

"I don't care," she declared as she wrapped a towel around her body and stepped out into the hallway.

Fight-or-flight mode took effect immediately when she saw a shadow cross the hallway opening into the living room. If Theron had come back again and waltzed right into the house like he owned it, she intended to give him a royal piece of her mind. She did a tiptoe dance to her bedroom, threw off the towel, and left it lying on the floor. She dug through her suitcase for underwear, a pair of cutoff jean shorts, and a tank top and dressed hurriedly.

When she stomped into the kitchen, she found Kate sitting at the table eating some of the same chicken casserole she'd had right out of the pan. "Well, good mornin', sunshine. I heard the shower going, so I let myself in. This is pretty good even cold."

"Thank God it's you. I had a speech prepared if it'd been Theron eating my casserole," Fancy said.

"Why would he be here?" Kate didn't wait for an answer. She wrinkled her nose and said, "Go dry your hair. It looks horrible."

"I'm going to braid it today, so it doesn't matter. I'm fixing the ladies' hair, remember? This is Wednesday."

"But Hattie died. Aren't you going to wear black and sackloth and ashes for at least a day?"

"Hattie made the rules. No funeral. No memorial. Get on with life. That's what I'm going to do."

"You tell your momma that?" Kate asked.

"I did. We went into Granny's room, and it freaked her out. She said she couldn't stay here," Fancy said, and she went on to give Kate a play-by-play of the whole night's events up to and including Theron's visit both the night before and that morning.

Kate laughed. "That man must have a thing for you, Fancy Lynn."

Odd, her momma had said much the same thing just the night before. "You remember what I said about a Greek god who promises me a forever thing?" Fancy said.

"Well, as Sophie said, the name *Theron* could be Greek, and he could give you a forever thing."

"I don't think so. Didn't you hear the part about his being a bachelor until his dying breath?"

"Methinks the man doth protest too much," Kate paraphrased. "So the ladies are coming around for hair-fixin' this mornin'? That must mean it's all right for you to go to the party on Friday, where I'm going to meet my knight in shining whatever from Australia. You won't be in mourning, will you?"

"I wouldn't miss the party for the world. Who knows? Your knight in shining whatever from Australia could have a friend with a forever thing in his pocket," Fancy said.

Chapter Seven

Fancy arrived at the party on Friday night in her hip-slung tight-fitting jeans, boots, and the white sleeveless shirt with pearl snaps. It should have been the day she attended her grandmother's funeral, not gone to a barn-dance party. But she'd had to ask the preacher's forgiveness and say that she and her mother were following Hattie's wishes: no funeral.

Everything in her steady world had turned topsy-turvy since she left Florida. She'd figured she would be going to Texas for a year of boring life with a barbed-tongued grandmother. Life in Albany had been anything but. Fancy stopped inside the big barn doors and looked around. A bar was set up in one corner. Waiters in black slacks and white shirts were everywhere at once. The buffet table was laden with barbecued ribs, chicken, brisket, and pork loin, along with potato salad, baked beans, chips and salsa, corn bread, hot rolls, and desserts of every kind imaginable, including turtle cheesecake.

Sophie crossed the barn floor and looped her arm through Fancy Lynn's. "You're here! Kate and I were worried you'd chicken out."

"I almost did," Fancy said honestly.

"It's all right for you to have a good time. Hattie didn't want any mourners."

"What do I do with the ashes?" Fancy asked as she let Sophie lead her across the barn to the table where Kate waited.

"We'll think of something later, but tonight you are here to have a good time, not fret about things you had no control over."

"Is that the voice of experience I'm hearing?"

Sophie nodded. "It truly is. Now, come and meet Kate's Aussie, whose armor isn't shiny enough to keep her attention."

Fancy giggled under her breath. "Only Hart Ducaine will ever do that."

"We know that, but she has to figure it out on her own."

Sophie introduced her to Edward Sussex, a tall, dark-haired man with twinkling blue eyes. A waiter asked if he could get anything special for Fancy, and she shook her head.

"So I hear you're the one who came from Florida," Edward said with his clipped accent. "Sophie hails from Arkansas, and Kate here with the deep-South accent from Louisiana. How did you girls ever get to be friends?"

"We went to high school together; then we were scattered to the three corners of the world, or so it seemed at the time, but we've kept in touch," Fancy said.

"I see. Well, oh, my, there's Maud. I must see her about that bull I bought. Will you girls excuse me?"

"You're letting your Aussie leave without a fight?" Fancy asked Kate.

"I am. No chemistry. If I close my eyes, his accent is nice, but it doesn't give me the chills I thought it would."

"I think it's because Edward didn't offer to kiss her feet or go all goggle-eyed over her black hair and her long legs," Sophie whispered.

Kate replenished her pint jar from the pitcher of beer. "Stop it. I'm not that vain. I just want someone who can't see anything but me. At least at first. After twenty years or so he can let his eyes wander."

"If you say so. Are y'all ready to hit the buffet? Dancing starts in thirty minutes," Sophie said.

"Yes, *chere*. And I'm not sitting out a single dance. Could be my knight will arrive and sweep me off my feet yet," Kate said.

"I'm starving. I haven't eaten anything but a slice of pizza all day. The ladies brought a pie and two desserts to the shop. It was their personal memorial for Hattie in the shop they'd all loved so much. They each said a few words about her," Fancy said.

"What did they say?" Sophie led the way to the buffet table.

"Leander said that Hattie was a good listener. Viv said she knew how to tease up hair really well and that it was hard to find a hairdresser these days who still knew how to make a hairdo that didn't lie flat on top of the head. Things like that."

"Strange eulogy, wasn't it?" Sophie said.

"*Hattie* was strange. She wasn't your normal, bake-the-cookies grandmother, was she?" Kate picked up a plain white platter and commenced filling it with food.

"It's still all so surreal," Fancy said.

Sophie's Aunt Maud joined them in line for food. "Hello, girls. I'm glad you could come to the party."

"Thanks for having us. We didn't buy a bull or even come to the sale," Fancy said.

"You're the window dressing." Maud laughed. She was a tall, thin woman with chin-length gray hair she wore straight and parted in the middle. That evening she wore jeans and an electric-blue satin western-cut shirt with bright red pearl snaps. Her red boots were round-toed, and her earrings were carat-sized rubies.

"Like in the old Las Vegas days when they hired showgirls to dress up a party? I always wanted to be a showgirl in feathers and those big old headdresses," Kate said.

Maud smiled. "Something like that. I'm sorry to hear about your grandmother, Fancy Lynn. But I stand by the idea that we old people should finish up the way we want, not the way society says we should. So if Hattie didn't want people crying over her dead body, then they shouldn't do it. Have some of that chicken, Fancy. It's absolutely scrumptious. The caterer is out of Abilene, and they use mesquite for their smoking process."

"I'm glad they can use it for something. It's a nuisance, isn't it?" Fancy said.

"Keeps me young. I'll go to my grave fighting mesquite out of my pastures," Maud said. "How'd you like the Aussie, Kate?"

"Like his accent. The man doesn't appeal to me."

"Still honest as the day is long," Maud said.

"Don't know any other way to be."

"Don't ever change." Maud finished loading her plate and carried it to a table where a dozen people were discussing raising longhorn cattle.

"She looks fine tonight," Fancy said as they carried their food back to their table in a corner of the barn.

"That's her barn-dance-slash-party outfit. She wears it to

everything other than church. For that she's got about five nice suits she alternates on Sunday, Sunday night, and Wednesday-night Bible study. She says God doesn't care what she wears so long as she's got all the body parts covered up. The rest of her closet is filled with jeans and work shirts. She hasn't changed much in twenty years," Sophie said.

"But you have?" Kate picked up a chicken leg and rolled her eyes in appreciation when she bit into it.

"Yes, I have. Aunt Maud and I make pretty good business partners now."

They'd barely finished their dinner when the band struck up the first chords for the dance. There were two guitar players, a fiddler, a drummer, and a mandolin player in addition to a woman lead singer who went into an old Anne Murray song, "Could I Have This Dance." It was a slow waltz that talked about always remembering the song that was playing the first time they danced and swayed to the music, holding each other, when they had fallen in love.

Theron Warren appeared out of the clear, warm night air and tapped Fancy on the shoulder. "May I have this dance?"

She was so stunned, she simply nodded and stood up. He wrapped one arm around her waist and executed a fine two-step around the dance floor.

"You're pretty good at this," she said.

"My daddy said a good rancher has to be able to dance. I hated it, but my sister and I were taught to dance just like we were taught to take care of cattle," Theron said.

The singer finished and went right into a slow George Strait tune. Theron wrapped his arms back around her and waltzed her into the middle of the floor. She fit so well in his arms that he could have danced the whole night with her.

Fancy laid her head against his chest and was amazed at the chemistry between them. Now, wasn't that horrid luck? To be drawn to a man who had sworn off marriage for all eternity. One who'd certainly never have a forever thing to offer.

The singer finished and went into a more modern mode, with songs from Shania Twain, Sara Evans, Taylor Swift, and Sugarland mixed in among Patsy Cline, Loretta Lynn, and Dolly Parton. Surprising enough, the young people danced to the old tunes as much as the newer songs.

Fancy danced with the Aussie twice, then again with Theron and a few older men. She couldn't remember all their names. She was sitting out a dance when Theron pulled up a chair beside her.

"What are you doing here anyway?" she asked.

"I might ask you the same thing. I bought a bull at the sale last night. What did you buy?"

"Nothing. I'm a showgirl," she said.

His face registered confusion.

"In old-time Las Vegas when there was a party, the host hired showgirls to keep the party lively. Window dressing is what Maud called it. You shouldn't be surprised. The first time you saw me, I was a drunk driver, remember?"

"Are you picking a fight?"

"If I am, I'll win, you can be sure," she said.

"Why?"

"Because I won't quit until I wear you down, and then I'll win," she said.

"No, why would Maud hire you for window dressing?"

"You don't think my friends and I are good-looking enough to be showgirls?" she asked right back.

"What'd she pay you? I might be interested in hiring you for my barn dance next year," he said.

"It'll cost you all the 'squite-smoked chicken I can eat and all the leather I can dance off your buyers' shoes."

"You work cheap, then."

Fancy struck a pose by batting her eyes and pursing her lips. "That's me. Fast. Cheap. Easy."

He waggled his eyebrows. "Really?"

She slapped his arm, amazed anew at the sparks that flew when her hand touched him. "No, not really. So don't be getting foolish notions."

"Not me. I'm just a bull buyer who's here for a good time. No foolish notions in my head. Tell me, what happens to the showgirls when the party is over?"

"They go home and read the Bible," she smarted off.

"Sure, they do," he said. "Save me the last dance. I want to ask Maud something, and I see she's sitting over there alone."

Kate slid down in the chair he left behind. "Whew! My feet are aching."

"Do you have to work a shift tomorrow at the café?"

"No, I've got to fill in for a sick officer tomorrow. That'll give me time to recoup before I work the lunch rush on Sunday."

"You find anyone interesting in the whole bunch of them?" Fancy asked.

"There ain't no one out there to make my heart do double-time. How about you? Theron Warren's been dancing with you a lot. You about to change your mind about him?"

"No!"

"That came out way too quick," Kate said.

"Listen when I talk. I told you about his wanting to be a bachelor forever, amen, right?"

"I wonder why he's so set against marriage?"

"Why are *you*?" Fancy countered.

"Two words. Hart Ducaine. May the devil put him on a barbwire fence on the back forty in Hades forever," Kate said.

Fancy fanned her face with one hand. "Remind me to never make you mad."

Kate poured a glass of cold beer and took a long gulp. "Y'all look cute together out there on the dance floor. You're about the right height, and you dance like you were made for each other."

"Dancing is the only thing we do well together, unless you count all the arguing. We do that really well."

"Maybe you're fighting against your hearts," Kate said.

"And maybe you've got cow chips for brains. Go dance away such crazy ideas. I'm not fighting anything. Besides, Momma says she's never stepping foot back in Shackelford County, Texas, again. How would I see her if I stayed in this gosh-forsaken part of the world?"

Sophie joined them. "What are y'all gosh-forsakin'?"

"We were gosh-forsakin' this part of Texas," Kate replied.

"And why is *that*?"

"First you tell me what you thought of Fancy and Theron out there on the dance floor."

"They look like they could be on that *Dancing with the Stars* thing on television. Smooth as silk."

"That's what I think too. Any two people who can dance like that should put their arguing aside and kiss a few times to see if that don't feel better," Kate said.

Fancy blushed so brightly, it lit up the area.

"See? She's been thinking about it, or she wouldn't look like she's sunburned."

"Stop it," Fancy whispered. "He's liable to hear you and think I'm interested. And I'm *not*."

"Why not?" Sophie said.

"Yeah, why aren't you?" Kate asked.

"Why should I be? He's already said he's never getting married, and he's content with his life's status quo. It would be a big waste of time. I'll just be a showgirl tonight," she said, trying to make light of the situation.

"And what does the showgirl do when she goes home?" Sophie asked.

"She takes a cold shower." Kate laughed.

Theron walked up behind her and chuckled. "According to this showgirl, she goes home and reads her Bible. I believe this is the last dance, and you promised it to me."

"I did not. You told me to save it for you. How do you know I didn't already promise it to someone else?" Fancy argued.

He held out his hand, and she took it. Kate was right. The sparks were dancing around like water droplets on a hot cast-iron skillet. But she chalked it up to the moment's festivities. She was wearing tight jeans and a fancy shirt, had her hair curled and her makeup on. He looked downright handsome in his starched green plaid shirt, Wranglers, and dress boots.

"Did you?" he asked as he led her out to the floor.

"What?"

"Promise this dance to another man?"

She shook her head.

"Good. Dancing with you is like floating on air."

"Thank you, I guess."

The slow dance ended way too soon, and Theron returned her to her friends with a simple "Good night, Fancy Lynn."

She and Kate both made a trip across the barn to thank Maud for a lovely evening, hugged Sophie, and headed for their vehicles, which were parked in an adjoining pasture.

"Your knight's not walking you to your car?" Fancy teased.

Kate looked down at her. "The Aussie? He wants some little follow-behind-me woman with no backbone. When I told him I was a cop, he stuttered and stammered around like a drunk facing a Breathalyzer test. Besides, you made a bigger splash with Theron than I did the Aussie. Why isn't *he* walking *you* to *your* car?"

"He doesn't have a forever thing in his pocket—or anywhere else—to offer," Fancy teased.

Kate looked at her and sighed. "See you later. We still on for Sunday afternoon, even though we had tonight?"

"Of course we're on for Sunday. We've got to gossip about tonight, don't we?" Fancy opened her car door and climbed inside. The smell of almonds still permeated the heated car's air, making her remember her first glimpse of Theron Warren's mossy green eyes.

"Don't get caught speeding, or we'll have to bail you out of jail," Kate said with a wave.

"I'll be careful," Fancy told her.

Kate laughed and drove away.

Fancy drove north into Albany from Baird and was passing the Hereford Inn when she noticed a pickup truck behind her.

She passed the courthouse before she realized the pickup was still following her. She sped up, and the truck behind her did the same. She turned the corner to Hattie's house on two wheels and slung gravel for half a block, stopping only in the driveway. She grabbed her purse and was halfway to the porch when Theron called out from the open window of his truck.

"Hey, are you in a big hurry to get to that Bible?" He climbed out of the truck and meandered to the porch. "What's the matter?" he asked when he could see that her face was ashen and her eyes wide as saucers. "What's wrong, Fancy?"

"You scared me, tailing me like that."

"I'm sorry. I didn't mean to. I didn't even mean to come home this way, but I pulled out behind you and got to thinkin' about one thing and another and didn't make my turn to the ranch."

She slid down the porch post until she was sitting with her knees drawn up under her chin. In spite of the hot night breeze, chills caused goose bumps on her arms.

"Go on inside, and I'll backtrack and go home. I know that the showgirl needs to read before she goes to sleep," Theron said gently.

"Don't tease me. I was really frightened."

"It's Albany, Fancy Lynn. You're safer here than you were in the big city."

"Sure, I am. You dragged me to jail when I'd been here less than twenty-four hours," she reminded him.

"Funny, tonight you don't look sixteen," he said with a gleam in his eye. "You look all grown-up."

"Scare me and then ruin my ego," she told him grumpily.

He stepped up onto the porch. "I intended neither of those things. I'll wait until you get inside and the lights are on."

She stood up, turned too quickly, and stumbled. He caught her before she wiped completely out and wrapped his arms tightly around her, pulling her close to his chest. He tucked one fist under her chin and leaned down. She rolled up on her toes and met him halfway. When their lips met, more than sparks danced. Her heart beat in unison with his, and she wanted the kiss to go on and on.

But he broke away, took a step to one side, and opened the screen door for her.

"Good night, Fancy. Thanks for the dances and the good time tonight. I'm going home now."

"Old men can't endure the late hours, can they?" she teased to cover up the fact that she really wanted him to kiss her again.

"Old women need their beauty sleep," he shot back. That kiss was a one-time thing that wouldn't happen again. It had stirred entirely too many emotions down deep in his heart.

"Okay, we'll leave it at that. Good night, Theron. See you Sunday morning."

* * *

Theron had actually planned to take Highway 576 across to Moran and then drive north to his ranch, which was located five miles south of Albany. But he'd been thinking about how much he'd enjoyed dancing and arguing with Fancy and missed the turnoff.

He wondered what his family would think of Fancy Sawyer. His grandma would have loved her, but she'd been gone for a long time. His grandparents had lived on a ranch in Decatur until they died within six months of each other two years ago. His dad inherited the place, then leased the land and the house. But the cabin set at the back of the property remained their hunting lodge. It was where he had taken Maria for their honeymoon, a nice quiet little log cabin sitting on the edge of the Trilogy River.

He parked the truck in front of the two-story house that his Uncle Joe had built years before, and half a dozen cats came off the porch to greet him.

"If you don't trip me and make me fall and break my neck, I'll bring a bowl of milk out to you," he told them.

He made good on his promise and sat on the porch for thirty minutes, petting first one and then another. If Fancy changed her mind and stayed in Albany, he'd give her first pick of the next litter of kittens. Or she could have two or three if she wanted.

But she wasn't going to stay around any longer than it took to straighten up Hattie's estate. Suddenly, he found himself hoping that the house wouldn't sell the first few weeks it was on the market. Maybe if she didn't leave, he could offer her a job the next fall. Mrs. Lowerly was retiring at the end of the year. She taught kindergarten, and Fancy already knew some of the children who would be enrolling in kindergarten from their Sunday school class.

Fancy tossed her sweaty shirt and jeans into the dirty-clothes basket and took a quick shower. She wrapped a towel around her head and another around her body and padded barefoot back to her room. The door across the hallway remained shut, and she went so far as to put her hand on the knob but couldn't open it. Kate and Sophie would have to help, because she could not do it alone. She was so grateful to have good friends.

When she was dressed in a nightshirt, she went to the kitchen for a snack. She found grapes and cheese in the refrigerator and put them on a paper plate. She sat down at the kitchen table, then stood up and carried the food to the living room. It was her house now, at least until it sold, so she'd eat in the living room if she wanted. She felt a little guilty, but she sat on the sofa and ate her snack by the light of the moon filtering in through the lace curtains. That kiss had knocked her socks plumb off her feet, but she'd learned that physical attraction didn't bring about lasting relationships. Look at how her relationship with Chris had turned out.

Fancy went back to the kitchen, tossed her empty plate into the trash can, and went to bed. She laced her fingers behind her head and, to take her mind off Theron, thought about the last night she had spent on her beloved Florida beach. The ocean had been tempest-tossed that evening. The salt spray from the turbulent winds had plastered her loose-fitting cover-up to her skin as she walked bare-foot through the sand.

Gulls with their white underbellies flew in a V as they tried to ride out the fierce wind. She felt like she was going backward as she battled against the wind that bent the sea oats and saw grass as well as the palm trees. The gods of the ocean were angry with her for leaving and telling her that she had no business forsaking them and going back to nothing but mesquite trees, heat, and mosquitoes.

An old couple, tired of walking against the head wind, sat down on the beach, laughing and talking about the huge waves. A couple of newlyweds sat not far from them. Their eyes were only for each other, and the man picked up the woman's ring finger and kissed it.

Past and future had been right there before her, and she hadn't fit with either. Her perfect world was changing, and if the weather was an omen, it wasn't a good one.

She looked at the clock. Three in the morning; thank goodness it was Saturday. No beauty-shop duties. No Sunday school to teach. She could sleep until she awoke. She finally slept, only to dream of Theron walking toward her on the white sugar sands of the Florida beach. His hand was outstretched, but the wind kept pushing her backward, closer and closer to an angry ocean.

Chapter Eight

Kate parked behind Sophie's truck and shivered when she got out of the cab. The first norther of the year hit early that morning, plunging temperatures from the eighties down to fifty-five in less than two hours. Fall had arrived, and the chilly wind whipped a long dark braid across her eyes.

"Y'all in the kitchen?" she yelled from the front door.

"No, we're in the hall," Fancy hollered back. "Get a cup of hot chocolate from the pan on the stove, and come on back here."

Kate found a mug, dropped a handful of miniature marshmallows into it, and poured in steaming hot chocolate. She carried it gently down the hall, blowing on the floating marshmallows the whole way. "So y'all waited on the boogeyman before you opened the door?"

"That depends. You the boogeyman?" Sophie asked.

Kate eased down to keep from spilling the hot liquid. "In the flesh. We going to have prayers or a séance or something before we blast in the door? Oh, rats, I forgot my ghost-buster apparatus. It's too early for cold weather in Texas."

"Global warming," Sophie said.

"Tell me about your week before we start this job," Fancy said.

"Procrastinating?" Kate asked.

"You bet I am."

Kate sipped the chocolate. "Okay, this week I had three nights of work at the police station. They asked me if I wanted to apply for the dispatcher's full-time job, but I turned it down. I can make more working as a waitress than that, and I want to be a policeman, not a dispatcher. Skip Anderson came into the café and flirted with me."

"Skip hasn't grown up, has he?"

"Not a day since high school. Still pretty and still has gorgeous blue eyes, but, darlin', one-was-a-borderline-fool ain't *that* big of a fool," Kate said.

Fancy frowned as she attempted to figure out what Kate meant. "Oh," she said after a few seconds.

"Remember, you're the one-was-pretty, Sophie is the one-was-smart, and I'm the other one," Kate reminded her.

"I'd almost forgotten that conversation," Fancy said.

"It's because you're stressing over opening Hattie's door and emptying out her room," Sophie said.

Kate set her cup down and quickly slung the door open. "Breckenridge police," she announced. "Open the door, or we'll break it down!"

Sophie and Fancy hopped to their feet, leaving their mugs on the floor.

Sophie peeked into the room. It didn't look as formidable as she'd figured it would. "You didn't even count to three before you opened the door, Kate."

Fancy peeped around Sophie's side. Nothing popped out of the room. Not an evil spirit. Not a wicked laugh. Not even a faint apparition with short gray hair and lifeless eyes. A cold breeze did flow out into the hallway, but that was because the room had been closed off from the heat.

"You going to open the closet, or am I?" Kate asked.

"Go ahead," Fancy said.

Sophie threw her arm around Fancy's shoulders. "This room really does terrify you, doesn't it?"

"Granny disappeared into this place every night after supper. Momma and I watched television in the living room, did homework, or played games at the kitchen table."

"What about the nights when your momma went out? She was a young woman. Surely she dated, no? Although, come to think of it, I don't remember her ever not being here when we came over to hang out," Sophie said.

"Momma never dated. Granny kept me in the beauty shop when Momma went to work at the bank, but when she got home, I was her responsibility." Fancy shivered.

Kate opened the closet door and threw hangers full of clothing onto the bed. "Box 'em up. I'll put them in the truck and take them to the church clothing bank over in Breckenridge. There's needy folk who'll be glad to have them."

Sophie removed shirts, skirts, slacks, and dresses from hangers and folded them into boxes that Fancy brought from her room across the hallway. She tied hangers together a dozen at a time with twine and put them into another box.

"Sit on that side of the bed, Fancy. There are things up here on the shelf you have to go through," Kate said.

"Just throw it all away."

"No, ma'am. There could be money or insurance papers or deeds up there," Sophie said.

Fancy sat cross-legged in the middle of the bed with boxes at her feet and clothing all around her. "Bring it on then, Dr. Psychiatrist Miller."

"That's a woman talking, rather than a scared little girl," Sophie said with satisfaction.

Fancy opened the first box as Kate sat before her. "No philosophizing. Let's just get the whole thing over with."

The box held pictures. Neatly organized in manila envelopes and labeled. Gwen's school photos. Fancy's school photos. Hattie's family. Orville's family. Fancy started with Hattie's family. She'd never even known her grandmother had family. Somehow in her mind Hattie had been born an old woman with gray hair who lived to fix hair. There was a baby picture of Hattie sitting on her mother's knee with her father standing proudly behind them. Then there was one of Hattie when she was probably about eight with her mother, who looked very sad. That would have been after her sister, Gwen, had died. The next one in the stack showed Hattie with other children. Fancy turned the picture over to see *Hattie, 12; Audra, 5; Mary, 7; Robert, 3; Milford, 2* on the back.

"Momma needs to see these," Fancy said. "I wonder what happened to all of them."

Kate set a shoebox on the bed. "You might find out in this box. It's marked LETTERS."

Fancy opened it to find yellowed envelopes. It didn't take long to discover that Milford had died in World War II and Robert in the Korean War. Their parents were gone long before that, and her two sisters died during the polio epidemic, leaving Hattie the sole survivor in the family.

Her phone rang, and she dug it out of her hip pocket. "Hello, Momma. We're knee-deep in Granny's room. Kate and Sophie are here with me. They're packing everything into boxes and toting them to Kate's truck. Is there anything you want? I found pictures. Your school pictures. Mine. I always wondered what she did with the ones we gave her. She kept them in a box on the shelf in her closet. The only picture out to see is the one of her and Grandfather on the chest of drawers."

"I'd like to have any pictures," Gwen said. "I have so few. Hattie never took any, so I have very few photos of the time before I started dating your father. There's one of me and him that I've saved for you, and, other than that, all the others were taken after you were born. Once I went to work at the bank, I bought a simple little camera, so there's more after you were two years old, but not many from before that."

"Okay, I'll box them all up and bring them to you. Anything else you want?"

"Just for you to get that place sold and come home. I miss you. I figured it would take a few weeks, but you've been there forever. If the place hasn't sold by Christmas, burn it down and come home," Gwen said.

"Will do." Fancy giggled, said good-bye. and hung up.

"That was a nice sound," Sophie said.

Fancy looked up quizzically.

"A giggle," Kate said.

"She said if this place hasn't sold by Christmas, I'm to burn it down and come home."

"I can see her point, but I'm hoping it doesn't ever sell. I don't want you to leave," Sophie said. "These Sunday afternoon sessions are the best therapy for me."

"You can both come with me. You'd love the beach. You can buy a big fancy house right on the oceanfront, Sophie. Kate, you can be a detective for the Panama City Beach police department. We might all even live together in Sophie's house," Fancy said.

"Remember what your momma said that summer when we were twelve and spent every waking minute together? We'd started bickering, and she sent me and Sophie home. Said we always got into some kind of trouble when we were together, so we couldn't play together for a whole week," Kate said.

Fancy put pictures into a shoebox to take to her mother. "We're grown now. We could do it."

"Aunt Maud has brain cancer that's inoperable. She's got a year at the most without treatment. Two, with it. She's decided she doesn't want to spend her last months sick as a mule—those are her words—so we're looking at a year," Sophie blurted out.

"Oh, honey, I'm so sorry." Fancy popped up onto her knees and scrambled across the bed to give Sophie a hug.

"Me too. You've got to stay to see me through it, Fancy," Sophie said, tearing up.

"A year?" Fancy said.

"If she makes it that long. If this house sells, you can move in with us on the ranch. I'm calling in your debt. You said you'd owe me for helping clean out this room," Sophie said.

"Are you serious?" Kate asked.

"It's a lot to ask, but I'd ask it of you if you were talking about going back to New Iberia," Sophie said.

"Can I go home for Christmas?" Fancy asked.

Sophie nodded. "But you have to promise you'll come back. I can't get through this without you two. The thing with Matt was too difficult all alone. Aunt Maud pulled me up out of the mire and set me on solid ground. I'll need you both to do the same thing when she's gone."

"Then we'll do it." Kate picked up a final box of clothing and carried it to the truck.

"Thank you," Sophie whispered. "I know it's asking a lot, but you don't have a job and . . ."

"I'll stay. It's a small price to pay for what you're doing for me today. And what you've been doing. Besides, this old house isn't going anywhere for a long time, from the look of the economy. I'll tell Momma we might have to give it a year. If it doesn't sell by then, we'll invite everyone we know and have a marshmallow roast when we burn it down."

Kate returned and took a long look around the room. "Y'all ready to load all the rest of this stuff into Sophie's truck?"

"Sure. We're tough and mean as your Louisiana gators, *chere,*" Fancy said with a laugh.

"And don't you forget it, ever," Kate said.

The storage unit Fancy had secured was a mile from the house, and they stacked the bedroom furniture against its back wall. Fancy would add to the pile later as she cleaned out other rooms in the house. After that, she could decide what to give away or sell. Maybe she'd open the big garage door and have a sale right there.

"Let's go eat banana splits at the Dairy Queen. My treat," Fancy said when they finished the job.

"Sounds good to me," Sophie said.

"I want one of those Peanut Buster Parfaits instead," Kate said.

"Sophie makes me promise to stay in Albany for a whole year, and all you want is ice cream?" Fancy said.

"That's just for today. I'm saving my big payback until some midnight when you're snuggled up to Theron after you marry him. Then I'll demand that you come help me out of some dire situation." Kate grinned.

"Then I don't ever have to worry about it. Theron and I are barely friends. We tolerate each other for Sunday school, but mostly we end up arguing. This morning we 'bout set the room on fire with our 'big-people discussion.'" Fancy hadn't told them about his sizzling kiss that night on her porch. If she did, they'd throw a veil onto her head, zip her into a white dress, and push her down the church aisle.

They all had their treats and left the Dairy Queen to go in different directions. Somehow Fancy wasn't even all that surprised when she saw a pickup truck tailing her again or when it pulled into her driveway right behind her.

"What are you doing in town at this time of night?" she asked when Theron got out of the truck.

"I just finished up some paperwork at the school and was on my way home when I saw your car. Hungry? Want to get a burger?"

She shook her head. "Just had a banana split with Sophie and Kate."

He looked . . . disappointed? Not possible, Fancy thought.

"I figured," he said. "Their trucks are here every Sunday afternoon."

Her blue eyes narrowed into slits. "Are you stalking me, Theron Warren?"

"Don't flatter yourself. I have to drive past your place on the way home from church."

She fought back the heat rising from her neck. "Anyway, Sophie and Kate came over, and we cleaned out Granny's bedroom. Amazingly, she'd kept lots of pictures, including some of my momma and me."

He looked thoughtful for a moment. "Hattie is a good example of the fact that we never really know anyone. That's another reason I'm never getting married again." He seemed to straighten his shoulders, as if waging some internal battle.

Fancy shrugged it off. "Well, Mr. Eternal Bachelor, want to come in for a pot of coffee?"

Again he looked thoughtful, then nodded. "Okay. It's starting to freeze out here. Strange weather for Texas at this time of year. Are you flying home for the Thanksgiving holiday?"

She nodded as she opened the door. "After the ladies get their hairdos on Wednesday, I'll fly out of Dallas that afternoon."

He shut the door behind him, removed his coat, and tossed it over the back of the sofa. "Be back for church on Sunday?"

"Oh, honey, I'd be afraid to miss church. You'd be declaring me dead and claiming the Sunday school class, possession being ninety percent of the law."

He sat down at the kitchen table and watched her make coffee, his gaze lingering on her lips. It wouldn't be right to kiss her again, he told himself. She'd think there was something there, and he couldn't offer Fancy Lynn Sawyer anything. Besides, she was going back to Florida as soon as Hattie's house sold, and he had a ranch in Texas.

She leaned against the cabinet while the coffee dripped. "I don't remember this kind of cold in November. I remember playing outside without a coat on Thanksgiving."

He nodded. "It's strange, all right. Maybe the storm they're predicting will bypass us, and we'll just get the edge. Weatherman said there's ice in this one and maybe snow in the one to come in the next couple of days. It might shut down the schools."

"I hated it when we had to shut down for hurricanes. It always threw my schedule off and made the kids even wilder when they came back to the classroom."

"Know just what you mean," Theron said.

She poured coffee into two cups and set them on the table, then sat down across from him. The phone rang, and she hurried to the living room to dig it out of her pocket. It was Sophie saying that she and Aunt Maud were planning a big Thanksgiving dinner, and if the weather kept her from going home, she was welcome to slide on down to Baird instead. She thanked Sophie and turned around, only to run smack into Theron's chest.

"Sorry," she mumbled.

"Thank you for the coffee," he said hoarsely, looking down into her mesmerizing blue eyes.

"You're welcome," she whispered.

He reached out with his right hand and traced her jawline. "You are a beautiful woman, Fancy Lynn Sawyer."

She didn't know what to say to that, but she didn't have to say a word, because his eyes slowly closed, and he leaned down for the kiss. It was every bit as earth-shattering as the first one had been.

"Good night," he murmured when he broke the kiss.

"Good night," she whispered.

Before she could say another word, he was out the door, and she could hear his pickup backing out of the driveway. She wrapped her arms around her body, hugging herself tightly. Her world was changing; the winds were blowing her sideways, and she wasn't sure that she liked it one bit.

Nervous energy surged through her veins, and it was too early to go to bed, so she dragged out a suitcase and packed for her trip to Florida. When she finished, she forced herself to eat a piece of string cheese with ham wrapped around it, blaming the jitters on too much sugar and caffeine. She'd just finished eating it when the house phone rang.

"Hello," she said cautiously. The phone hadn't rung one time since she'd been there; it was probably a telemarketer.

"Fancy, it's Theron. I've got a big, big problem, and I need help. I didn't have your cell number, and I was afraid Hattie's phone had been disconnected. I'm glad you picked up."

Theron was talking too fast, and she could hear fear in his voice. "What's wrong, Theron? Tell me what's going on."

"I need you to come with me to Decatur. Can you please, please come with me? The weather is getting bad, so it might involve an overnight, so pack a bag. I can have you back early tomorrow morning, if not tonight. The bag is just in case we absolutely have to stay overnight."

"Theron, what are you talking about?" she asked again.

"I'll have to explain on the way. It's my ex-wife, and she's barely given me enough time to get there. Will you help me?"

She made a decision with her heart, bypassing her head. "I'll be waiting on the porch," she said.

She turned off all the lights, put the heater on low, and set her already-packed suitcase out on the porch. The temperature had dropped again, and a cold mist stung her warm face.

In seemingly no time, truck tires crunched the cold gravel of the driveway, and she locked the front door. Theron hopped out, grabbed her suitcase, and rushed her to his pickup.

"We've got to hurry. That mist is going to slow us down. It's freezing on the windshield so fast, the wipers are having trouble keeping up," he said.

She buckled herself in. "Theron, what's going on?"

"It's a long story, and I'm scared to death. I'm glad you're going with me. Even an argument would keep my mind off what's going on. I'm in shock."

"Then you'd better start talking. We can't fight if you keep talking in circles, because I can't make heads or tails out of what you're saying. Do you know you're as white as a sheet? Did she murder someone or what?" Fancy asked.

Chapter Nine

Theron pulled out of Albany headed east on Highway 180 at a speed that did not take the freezing mist into consideration. Something horrible had happened, and Fancy's curiosity was on high alert, but she kept her silence, giving him time to put his thoughts into sentences.

"Maria called," he finally said.

"I got that much. Is she dead or something?" Fancy asked.

"She wouldn't be calling if she were *dead*," he said. "You remember how you felt that night you told me about Hattie? How stunned and shocked you were?"

She nodded.

"Multiply that times a thousand, and you'll understand the turmoil I'm in right now. Maria suggested I bring someone with me, and I could only think of you. You're so good with the little kids at Sunday school, and you've taught first grade all these years. I don't know a blessed thing about three-year-old girls."

Three-year-old girls? "Slow down, Theron. Start from the beginning. Do you want me to drive?"

"No, I can drive. It's two hours to Decatur in good weather. If I'm not there by eleven, all deals are off."

"Okay, we'll get there by eleven if we have to stick our arms out the windows and fly. Now tell me what Maria said when she called. Go slow," Fancy said. So it had something to do with a three-year-old, and he couldn't tackle the job on his own.

"Maria left me a message. Evidently she finally got someone to tell her where I was, and she found a number. The ranch is still in Joe's name. He's my grandmother's brother, so his name isn't

Warren; it's Frank. Anyway, she found the number after asking enough people up in Shamrock." He paused.

Fancy had told him to go slow, but she didn't mean that he should start out with "In the beginning God created . . ." and go from that point. So far he had established that Joe Frank was his great-uncle on his mother's side.

"She's been in and out of Shamrock for a couple of months. My sister, Melissa, called a few weeks ago and told me Maria was around town asking questions."

So now Fancy knew he had a sister named Melissa. Was his mother Mary? That way all the women in his life would have *M* names. She waited patiently for him to continue.

"In the message she said it was a matter of life and death, so I called. She said that when she left me, she was pregnant, but she wasn't sure she was going to keep the baby, since she didn't want to be married anymore. Her brother and sister-in-law talked her into keeping the child by offering to help with the babysitting. She moved in with an old boyfriend after she had the baby. But he's been out of the picture for a few months, and now she's going to get married again. Trouble is, she doesn't want to take the child with her. And she's flying out tonight. Remind you of Hattie's story, only in modern times?"

"Wow!" Fancy whispered. "How . . . cold," was all she could think of to say.

"She's at the old hunting cabin where we spent our honeymoon. It's on my grandparents' property and way out in the middle of nowhere. She's threatened to give the child to her sister-in-law if I don't get there tonight. She said Kayla didn't really want her because she's expecting twins herself now, but she said she'd take her if I didn't want her."

Fancy gasped. What was wrong with these people, discarding a child as if she were an outgrown toy? "So . . . why am I here?" she managed to ask.

"To begin with, I don't know much about suddenly taking care of a three-year-old on a twenty-four-hour basis. And I'm hoping that having a woman with me when I go to get her will keep her from being afraid. She doesn't know me. Her own father is a stranger to her," he groaned. "And I guess I need a friend right now."

Fancy smiled. So she was his friend? "Settle down. Breathe easy. It won't do that baby a bit of good if her father has a heart attack and dies at the age of thirty."

"Thirty-one," he corrected.

"Okay, then, thirty-one. We'll get through this, Theron. I'll help."

"Thank you, Fancy. I . . . I just didn't know who else to call." He fell silent for a moment, then said, "This weather is getting worse. We'll probably do best to stay in the cabin tonight and drive back early tomorrow morning. I'll call in and take a personal day." He made plans as he drove.

"What's your daughter's name?" Fancy asked.

Theron shrugged, looking miserable. "I don't even know. Maria said she was leaving a packet with her birth certificate and vaccination records. I didn't even ask her name. I was so confused and shocked, I could barely see straight."

"Quite a lot to throw at a self-confirmed bachelor," Fancy said.

"Yes, it is. Just more reason to be one too. Women!"

Fancy fought back a smile. "Not all women are like Maria."

"How would I ever know the difference?" he moaned.

"You'll know when the time comes, Theron. For now just concentrate on keeping this truck on the road and out of a ditch."

Theron kept silent for the next hour. When they reached Mineral Wells, he stopped long enough for them to dash into a convenience store, use the restrooms, and grab two large cups of coffee. Having something warm to wrap her hands around helped calm Fancy's nerves.

"What would you say to her if you were in my shoes?" Theron asked thirty minutes later when they headed north on Highway 51. The weather was getting serious. The road was covered with black ice, and the oncoming traffic was moving very slowly.

"I have no idea. I was so stunned myself at Granny's news, I hardly knew what to say to her. And this is so much bigger. It involves a little girl who's going to be terrified to be left with strangers," she said.

Carolyn Brown

Theron moaned. "Do you think she'll ever recover without a lifetime of therapy?"

"You can worry about that later. Tonight you just face the first step of meeting her."

He sighed. "Thank you," he said softly.

Fancy checked the dashboard clock. It was already ten, and she had no idea how much farther it was, but Theron had slowed the truck down to fifty miles an hour.

As if he could read her mind, he said, "Thirty-three more miles. The ranch is a few miles south of Decatur, and the cabin is a good two or three miles farther down a gravel road."

"Will we make it before Maria leaves?" she asked.

"I think so."

"Will she even make it to the airport in this kind of weather?" Fancy wondered aloud.

"She's not staying at the cabin. She can run off the road and freeze to death, for all I care," Theron said.

"Okay, you've got a right to your anger. I'd have it too. But remember something. Maria is that child's mother, and you'll do well to be quiet around your daughter when it comes to your personal opinions about her other parent. She'll figure it all out soon enough without your help."

"Please don't preach to me right now," he said.

Fancy shook a finger at him. "I know you're mad, and rightly so, but don't be foolish. I'll stay with your daughter in the cabin, and you take Maria to the car. Once outside, you can yell or cuss and rant until your face turns blue and her ears burn off, but don't you let that baby girl hear a word of it."

According to the sign on the road, they were entering Springtown, population 2062. The lights from the houses bounced off bushes already laden with ice. Tree branches looked as if they were draped in diamonds.

If Fancy hadn't been in a moving vehicle, she might have enjoyed the sight. Looking at it from a living room window with a cup of hot chocolate in her hands and warm slippers on her feet would be a lot better than glimpsing it between swishes of the overworked windshield wipers. It was ten thirty when they passed a sign saying that Boyd was off to their right and Paradise to the left.

"Paradise, on a night like this?" she asked.

"Does sound strange, doesn't it?"

"Mind if I turn on the radio and see if this is going to melt tomorrow?" she asked.

He reached out and pushed a button.

". . . if you're out in this wintry mix, go home. If you are home, stay there. All of Parker, Palo Pinto, Stephens, and Shackelford schools have been closed tomorrow. Wise County schools haven't checked in with us yet, but I'll be surprised if the buses can run on this ice. Temperatures tomorrow are not expected to get above twenty degrees. It will probably be days before we see a melt . . ."

She turned it off. "Guess I got my answer."

"The sand trucks will be out early tomorrow. By afternoon we can be out of the woods," he said.

"I just need to be home by Wednesday morning. My ladies will want to be pretty for the holiday. That and I've got a ticket to fly home Wednesday afternoon," she said.

"No problem. We'll get you there."

It was ten forty-five when he left the main highway and made a left turn.

"Ten minutes, tops. We'll be there on time," he sighed.

A couple of more turns and he eased the truck into a narrow lane. Seconds afterward, car headlights started toward them. Theron swore as he eased the truck far to the right to let the other vehicle pass.

It pulled up beside him, and the driver's side window lowered. A woman called, "There's a letter on the table with her things."

"We need to talk," Theron called back.

"Nothing to talk about. She's your child, so you can have her," Maria yelled as the window closed and she drove off.

"She's left her alone, Fancy!" Theron sputtered. "What does that tell you about her mothering instincts?"

"Right now I'd like to slap her silly," Fancy said through gritted teeth.

Theron laughed. Granted, it was an edgy laugh born of sheer nerves, but it lightened the tension in the truck.

When he gently hit the brakes in the yard, the truck kept right on sliding. It came to a sideways stop with the porch blocking the passenger door.

"How on earth did she drive out of here?" Fancy asked breathlessly.

"Chains," he said.

"You got any?"

"In the barn back at the ranch. Didn't even think about bringing them along."

Theron opened his door, and Fancy slid across the seat. They slipped and slid several times on the frozen earth and up the three steps to the porch. When it came time to open the door, Theron stopped in his tracks.

"Go on. Standing out here won't solve anything," Fancy said.

He tiptoed inside with Fancy right behind him. They found the little girl on the sofa. She wore pajamas with feet and was covered with a heavy quilt. Long lashes feathered out on her rosy cheeks. Dark, curly hair spread out on the pillow beneath her head. Her features were delicate, and she looked small for a three-year-old.

"She's the image of my sister, Melissa, except for the skin tone," he whispered.

"Let's get some warmth into this place before she wakes up." The cabin was almost as cold as outside, and Fancy's breath came out in a puff of mist.

"Woodstove and fireplace. I'll get both started if you'll sit right there and make sure there's a face she can see if she wakes up," he said.

Fancy shook her head. "This place is so small, she can see us both. I can help."

Together they got a blaze going in the fireplace and a warm fire set in the small woodstove in the back corner near the kitchen area. The cabin was one large room with a doorway into a bathroom on one side. An outdated brown carpet designated the living area with its sofa, an easy chair, and a wooden rocker. The bedroom area consisted of two sets of bunk beds built against a wall. All four twin-sized beds were made up with patchwork quilts in various colors. The kitchen was located on the other side of the living area. A few open-front cabinets showed off dozens of cans of food; a small freezer sat in one corner; a dormitory-sized refrigerator with a microwave on top of it and a chrome table with four chairs around it made up the rest of the kitchen.

It was cozy enough, but why on earth would a man bring his new bride to a cabin with bunk beds? Fancy wondered.

"When we came here for the honeymoon, it looked very different. I had a big four-poster bed with a white lace coverlet on it, and every rose I could find in the area had been commandeered to turn the place into a honeymoon suite," he said.

"I didn't say a word," she protested.

"You didn't have to. It was written on your face." He looked at the big manila envelope on the table. "I guess it's time to look at that. Will you join me?"

She pulled out a chair near the stove. "In for a dime, in for a dollar."

He pulled out the first piece of paper, and shock covered his face. "It's the birth certificate. Good Lord!"

"What?"

"Her name is Echo. It's so . . . cutesy. Like . . . like something you'd name a horse."

"Like Fancy?"

"You got it," he snapped.

"Well, thank you so much," she snapped back. She'd ridden on ice with him in a bearish mood for more than two hours, just to have him say he hated her name.

"I'm sorry. I—"

"What's the rest of it?"

"Rest of it?"

"Her name," Fancy said testily.

He looked down at the birth certificate again. "Echo Martina Santoya. I'll have to get her last name changed. How much trouble will that be?"

"Ask a lawyer. You'll need one anyway to document all that's gone on tonight. Just in case Maria ever comes back and says she wants Echo again, you need documentation that she abandoned her in this cabin all alone."

"We were just minutes away," he said.

"Did Maria know that before she got ready to leave? Could she even tell through the freezing rain that it was you arriving in the truck?" Fancy asked.

"I see your point." Theron nodded grimly.

He handed the next piece of paper to Fancy. "Letter from Maria. Will you read it?"

"You sure you want me to? It could be personal."

"Please. You can read it out loud to me. My head hurts—maybe from all the driving and stress."

"Okay, here goes," she said.

The letter revealed that Maria had often left her daughter for weeks at a time with her sister-in-law, Kayla, from the time she was born. Maria justified her behavior by saying that her fiancé was frequently on the road for business and that she had to work to make ends meet. They'd lived in Amarillo, and it was easier to leave Echo with Kayla from Sunday night until Saturday morning each week.

She knew Theron would make a wonderful father, and she hoped he would be very happy to have Echo in his life. But if he didn't like the arrangement, he could put her up for adoption or let his sister, Melissa, raise her if she was willing.

"That's it?" Theron asked. "It's not much more than what she told me on the phone."

"Well, it's in writing, and it's documentation you can use as leverage if she ever comes back demanding child support or Echo back." Fancy folded the letter gently and put it back in the envelope.

"When is her birthday?" she asked.

He looked at the birth certificate again. "December 31. She weighed five pounds at birth and was eighteen inches long. She'll be three next month."

"If you'll bring in the suitcases, we can at least have a shower and get some rest for a few hours before she wakes up," Fancy said.

Theron looked as if he were about to faint.

"Don't I need to be awake when she opens her eyes so she won't be afraid?"

"My guess is that Maria brought her here several hours ago, so she already knows the place, and she's used to her mother not being around," Fancy said.

"You do look a lot like her Aunt Kayla. She's taller than you are, but she's got brown hair and blue eyes. Maybe there's enough resemblance that she won't be so afraid."

"Good, now get the suitcases inside, and let's get a few hours of sleep."

"I'll stretch out on a bunk, but I'm too wound up to sleep. You really want a shower in this cold cabin?"

"Maybe I will wait until morning if you'll guarantee me that the pipes won't be frozen," she said.

"They've never frozen before, and we've been here when it's been pretty cold. The hot-water tank is propane powered. The cookstove in the kitchen is the same."

"Where's the stove?"

Theron stood up and lifted a section of countertop to reveal a small cooking range. "The oven is here." He opened a cabinet door. "Sometimes we need the countertop more than the stove, especially if we're only boiling beans or chili on the woodstove, so Grandpa made it double duty."

Theron brought in the bags, went into the bathroom, and came out in flannel pajama bottoms and a long-sleeved thermal-knit shirt. He stretched out on a bottom bunk and laced his hands behind his head.

Fancy had changed into boxer shorts and a tank top, wishing that she'd brought warmer pajamas. She was under the covers in the bunk closest to the sofa when he returned.

"Thank you, Fancy," Theron whispered into the semidark room.

"You're welcome. Good night again, Theron," she said. No kiss this time, but it was for the best. With glowing embers in the fireplace and ice surrounding them, one kiss could lead to two, and they had an abandoned child to think about.

"'Night," he whispered.

She wished she didn't like the deep timbre of his voice or his beautiful eyes or the way he looked at her just before he was about to kiss her. All those things kept her awake long after he began softly snoring.

The next morning Fancy awoke to dark curls in her face and a little girl snuggled up in her arms. She didn't move a muscle but looked around the room slowly, getting her bearings and remembering why she was there. When had Echo awakened and gotten into bed with her?

Little brown eyes opened wide, and the girl smiled. "Mornin'. I'm Tina. You're not Kay-Kay," she said innocently.

"No, I'm Fancy. I'm going to help take care of you today. Okay?"

"Momma's gone," Tina said.

"Yes, she is. Is that all right?"

Tina nodded her little head. "Kay-Kay's gone too?"

"Yes. But I'm here now for you."

"Tina will be a good girl," she said brightly.

Fancy's heartstrings stretched so tightly that she fought back tears. How could anyone leave something as fragile and precious as this child?

"Good morning," Theron said softly as he crawled out of bed and kneeled beside them.

Tina studied him a full minute, staring so intently into his eyes that it was eerie. "I'm Tina," she said.

"Tina," he said softly. "I thought your name was Echo."

"No. No one calls me that. I'm Tina."

Theron glanced up at Fancy, who smiled. Then he looked back to Tina.

"I'm your daddy," he said.

"Johnny?" She cocked her head to one side just like Theron did when he was thinking; there was no doubt about her parentage.

"No, I'm your real daddy. Do you understand?"

"Gone," she said.

"No, I'll come home every night," he promised.

"Okay," she said.

"What did you say your name is?" he asked.

"Tina. Momma is gone. Kay-Kay is gone."

"I like your name, Tina. Are you hungry?"

She nodded. "I need to pee-pee."

Fancy threw back the covers and set her on the floor. "Then let's go."

Tina raced to the bathroom.

When she finished, Fancy brought her back to the living room. "Get warm with your new daddy, and I'll make us some breakfast. What do you like?"

Tina's eyes glittered. "Pandy cakes."

"Then pandy cakes it will be. We do have things to make those, don't we?" Fancy asked Theron, who sat on the sofa in silence.

"In the cabinet. The frying pan is in the oven. Can I hold her?" he asked.

Fancy lifted her into his arms and covered them both with a quilt.

"I cannot believe something this precious is mine," he whispered.

Tina wiggled down into his arms, looking up at him quizzically as if trying to decide if she was really going to believe that he was her new daddy. Finally she said, "Read to me?"

"Of course. Did you bring your books?"

She hopped out of his lap and skipped across the room to a small tote bag full of her most precious toys. She gathered several books up into her small arms and carried them to the sofa, where she unloaded them with a gush of air as if they weighed a ton. "I like all of 'em," she said.

Theron picked up the nearest one. "Okay, then let's read this one."

"I like this one better." She handed him a Little Golden Book about Cinderella and sat close to his side.

"Okay, then, we'll read *Cinderella* while Fancy makes breakfast."

He looked over his shoulder at Fancy. "I'm in awe. She likes books."

"Enjoy it," she teased. "There will be days when she's not so precious, and you'll wonder if you'll ever get her raised."

He opened the book and read, "Once upon a time . . ."

Chapter Ten

In the middle of the morning Theron called his superintendent and found out that school had been canceled for Tuesday as well. The Thanksgiving holiday began on Wednesday, so if there was going to be bad weather, it was at least the best time, because they'd only have to close down for two days. Theron called the high school boy who helped him occasionally on the ranch and hired him to feed the cattle twice a day and to remember the cats and dogs with water and food.

Fancy called Kate and asked her to call the ladies and tell them she most likely wouldn't be home in time to do their hair on Wednesday.

"Honey, you won't be home until the weekend. There's another cold front coming in, this time with an inch or two of snow, and the sun isn't going to shine until Friday or Saturday," Kate said.

"No! I'm flying home tomorrow night."

"The airport isn't flying anyone in or out until it thaws. You wouldn't be going anywhere if you were in Albany either, so suck it up. Remember the fifteen-minute rule," Kate said.

Fancy literally stomped on the floor. Theron looked up.

"So you're in a remote cabin with Theron? How did you get there?" Kate asked.

"By truck," Fancy said.

"Stop pouting. You know you're warming up to him, or you wouldn't be there, so make the most of it."

She whispered into the phone. "He found out he's got a daughter, and she was left here for him to claim like a . . . oh, I don't know what . . . an abandoned puppy or a stray kitten. He didn't even know he was a father, and now he's got a child who's almost three years old. It's a shock. So don't tell me not to complain. Just hush and call Momma and the ladies, because I forgot my battery charger, and my phone is about to go dead," Fancy said.

"Sounds pretty cozy to me," Kate teased. "Is Fancy maybe protesting too much? But don't worry. I'll make the calls. Since you can't call out anymore, let's get serious. Is there anything at the house that needs to be done? Pipes freezing a problem? Anyone else I need to call?"

"No, that covers it. I'm hanging up now to save what I've got left in case of an emergency."

"One other question. Why didn't you call your momma? Did you not want her to know you're holed up in an ice storm with Theron Warren? I won't tell her if it's a secret."

"The detective is coming out in you. But, no. I tried but couldn't get reception to her. I was surprised when I got through to you," Fancy said.

"Find some paper, and write down all the details. I want to hear the whole story when you get home. A kid? I bet he was freaked out. Bye, and happy Thanksgiving!" Kate said.

The phone went silent. A loud crack close to the cabin startled her.

"Who's shooting?" she asked.

Another loud crack sent a huge pecan limb tumbling down to land barely a foot from the porch. Theron opened the door and peeked out through the screen. "Guess we'll be cleaning up a mess come spring. Sounds like the trees are loaded with ice and are breaking down."

She put the phone in her suitcase and held her hands in front of the fireplace. The warmth was wonderful, but it made her fingers tingle.

"You bring a charger for your phone?" Fancy asked Theron.

"Oh, no!"

"Got one of those cigarette-lighter kinds in your truck?"

He shook his head.

"Then you'd better make all the calls you want to pretty quick. Reception is horrible, but we won't have any when the batteries go dead," she said.

"I've got to call my folks to let them know there's a possibility I won't be there for the holiday," he said.

"We won't be anywhere but right here," she groaned. "Kate said the airport is closed. There's snow on the way, and the sun won't be out until the weekend," she said.

"Snow?" Tina's eyes lit up. "Snowman snow?"

"Maybe," Fancy said.

"Or snow ice cream," Theron said.

Tina and Fancy looked at him.

He laughed. "You make it out of clean snow, sugar, canned milk, and vanilla. We only had it a couple of times when I was growing up. Granny made it for us once when we were down here on a hunting trip."

"Okay, then snowman and snow ice cream if we get enough," Fancy promised Tina.

The little girl giggled and jumped up and down

"This isn't right," Fancy whispered to Theron.

"What? That she can jump at her age? Is something the matter with her? Do I need to take her to a doctor first thing?" he asked.

"No, that she hasn't cried for familiar surroundings or people. That she accepts us the way she does. I've had first-graders cling to their mothers and scream at the top of their lungs at the thought of being separated from them. Someone should be shot right between the eyes for doing this to her. She's like a child in the system. She's been scuttled around so much, she doesn't have any stability. Sure, you're her new daddy, but that can't possibly mean much to her this soon," Fancy said.

"Yes, it does. She's my daughter!"

At Theron's raised voice, Tina put her hands over her ears and ran to the nearest corner, where she sat down facing the wall and curled forward. Sobs shook her tiny shoulders.

"That's not what I meant, and don't you ever yell like that in front of her again," Fancy hissed. "Go over to her and reassure her that everything is all right."

"I'm sorry I raised my voice," Theron said as he knelt beside Tina and touched her shoulder. She flinched but didn't look at him. "Fancy and I were just having a grown-ups' discussion."

She nodded but wouldn't take her hands from her eyes. "Don't yell like Johnny."

He gently rubbed her stiff shoulders. Theron looked up at Fancy with questions written on his face.

Fancy had tears flowing down her cheeks. She crossed the floor and sat down on the other side of Tina. "Daddy won't yell anymore, and neither will I. Can you come out of the corner now?"

Tina turned around, drew her knees up under her chin, and studied both of them. "I'm hungry."

"Then we will cook lunch, won't we, Daddy? What can we make?"

"Chicken noodle soup?" Tina asked.

"You really talk well," Fancy said.

"Not a baby anymore."

Fancy took her hand and led her to the kitchen area, where she drew a chair up to the cabinet and let her pour the soup from the can into the saucepan.

"Do you take a nap after lunch, Miss Tina?" Fancy asked.

"On a towel on the floor," Tina said.

"So you went to the babysitter's every day?"

"Kay-Kay and me. Where the kids play."

"Why did Maria leave her with Kayla if she was just going to take her to a sitter anyway?" Theron mumbled.

"Night job, remember?" Fancy said out of the side of her mouth.

"Don't touch the stove. It's very hot," she told Tina when she turned on the burner.

"Okay," Tina said seriously.

She ate a whole bowl of soup with crackers crumbled in it and looked up. "Jell-O?"

"Not this time, but maybe if we can find some in the cabinet, I'll make it for supper. How about peaches?" Fancy asked.

"Yes, yes, peaches," Tina said excitedly.

Fancy opened a can and cut up two halves into a small bowl. Tina finished them and promptly started looking around. Finally she crawled down off the chair and went to the bathroom, brought a towel out, and laid it on the floor in front of the sofa.

"Since you're the only little kid we've got here, why don't you sleep on a bed or the sofa?" Theron asked.

She thought about that for a second, picked up the towel and handed it to Fancy, and hopped up onto the sofa with her doll and shut her eyes.

"She's trained well," Fancy said.

"It's kind of sad," Theron said.

"I agree. It's plain she's spent her whole life in day care. Worse, Maria and Johnny fought a lot, and Johnny's yelling scared her."

"That makes me sick. My three-year-old daughter should never feel like that," Theron said.

"Then change it. Chances are she won't remember a lot about those days when she's older. You can start now to make her life happy," Fancy said.

"I taught seventh-grade math before I became a principal. Little children are not my . . . my . . . ," he stammered.

"You'll learn. Just be patient with her," Fancy said. "Boy, you sure do know how to pick a wife."

"Look who's talking. You were involved with Chris Miller," he shot right back at her.

"But I didn't marry him."

"And was that your choice at the time?" he asked.

"Why are you picking on me? I just meant that I can't see you married to someone like Maria. You seem so much more . . ." She couldn't find the right word.

"What?"

"Intelligent," she finally said.

"It's been said that when a person is in love, everyone looks like an angel. I guess I wasn't too intelligent after all," he said.

"And I guess she wasn't an angel after all," she countered.

"You'll never know how right you are. But I won't make the same mistake twice."

"Good for you. What'll we do for supper? More chicken noodle soup?"

"I make fantastic spaghetti. There's always meat in the freezer and sauce makings in the cabinet. Those are things that keep. We make spaghetti and chili and big pots of vegetable soup while we're here on a hunting trip."

"Then you can be the chef tonight. Are we having chili for

Thanksgiving?" The thought of not being with her mother on a holiday for the first time in her entire life almost made her weep.

"No, there's also a chicken in the freezer. We'll do the best we can to make a nice dinner, since it's our first with Tina."

Fancy caught that "our first," but she let it slide.

Theron opened the freezer and brought out a white-wrapped package labeled VENISON SAUSAGE and laid it on the cabinet to thaw. He rustled around in the cabinet and found tomato paste, two cans of diced tomatoes, an onion that had three-inch sprouts on it, and a can of mushrooms. From there he went to the space under the sink and pulled out a bottle of Merlot.

"Wine?"

"It's not a great brand. We just keep a couple of bottles under there for spaghetti sauce," he said. "But there's no real milk or eggs, so our Thanksgiving dinner might be very limited."

"We'll simply have to be creative. And, buster, you're going to owe me one big favor when we get back home, because I'm missing a real feast," she said.

"You couldn't have gone to Florida anyway. You said the airport was iced in," he reminded her.

"But I could have driven far enough to eat with any one of the ladies who come to the shop for their hairdos, or I could have made a dinner at home for just me. At least I have milk and eggs," she said.

"Okay. I owe you. One big favor of your choosing. Up to but not including a walk down the aisle in a church."

"That wouldn't be a favor. That would be a jail sentence," she said.

"So glad we agree on something today," he said. He diced the onion and sautéed it in cooking oil. When that was done, he added the tomatoes, mushrooms, and paste.

"When does the Merlot go in?" Fancy asked from the table, where she watched each step. The cabin was beginning to smell delightful.

"This simmers half an hour, and then I add the meat. When the sausage is in the pot, then I add the wine and simmer the whole thing for two hours."

"Venison?" She couldn't keep her nose from wrinkling.

"Don't condemn it until you try it. You'll be pleasantly surprised. I promise."

I just bet I will, she thought. Her saliva glands dried up just thinking about eating a beautiful deer. At least he had mentioned a chicken for Thanksgiving dinner, thank goodness.

Tina awoke in exactly thirty minutes. She didn't move anything but her eyes for several seconds as she remembered where she was. Then she looked at Fancy and gave her a brilliant smile.

"Good nap. Outside now?" She peeped over the back of the sofa at Theron in the kitchen.

"It's really cold," Fancy said.

"Coat and boots," she said.

"Daddy, help me," Fancy said.

"Coat and boots and only for a few minutes. You'll freeze your little fingers off if you stay out very long."

"What's cooking?" Tina went to the second tote bag and brought out a pink sweat suit and a faded red jacket.

"Spaghetti for supper," Theron said.

She dropped the clothing and clapped her hands. "Busgetti. I love it."

"That's good. Let me help you out of your pajamas and into those warm britches," Fancy said. "Need to go to the bathroom first?"

Tina nodded.

Fancy dumped the tote bag out on the sofa—two sweat suits, one pair of jeans and a T-shirt, a faded coat, a pair of well-worn tennis shoes, and a pair of red boots. She found two sets of underpants and socks in the outer pocket.

"We'll be going shopping on the way home," she said.

Theron looked at the meager pile. "Is that all of it?"

"That and the pair of pajamas she has on."

Tina made a dash to the bathroom. "Got to go."

Fancy hurried to follow her, getting her onto the potty just in time. She'd have to wear the one pair of pajamas every night, because if Fancy washed the heavy flannel by hand, they'd never be dry before she'd need them again.

When she and Tina came out of the bathroom, the child wore

only her underpants, and Theron saw just how tiny she was. She didn't look malnourished or fragile. Her skin was pink, and she appeared to be healthy; she was just small, like him. Pride welled up in his chest along with the fear that he would never know how to raise a little girl properly.

Fancy set about putting socks and a sweat suit on her, along with the coat and boots, which turned out to be on the verge of being too small. She silently added a pair of boots to her mental list of what Tina would need. Theron could get her a few things at the Wal-Mart store on the way back to Albany, and later he could take her to the right stores and buy her clothing for church and for day care.

Fancy's heart stopped.

Day care! That baby didn't need to be shuffled into yet another day-care center. She needed stability. But Theron couldn't quit his job and stay home with her. Fancy couldn't keep her. She had a beauty shop to run, and the house would sell soon, and she'd only promised Sophie a year at the most. After that Tina would have to be sent to day care anyway, so why start something that would simply break Fancy's heart when she had to walk away from it?

"Are we ready, ladies?" Theron asked from the door.

Fancy hurried into her own jacket.

Tina ran ahead and slipped and fell on her hind end the first time she stepped out the door. She scooted across the porch and down the steps without getting up, giggling the whole way. That gave Theron an idea, and he went back inside and came out with a big round dishpan edged with a red rim. It had a hole in one side to hang it on the wall. He brought twine with him and attached it through the hole, picked up Tina, and set her down in it. Her feet and legs dangled over the edge, but she squealed with delight when he pulled her across the ice.

Her brown eyes lit up as she wiped her long dark hair out of her face. Her little hands were pink in no time. Fancy went back inside and brought out a pair of her socks and put them on Tina's hands like gloves.

"More. More. Again," she begged.

Theron had trouble keeping his own footing, and the dishpan

that should have been trailing behind him kept bumping into his legs. Fancy sat on the porch and laughed until she got the hiccups.

Theron motioned toward her. "Okay, smarty-pants, it's your turn."

"Oh, no, you're not putting me in that. Besides, Tina would be upset if you took her out."

"I'm not ending her turn. You're going to sit in it, and she's going to sit in your lap," Theron said.

Fancy shook her head.

Theron laid the rope down, whispered into Tina's ear, took two running steps, and then skated all the way to the porch, where he scooped Fancy up in his arms and carried her to the dishpan. Tina hopped out, and Theron set Fancy down inside the big round pan. He didn't have to put Tina in Fancy's lap. She was there before Fancy could try to get up.

"You are wicked," she laughed.

Tina laughed with her. "No, he's new daddy."

"See that tree down over the rise?" Theron pointed.

"Don't you dare," Fancy said.

"Yes, I do dare. Lean to the left, or you'll hit it." He gave them a push instead of tugging them around the yard.

The dishpan sailed like a sled on the slick ice. The slight slope let it build up speed. Tina giggled with excitement, and Fancy barely remembered to lean to the left in time to miss the tree. Tina was screaming for more. The only thing that saved Theron from at least a good tongue-lashing about the dangers of what could have happened if they'd hit that frozen mesquite tree was the fact that he fell flat on his rear end when he started down the rise. He slid all the way to the bottom on his back, only stopping when he hit the edge of the dishpan with his foot.

Tina clapped her sock-covered hands together. "Do it again, new Daddy."

"Yeah, do it again," Fancy agreed.

"What a ride." Theron grinned.

"And who's going to get us back up that hill?" Fancy asked.

"No one. We're going to pull Tina around it and to the house the back way. Should take about fifteen minutes, and by then she'll have been out plenty long enough," he said.

"Me too. That dishpan is cold through my jeans."

"Then it's probably really cold through her little sweatpants. Don't get up. You can let her sit on your lap so she'll be warmer."

Fancy nodded.

Theron was going to make a wonderful father. Too bad he would never make a wonderful husband.

Chapter Eleven

The table was laden with whipped sweet potatoes, made from a can rather than fresh; chicken and dressing, made from boxed corn bread and onion powder, celery salt, and sage; giblet gravy from one tiny chicken liver and broth; green beans with a little bacon to season them, and canned cranberries. The yeast-roll recipe substituting mayonnaise for eggs worked well. Fancy could barely detect the faint taste of mayonnaise in the hot rolls and couldn't taste it at all in the pumpkin pie or the chocolate cake.

Theron gave thanks.

Since it was a holiday, Fancy put only what Tina wanted on her plate. When Fancy was growing up, her momma said that she didn't even have to eat vegetables on holidays. Granny Hattie always said Gwen was doing the wrong thing, but Fancy had always been glad for the rule.

"In our family we all tell one thing we are thankful for at Thanksgiving dinner. Tina, what are you thankful for today?" Theron asked.

"I like mean beans today." Tina jabbed her fork into three and popped them into her mouth.

"Is that all?" Theron asked.

Tina's brow furrowed as she thought. "I like ice too."

Fancy pondered that. How could a three-year-old like ice? The frosty weather meant she was confined to a one-room cabin and two people she didn't even know.

"Why do you like ice?" she asked Tina.

"It's pretty, and you play with me. More mean beans, please?"

116

Fancy put another tablespoon of beans onto her plate. Amazing. A tyke who actually liked her vegetables!

"Anything else you like today?" Theron asked.

"New Daddy and Fanny. I like them." Tina went back to eating as if she'd just said that she liked her doll.

"We've made a lot of progress, haven't we?" Theron looked at Fancy.

Fancy's heart ached. It wasn't fair that when the sun finally came out and melted the ice that Theron would take Tina home with him, and she would be out of the picture.

"So what are you thankful for?" Fancy asked Theron.

"I'm grateful for a daughter I didn't know I had but who will be a big part of my life from now on. And I'm especially thankful for you."

Fancy pushed a strand of hair back behind her ear. "Me?"

"You dropped everything when I called. You've made this . . . transition much easier for Tina and me, even though you would much rather be with your family today than stuck in a one-room cabin with us. So today that's what I'm thankful for," he said.

"You're welcome," she murmured, somewhat stunned at his graciousness.

"You?" Theron asked.

Fancy looked up, expecting to see a platter of whipped sweet potatoes coming toward her. Instead, Theron was looking at her with a question in his mossy green eyes.

"What?"

"Do you have anything you're thankful for today?"

"A jar of unopened mayonnaise that wasn't outdated," she said, oddly uncomfortable with the question and needing to keep things light.

"Mustard. Not 'naise. It's yucky," Tina said.

Fancy giggled. "Mayonnaise, because without it we wouldn't have this meal. It was my egg substitute. And I'm thankful for condensed milk in a can, because without it we wouldn't have chocolate cake or whipped potatoes."

"Then so be it. Mayonnaise is your hero today," Theron said. He would never understand the way a woman's mind worked. They were a different species altogether.

"We're from Venus, you know," Fancy said as if she'd read his mind.

"What are you talking about?" he asked.

"You can't hide much. Whatever you're thinking is written all over your face." She pointed at him. "Les is the same way. You were disappointed that I didn't get all mushy because it's a holiday. Momma didn't raise me to be mushy. I speak my mind. I wouldn't have come to Texas if Granny hadn't broken her hip. I wouldn't be staying in Texas if Sophie's Aunt Maud wasn't dying with cancer and Sophie didn't need me to help her through it. I don't like Texas. It's nothing but mesquite trees, mosquitoes, and bad memories. And now I can add ice storms to that list. So I'm thankful for mayonnaise," she said.

"Whew! You do speak your mind, and the new commandment of the cabin is to always have a spare jar of mayonnaise and an extra can of milk. Shall I carve it in the ice on the porch?" he asked.

"It would just melt, and you'd forget. Besides, the next woman you bring up here might not even know how to make substitutions."

"I like orange potatoes." Tina joined the conversation.

"Do you like broccoli?" Fancy asked.

Tina wrinkled her nose. "Yucky. Little Foot likes tree stars."

Theron looked at Fancy.

"Leaves?" she guessed.

"What do you want to do after dinner?" Theron asked Tina.

"Nap," she said.

"Is that good?" he quietly asked Fancy.

"Very, but most kids fight it. She's obviously been trained since birth, so it's all she knows."

"Then we'll have a nap after dinner, and then what?"

Tina blew out her breath as if to say that sometimes big people didn't know much. "Make a snowman."

"I'm sorry, sweetheart, but it didn't snow. We just have ice, so we can't make a snowman," Theron explained.

She tried the second best thing. "Feed the birds?"

"That we can do. I bet they'd love some dressing."

"So my dressing isn't good enough to put up for leftovers?" Fancy raised an eyebrow.

"It's wonderful." Theron grinned. "Isn't that written across my forehead in flashing neon letters?"

"Yes, but it's spelled L-I-A-R."

"You believe every neon sign you read?"

"What's neon?" Tina asked.

"It's . . ." Fancy started to tell her that it was a gas inside tubes that made lighted signs. "You tell her. You're her daddy."

"It's the stuff they make pretty signs out of. Like McDonald's signs."

"Burger with no un-uns and Coke and a toy," she said.

"That's right," Theron said. "So did you eat at McDonald's a lot?"

She shook her head. "But I like it."

"Where did you eat burgers most of the time?" Theron asked.

She nodded. "SONIC. 'No macky cheese, Tina. Chicken or burger. Make up your mind,'" she said in a stern voice.

"Did your momma say that?" Fancy asked.

"Kay-Kay. Chocolate cake now?" Tina asked.

"Yes, yes, yes," Fancy said.

Tina giggled. "You are Sarah, not Fanny."

Fancy touched her shoulder. "You were Kay-Kay, not Tina."

Tina drew her eyes down. "Pick up toys, Tina."

Fancy remembered lines from the old movie *The Land Before Time*. "Three-horns don't play with long-necks."

Tina folded her arms across her chest. "Go to bed, Tina."

Fancy laughed with her at the new game.

"What are you two talking about?" Theron asked, clearly mystified.

"It's a kids' movie about dinosaurs. One dinosaur is Little Foot, and one is Sarah. One is Petri, and one is always saying, 'yes, yes, yes.' It must be one of her favorite movies," Fancy explained.

"I'm calling my ex-mother-in-law as soon as we get home. Maybe she can shed some light on the whole situation."

"It might be a good idea. Where's she from?"

"Pampa."

"Panhandle, huh?"

"That's right. I grew up in Shamrock. Maria, in Pampa. She came to work at the bank in Shamrock. Had a friend who helped get her the job, but her folks have lived in Pampa for years. I just assumed that's where she went back to after the divorce," Theron said.

"Pie or cake?" Fancy asked as she carried the desserts to the table.

"Both. It's a holiday," he said.

Tina finished her cake, went to the bathroom with Fancy's help, and curled up on the sofa for a nap.

"Right now I miss that remote control," Theron said.

That caused Fancy to think about what she missed. "I'm going out for a walk. I'll be back after a while."

"Cabin fever or kid fever?"

She put on his coat over her T-shirt and found gloves in the pockets. "Cabin. Tina is precious."

"Don't stay out too long. Those tennis shoes won't keep your feet from freezing," he said.

She nodded and opened the door to a blast of still-icy wind and looked up at a sky the color of fog. Snapping twigs could still be heard across the pastures. Every so often a big branch had all the weight it could endure, and the break was louder than a shotgun blast.

She walked around the house to the back and down a path toward an old barn. The ground was slippery, but she quickly got her bearings on how to travel on ice without falling. A black cat darted out of the barn when she started inside to inspect it. She jumped and remembered the black cat that had started her downhill slide into bad luck. The barn was as cold as the outside even if it was free of ice. Loose hay was strewn around the floor. A rat scampered across a rafter, but she didn't see anything else. She started to climb the ladder to the loft, but the idea of more rats kept her on the floor.

She picked up a hoe handle to use for a walking stick and meandered on down the pathway toward the trees in the distance. It wasn't anything like walking on the beach, barefoot in the sand and listening to the surf, but it wasn't all that bad. The ice made everything glitter and glow. She could imagine the shine it would have if sun rays were bouncing off it.

A single bright red cardinal lit up the black-and-white world in front of her. It hopped around on the ice, flew up to land on an ice-covered twig, and sang as if the day were bright and beautiful. She guessed the bird only had one song and used it no matter what the circumstances.

Fancy gave herself a stern lecture. She had many things to be thankful for that day. She was alive and had friends and family who loved and needed her. It didn't matter if it was raining or sunny, they didn't change their attitude toward her, so what right did she have to carry around a chip on her shoulder?

The pathway narrowed in and around the mesquite trees. She continued to walk, sometimes climbing up a slight incline, sometimes nearly falling on her rear end when the slope went downward. By the time she reached the edge of a creek or river, she was tired. She used her hoe handle to chip away enough ice from a frozen log to sit down to rest.

A squirrel scooted across the ground not two feet from her. A raccoon lumbered down to the water and pawed at the edge. She felt sorry for the old boy. Water all around him on everything, and yet he couldn't find a drop to drink. Two deer walked up behind her with their heads hung low. Lucky critters; it was too cold and the roads too slippery for the hunters to be out with their guns that day.

The cold began to seep into her bones. It was time to make her way back to the cabin before she really did have a problem with frostbitten toes. She stood up, took one step forward, and her numb feet flew out from under her as if they had a mind of their own. She could have been watching the whole thing on an old black-and-white television show running in slow motion. She threw her hands out to break the fall, but she wasn't going forward. The back of her head hit the log she'd been sitting on, and for a split second it hurt like the devil. Then everything slowly faded to black.

Theron picked up a book and stretched out on a bunk. His eyes grew heavy, and he dozed until Tina crawled in beside him and wiggled around until she was in the crook of his arm. They slept that way until he awoke with his arm asleep and her eyes prying holes in his face.

"Did you have a good nap?" he asked.

Her eyes were huge, and she shook her head from side to side.

"Why not?"

"Scary things."

"What scary things?" Theron asked.

"Monsters."

"I'll chase those scary monsters out of here. They won't live in our house," he said.

"Promise?"

"I promise. No more monsters."

"Where's Fanny?" she asked.

"She went for a walk. She'll be back soon, though."

She slid out of his embrace and set about getting her boots on. "I want to go."

"We'll go out in the yard and feed the birds, then come back inside and watch them from the window. Your clothing isn't warm enough to be out long, and Fancy wore my coat," he said.

"Okay," Tina agreed.

He looked at the clock before they walked out the door. It was after three, and Fancy had left just before one. The back of his neck prickled with fear. He had no coat. Tina's clothing wasn't warm enough for a hike. But they had to find Fancy. He checked the porch to see if she'd just stepped out for a breath of air while they slept, but she wasn't there.

"Tina, we're going to go find Fancy. We'll take the dishpan sled and wrap you in a blanket." He talked as he put both pair of sweat pants on her and an extra pair of socks.

He remembered his father's lucky hunting jacket in the bathroom closet and tugged it on over two extra shirts, and he picked up another blanket in case Fancy was sitting somewhere with her feet frozen to the ground. He grumbled as he settled Tina into the dishpan and wrapped the blanket firmly around her. She giggled and squealed at the idea of another ride in the homemade sled.

The barn caught his eye, and he hoped he would find Fancy settled in a corner playing with a nest of kittens, so he headed in that direction. When he got there, he yelled several times, but there was no answer.

On his way out he noticed the round holes poked every two to three feet in the ice. He stopped and studied them. No animal he knew made a track like that, but a walking stick could.

"Good girl," he mumbled as he followed the tracks.

"Tina's a good girl?"

"Yes, yes, yes," Theron said, but his heart wasn't in the joke.

"Look, Daddy. Red bird."

"It's beautiful, isn't it?" he said.

"Yes, yes, yes," Tina quipped.

The tracks led him to and through a copse of mesquite trees so thick, he could barely drag the sled among them. According to the tracks, Fancy was headed for the river at the back side of the property, and that was not a good sign. Right then he didn't care that he couldn't hide his feelings; he just wanted her to be safe and back inside the warm cabin. The holes stopped on the side of a log—and Fancy was lying in a frozen pool of blood on the other side.

"Fancy, can you hear me?" he called out.

No response.

He stretched the blanket out on the ground, gently picked her up, and laid her in the middle of it. Then he tied a knot in both ends, leaving her inside the cocoon, hoping he could carry her over his shoulder. He quickly saw that that plan wasn't sound. What if he injured her further?

"Fanny asleep?" Tina asked.

"Yes, she is, and we have to get her back to the house. Will you sleep with her?"

Tina nodded.

"Okay, I'm going to put you in the blanket and pull you both back to the cabin. You won't be afraid, will you?" Fancy was still breathing, so the important thing was to get her back to the cabin and warm her up.

After he undid the cocoon, Tina slung one arm over Fancy's chest and hugged up to her side. "Shh. Fanny is 'sleep."

It took him thirty minutes of slipping and sliding to get them home. His fingers and feet were numb with cold, but he kept moving.

When they reached the porch, he carried Tina inside and set her in front of the blazing fireplace.

"Take all your clothes off, and put on a pair of panties. Can you do that?" Theron asked.

"Yes, yes, yes," she said.

Theron raced outside and gently picked Fancy up from the blanket. She didn't make a sound and was limp as a dishrag. He liked her much better with fire in her eyes, fighting him on every front.

He carried her inside and kicked the door shut with the heel of his boot. He laid her on the sofa and removed her shoes and wet socks. Her toes looked pink and healthy. Then he slid off her jeans and T-shirt. He grabbed a pair of flannel pajama bottoms, a thermal knit shirt, and socks and redressed her. He wrapped her in a clean blanket before he rolled her over to check the wound on her head.

"Fanny still 'sleep?" Tina asked from the fireplace.

"Yes, she is," Theron said.

"I'm cold, Daddy," she said.

Theron hurriedly dressed her in her pajamas, then went to the kitchen, ran a basin of water, and rustled under the sink for the first-aid kit.

The wound had bled, and Fancy's hair was a complete mess. He poured a cup of warm water over it, letting it run back into the basin. When it was clean, he poured hydrogen peroxide over it. It bubbled and worked its cleansing magic. He wasn't sure how to proceed from there. He tried to put a gauze pad over the wound, but the tape had nothing but hair to stick to.

"Guess we're going to have to shave a spot, and she's not going to like it," he told Tina, who was watching, wide-eyed, from the end of the sofa.

She pointed at the bloody water. "That's yucky."

"Yes, it is. Why don't you go read your doll a book by the fire? I bet she's cold."

"Bambi. She wants me to read 'bout Bambi."

"Good. You do that, and I'll get Fancy's head all fixed."

He found scissors and a razor in the bathroom and clumsily but meticulously shaved half an inch all around the wound. He didn't remove any more than necessary, but still the results were disastrous. He cleaned the wound once again with hydrogen peroxide and then stretched Steri-Strips across it, hoping they would help pull the scalp back together. After that he applied a gauze bandage. He didn't know what to do with the rest of her wet hair. Let it hang over the bandage? Pull it up in some fashion?

"I'm not a hairdresser," he moaned.

Tina spoke so close to his elbow that he jumped. She pointed to her pigtails. "Make it like mine."

Sure enough, if he parted Fancy's hair down the middle, the wound lay perfectly in the part.

Tina removed her purple hair bands and handed them to him, and he wrapped them around the clumps of hair. He made a neck pillow of a blanket and positioned Fancy's head so that the bandage had no pressure on it when he rolled her back over. She was still frighteningly white.

He checked her pulse again, and it was strong. While he cleaned up the mess, Tina sat beside Fancy, holding her hand. Theron sat down beside his daughter on the floor and stared at Fancy. She looked even younger than sixteen with her hair pulled back away from her face in pigtails.

"Fanny still 'sleep?" Tina asked.

"Maybe for a long time. She bumped her head."

Tina kissed her on the cheek. "Wake up, Fanny. Time to eat."

Fancy didn't wake up.

Tina leaned down and whispered in her ear, "Chocolate cake."

Still Fancy didn't stir.

"Are you hungry, Tina?" Theron asked.

She nodded.

He checked the clock above the mantel but couldn't see it. How did it get dark so quickly? When he lit the lanterns, he was more than surprised to find that it was six thirty. No wonder his child was hungry.

He pulled leftovers from the refrigerator and started heating them in the microwave. Then he remembered that she liked macaroni and cheese, so he filled a small saucepan with water and set it on the stove.

By the time he had food on the table, she was sitting in her chair. No whining or fussing, just waiting patiently.

"Macky cheese!" She grinned when she saw it.

"That's right, and if you eat a good supper, there's more chocolate cake."

"Yes, yes, yes," she said.

Theron couldn't find a smile, so he turned his back for a moment.

Fancy smelled food cooking. It had to be coming from inside the motel, because she was on the beach. Only something was terribly wrong. The ocean was frozen. The white sand looked like an ice-skating rink, and the man who rented chairs and catboats wore a fur-trimmed parka. He was barefoot like always, but his toes were black.

She yelled at him that everything wasn't what it was supposed to be, that he needed to put on boots and socks, but he only smiled and waved. An elderly lady approached her from the east end of the beach. As she got closer, Fancy recognized Hattie. She was bundled up in a gray wool coat in a late-fifties style. Her hair was dark and wavy, and she was smiling. She motioned for Fancy to go with her on down the beach, but Fancy shook her head.

Her eyes fluttered open, and she heard Theron and Tina talking at the table. Something about cheese, but that was crazy. It was Thanksgiving, and she was in Florida. It was just a crazy dream she'd had after she'd eaten too much turkey and dressing for lunch. She had a headache. That's probably what had brought about the dream.

Momma must have bought a new sofa, because she didn't recognize the pattern. She tried hard to focus, but it still looked like brown plaid. Momma never would have picked that kind of pattern; she liked solid colors with floral touches.

Tina said something about chocolate cake. She really should get up and fix the baby something to eat. She'd be starving by now. Theron wouldn't know how to feed her properly. He'd never really been around children except at recess and Sunday school. He could push her on a swing or give her a ride on the merry-go-round, but he wouldn't necessarily remember to keep her on a good schedule.

Everything she looked at was foggy. Where was she anyway? She shut her eyes, and a black cat chased across her dreams. The smell of almonds filled her nostrils, and she brushed at her face to make it go away. She blinked and saw that her hand had bypassed her face and landed on a blanket covering her.

Was she still in jail? She had to concentrate. The black cat was the answer. It ran in front of her car, which was in a barn. Surely that was bad luck.

Then it was cold, and she was coming back home, only she fell and hit her head, and everything went black. Had she died and was drifting around in the afterlife, trying to find her way to heaven?

Chapter Twelve

The sun was a big orange ball peeping up over the windowsill, yellow rays sneaking through the miniblind slats. Fancy threw up an arm to cover her eyes. She'd been dreaming of walking on the beach in the rain, the soft drops making a pinging noise when they hit the chaise lounges and the catboats.

She blinked a few times, reminding herself that the beach was a dream and she was really in Albany, Texas. When she could really focus, she moaned. She was still in the cabin in Decatur, Texas, in an ice storm.

"Good mornin'," Theron said in a lazy drawl from a chair not two feet from her. "Welcome back to the land of the livin'."

It took a few minutes before she remembered how cold she'd been, slipping and falling. "Did I break anything?"

"Just your head. You're going to hate me, but I took care of it," he said.

She reached up to find her long hair in pigtails.

"That was Tina's idea, when she saw that I couldn't do anything with your hair. I was going to pull part of it up on top of your head and the rest down at the nape of your neck. Her idea worked a lot better."

She felt her forehead and groaned when she attempted to sit up.

"I'm thirsty. What time is it, and is that the sun?"

Theron headed for the sink to get her a glass of water. "It's six o'clock in the morning, and that is the sun."

"Morning? How long have I been asleep?"

"Fanny's awake!" Tina bounded out of bed and snuggled up against Fancy.

Fancy tried to remember what had happened, but everything was all too foggy. "What happened?"

Theron explained, "You went for a walk yesterday after we had lunch. Do you remember that?"

"I remember falling. That's all. I don't remember where I was or how I fell. It was cold, though." She sat up, and the room did a few spins before she got it under control.

Tina wrinkled her nose. "New Daddy fixed it."

Fancy's blue eyes were frantic when she looked at Theron for an explanation.

"You slipped and fell on the ice beside the river," he said. "You remember using the hoe handle as a walking stick on the ice?"

"Black cat in the barn. Should have come back to the cabin," she said.

"I love cats," Tina said. "Can I have a cat? Momma said no. Kay-Kay said no."

"I have cats, so you will too," Theron said.

"Not a black one," Fancy said.

"You hit your head on a log, and that's where we found you," Theron explained.

"New Daddy dragged us home," Tina said.

Fancy looked at Theron for more of an explanation.

"I fell asleep and awoke two hours later. You weren't back from the walk, so I figured something was wrong. Tina and I went looking. I took an extra blanket just in case you'd gotten cold."

"And then?"

He went on. "You had a scalp wound and, likely, a concussion. So I cleaned it with soap and hydrogen peroxide and put Steri-Strips and antibiotic cream on it."

"And he cut your hair off on the floor," Tina said seriously.

"You cut my hair?" Fancy groaned.

"Just half an inch around the cut. The bandage wouldn't stick, so I had to cut and shave the hair away," Theron said.

"You shaved my head?"

Tina patted her arm. "It's not yucky anymore."

"How long have I been asleep?"

"It's Friday morning. You fluttered your eyes a few times last night, and you muttered something about Kate, and once you told Hattie no about something."

"It's melting. I can hear the ice melting." She'd think about the back of her head later.

Tina ran to the end of the sofa and touched the gauze. "No more blood."

"We can probably go home tomorrow morning," Theron said.

"Not right now?" Fancy asked.

"The road out of here will take a while to be passable. The ice has been melting all day. If we tried to go now, we'd have to deal with several inches of mud. We'd only get stuck and have to wait until someone finally found us and came to rescue us. If it freezes over again tonight, we can get the truck out by early morning riding on the frozen mud. There's chains out in the barn," he said.

It made sense, but she wanted to go home.

"Don't cry, Fanny," Tina said.

Fancy swallowed twice before the lump in her throat finally subsided. "I'm fine, but I'm kind of hungry. Think we could have breakfast?"

"Pandy cakes?" Tina's eyes glistened.

Theron raised an eyebrow at Fancy.

"With sausage?" she asked.

"Tina, you watch the patient, and I'll cook," he said.

Fancy slowly began to remember her mishap as she mentally replayed everything after the black cat in the barn. She stood up, and the room just swayed a little bit.

Tina pointed toward the chair where Fancy's clothes were drying. "New Daddy washed 'em in the bathtub."

"Are you blushing, Miss Sawyer?" Theron joked.

"Don't you tease me, Theron Warren," she said.

Tina giggled. "Three-horns don't play with long-necks," she said, getting into the fun.

"You are right, darlin', they don't," Fancy said as she gingerly made her way to the bathroom. One look in the small mirror showed black circles rimming her eyes, pigtails hanging limp on her shoulders, and some dried mud peeking out from behind an ear. She bent forward and rolled her eyes upward but couldn't see the bandage. It had felt like a goose egg when she touched it; she hoped the shaved part wasn't that big. She checked in the cabinet and found a tiny mirror inside a compact and turned around. She bit back a moan. It would take years for that hair to grow out. Thank goodness the rest of her hair would cover the bald spot while it caught up.

Theron knocked on the door. "Are you okay in there? Your pancakes are ready."

She opened the door and leaned on the jamb. "I'm fine. Thank you for taking care of me, but did you have to scalp me?"

She took one wobbly step before the room spun again. He reached out and scooped her up in his arms, carried her to the table, and set her in a chair.

"You need food and liquid. I was afraid you had a concussion, but maybe you just lost a lot of blood. Scalp wounds always bleed a lot. As soon as we get out of here, you are going to a doctor," he said. "If our cell phones had been working, I'd have called 911."

"Don't tell me what I'm going to do."

"No doctor. No shot," Tina said.

Fancy held her fork tightly and concentrated on getting food from her plate to her mouth. "See? Even a three-year-old knows what she wants. Thatta girl," she said in solidarity with Tina.

Tina watched her carefully. "Good girl," she said.

Fancy smiled.

"There's no telling how much blood you lost. You might even need a transfusion," Theron said worriedly.

But Fancy's hands shook less with each bite. "I'll be fine in a few days. I might need a tetanus shot, but that's it. What's on the agenda today?"

"What's 'genda? Is it like macky cheese?"

"No, it means what are we doing today?" Fancy said.

"Outside?"

"I don't think so," Theron said. "Fancy is going to rest. Maybe she can read to you if it doesn't hurt her head, and when she gets her sea legs back, maybe she can take a shower."

"Bossy, bossy," Fancy mumbled.

"Yes, yes, yes. Bossy! Read Bossy Cow to me," Tina said.

Theron laughed until he lost his breath. Mostly it was pure relief that Fancy had awakened with an appetite and her memory intact. He'd feel even better once a doctor said she was fine.

Fancy sipped orange juice. "What is so funny?"

Theron wiped his eyes on a dish towel. "Everything, through a three-year-old's viewpoint."

"She will keep you entertained and free of boredom," Fancy said.

"You are so right," he said.

Tina finished her breakfast and went straight to her little satchel of toys, brought out a Bossy the Cow book, and carried it to the sofa.

"Think maybe you should get dressed first and let Fancy finish her food?" Theron asked.

Tina sighed. "Okay."

She unsnapped the tab at the top of her pajamas and unzipped them. Then she pulled her sweat pants and top from the drying chair. When she finished dressing, she picked up a pair of socks and carried them to Theron.

"Need help," she said.

"Did Kay-Kay help you get your socks on in the morning?" he asked.

"No. Mar-Daddy did."

Fancy held on to the chair for a moment to get her bearings when she stood up, then slowly made her way to the sofa, where she eased down beside Tina, who waited with her book open and ready. Fancy slung an arm around Tina's shoulders and began to read, "Bossy was a black and white cow who thought the whole barnyard belonged to her . . ."

Tina listened intently to every word.

By the time Fancy finished the book, clouds covered the sun and thunder rolled in the distance. Lightning lit up the cabin in flashes, and rain began to pour in great sheets. At least it wasn't freezing drizzle and they wouldn't have to spend the whole winter in the cabin.

Theron mumbled curses under his breath. Fancy caught a *damn* or two and a couple of *hell*s.

"So, suffice it to say that you hate rain?" she asked.

"Suffice it to say that we're going to be packing up and getting out of here in the next hour. I'll get the bags ready. You get dressed. We're going to get out of here and check into a motel in Decatur for the night," he said.

"Why?"

"Because it's fifty degrees out there, and it's not likely to refreeze. That means the rain will turn the dirt road into a muddy mess that will be worse than ice. If we don't get out now, we'll be stuck here until the road dries out, which could be a week or more," he said.

"I'll get ready and put Tina's shoes on. What about all the towels and bedding and food?" Fancy said.

He took care of things as he talked. "Linens and towels stay here. Dad will bring in fresh and take the dirty ones out when he comes to hunt or fish. Leftover food goes out in the yard for the animals and birds."

Fancy gathered up her underwear, jeans, and T-shirt. "Why a motel?"

"Because the highways will still be slick, and we need to shop for Tina. And because once I get us out of this mess, I'm going to be too uptight to drive two hours back to Albany," he said testily.

Tina curled up on the end of the sofa and looked at them with wide eyes.

Fancy sat down beside her. "We're going to a motel tonight. Do you know what that is?"

Tina shook her head.

"It's a place that has rooms something like this cabin. And we're going shopping."

"Wal-Mart?" Her dark eyes danced.

"Maybe. And maybe we'll find you a new book," Fancy said.

Tina threw her arms around Fancy's neck and hugged her so hard, it made her head throb. "Cake?"

"No, a book."

"Cake and a book. Happy Birthday to Tina," she singsonged.

"Maybe Maria or Kayla talked about her upcoming birthday?"

Theron wondered aloud. "Okay, Fancy, you can have the bathroom first to get dressed. I'm going to get the bags ready and out to the truck. Oh, no, I don't have a safety seat for Tina."

Fancy wondered at the mother who hadn't thought of that. "We'll buy one at the store. If we get stopped, you can tell the officer exactly why you don't have one yet," she said from the bathroom doorway.

By the time she came out, the bags were gone, and Theron's jeans and shirt were laid out on the sofa. Tina sat on the sofa holding her pitiful-looking doll.

Theron grabbed his clothing and headed for the bathroom. "My turn."

"What do we do?" Fancy asked.

"Pray."

"For what?"

"That my truck can get us out of the mud. It's already getting deep."

Tina steepled her fingers under her chin, looked up toward the ceiling, and said, "Now I lay me down to sweep . . ."

Fancy saw Theron stop in his tracks.

"Hey, the Good Book says that if the Big Man upstairs is going to hear a prayer, you can be certain he'll hear hers before he will ours," Fancy said.

Theron shook his head, then shut the door without a single retort.

When he returned, he picked Tina up, wrapped his father's old camouflage coat around her, and hurried her out to the truck, where he deposited her in the backseat. He turned to help Fancy in, only to find her two steps behind him. He trotted back up to the porch to lock the door.

Fancy strapped Tina and herself into the backseat of the club-cab truck.

"Car seat?" Tina asked.

"We're going to buy you a new one," Fancy said.

The big truck probably was yet another strange thing in Tina's young life. First she woke up in a cabin where she knew no one, then had to adjust to a brand-new father and Fancy Lynn, and now she had to make a mad dash somewhere in an unfamiliar vehicle that didn't even have a safety seat for her. The poor little thing probably felt as if she were being tossed by the four winds at once.

"New seat and new book?" Tina asked.

"And some new clothes," Theron said as he backed the truck out and started down the muddy road.

"But for now we have to be quiet and let New Daddy concentrate on getting us out of here," Fancy whispered.

"Will he get loud?"

"No, he won't ever get loud," she assured Tina.

Tina put a finger over her lips. "Okay, shh."

They'd barely cleared the yard when the truck bogged down in the mud and the tires spun. Theron eased up on the gas pedal, and the truck fishtailed from one side of the dirt road to the other, but he got control of it quickly and proceeded on.

Fancy let her breath out in a whoosh.

"Had you worried there, didn't I?" Theron said.

"You did," she admitted.

Tina shushed them. "Shh. New Daddy is busy."

The ten-minute trip to the highway took half an hour and lots of maneuvering, but finally the tires got a little bit of traction, and they headed north on the highway. Five miles later they reached the outskirts of the south side of Decatur, and Theron pulled into a Wal-Mart parking lot. "First stop. Car seat and . . ."

"A book," Tina said.

"That's right. You let her buy whatever she wants—my treat," Fancy said.

"Oh, no, in for a dime, in for a dollar. I know nothing about car seats, girl books, or girl clothing. You have to come with us," Theron said.

"I thought I'd get to just rest here in the truck," Fancy whined.

"I'll get a wheelchair at the door. I'll put you in a cart and push you. I'll even carry you, but you are going to help me with this. I'll owe you big-time. Whatever you say, whenever."

"Pleeeeeease," Tina begged.

"Is there a remote chance we'll see anyone we know?" she asked, reaching up to touch her mangled hair.

"Not in a million years. And from here we're going to the emergency room."

Fancy groaned.

"You're getting a tetanus shot. You don't want some wicked infection, do you?" he reminded her.

She unlocked the seat belt and whined some more. She was due her fifteen minutes and hadn't had it yet. She looked horrible already, and by the time they reached the doors, her hair would be even wetter.

Theron pulled an umbrella from under the backseat and picked up Tina. He looped an arm around Fancy's waist and hugged her close enough to keep the rain off their heads.

"I feel like a drowned rat," she said.

"Not a rat. A kitten, maybe. And you are a beautiful drowned kitten," he said, and he pulled her even closer.

Jolts of pure electricity that had nothing to do with the rolling thunder shot through Fancy's body at his touch. It didn't disappear even when they were in the store and had Tina in the basket seat of a cart.

"You want to push so you'll have something to lean on?" Theron asked Fancy, reluctant to remove his arm from around her. It felt so right and natural there.

"Yes, I would. We'd better have two carts, though. The car seat will take one all by itself, and the toy and clothes will take another."

Theron picked out a car seat, and they moved on to the children's clothing section. He looked inside the neck of Tina's sweatshirt and found that she was in a size three, so Fancy steered them in that direction.

"What do I buy?" he asked.

"Playclothes first. Jeans, pants, and then tops to match. Pajamas that aren't so heavy, because your house will be too warm for those things she has. Besides, I don't like them," Fancy said.

"Why?"

"They're ugly," she said.

"Well, then, we'll throw the old ones away," he said seriously.

"Don't make fun of me. I've hated that kind of pajamas since I was a little girl. Buy her pretty things, Theron. Make her feel special."

"Okay, help me," he said.

Fancy held up two outfits. The pink one had a cartoon character on the front; the bright blue one was decorated with sparkly fake diamonds in the shape of a heart.

"Tina, which one do you like better?"

She studied the outfits for a moment and pointed to the blue one.

"She's a girly-girl. Buy her diamonds and glitter," Fancy said.

"Jeans?" he asked.

"Sure, for feeding the cows or playing in the barn so she doesn't ruin her pretty things. But mostly at her age she needs elastic waistbands so she can get her pants up and down in the bathroom." She selected two more outfits. "How about these, Tina? Which one?"

Tina giggled and picked another set.

An hour later they had a cartful of clothing, including two Sunday dresses and a new pair of shoes plus a pair of rubber boots. Tina clutched a small teddy bear in her arms. That was what she wanted, even more than a book, and nothing could change her mind. Fancy picked up a couple of children's books anyway and at the last minute a combo bottle of shampoo and conditioner and a cell phone charger.

It was a hoot watching Theron remove the safety seat from its bulky packaging in the front seat of the pickup so it wouldn't get wet. He wrestled with the big box and finally ripped it to pieces to get the thing out. It was a narrow fit to get it over the front seat and into place on the passenger side of the backseat, but finally it was secured and Tina was safely in it.

Then Theron headed toward the hospital. Fancy was surprised when they walked into the emergency room and were taken straight to a cubicle. The doctor took the bandage off the wound, informed them that he couldn't have done a better job, redressed it, and said that he'd order a tetanus shot plus an X-ray, just to be on the safe side.

Fancy moaned.

Theron grinned.

"I hate shots. I mean, I really, *really* hate them."

"As much as ugly pajamas?" he asked.

"Almost." She pouted.

"Payback is the devil, isn't it? That's what you get for laughing at me with that vicious car seat. The thing tried to murder me, and you just sat back there and giggled," he reminded her.

"But it didn't hurt like a shot."

The doctor returned with a needle, and Tina put her hands over her eyes. Fancy wanted to too.

After they had a scan of her head, the attending came back into the room. "I'll send the results to your doctor, but I don't see any problems," he said.

"I told you it was just an unnecessary expense," she said.

The doctor patted her on the arm. "You can't put a price on peace of mind. Have your husband help you wash your hair. The way you're wearing it is the best way I could think of for at least ten days. He can wash one side and then the other, being careful to keep the bandages dry. Change them every day, and keep antibiotic ointment on the wound. If it gets red streaks or infected, see your doctor," the attending said.

"Thank you," Theron said.

They went to the desk to sign insurance forms and were back in the truck in less than an hour.

"I'm hungry," Tina said.

"Why didn't you tell him I wasn't your wife?" Fancy asked.

"Why didn't you?"

"Macky cheese?" Tina asked.

"I'm not sure where to get macky cheese. How about pizza?" Theron said.

"Pizza, yes, yes, yes." Tina clapped her hands.

"All right with you, Mrs. Warren?" Theron asked.

"Are you talking to me? I'm Miss Fancy," she said.

"Then, Miss Fancy, is pizza all right with you?"

"I love pizza. We could maybe even hit a noon buffet. I could eat a bushel of salad with French dressing right now."

"No salad," Tina said. "It's . . ."

Theron and Fancy chimed in together. "Yucky."

While they ate, another rainstorm hit the area, and they had to use the umbrella to get back to the truck. Fancy was glad she didn't have to drive. She was still more than a little jangled.

Tina had been quiet while she ate, but when she was strapped into her seat, she piped up, "New Daddy is a good daddy."

"You are right," Fancy said.

Tina held her new bear tightly and sang "Twinkle, Twinkle, Little Star" to it.

Fancy touched her pigtails and sighed. "So, Mr. Warren, are you going to wash my hair when we get there?"

"I surely am. One side at a time, just like the doctor said."

"Wash my hair too?" Tina asked.

"Yes, I will," Theron said softly.

He parked under the awning in front of the motel doors and went inside to register. He returned with one key, apologizing that only one room was available but that it was large enough to be a suite.

When they got there, they saw that it had two queen-size beds and a big bathroom with a Jacuzzi tub.

Fancy swooned at the sight of the tub.

Tina squealed about the big plasma television.

Theron sighed deeply at the sight of a bed, but it didn't take all the tension from his body. Not by a long shot.

Chapter Thirteen

Fancy opened her bag and removed a long nightshirt and a pair of boxer shorts.

Theron fell back on a bed and shut his eyes.

Tina stood in the middle of the room and hugged her bear. "It's a castle," she breathed.

Theron chuckled. "And I'm the king."

Tina twirled around, taking it all in. "Fanny is the queen."

"And you are the princess who hasn't had a bath. The king can sleep for one hour while we pamper the princess, and then he has to wake up and wash the queen's hair for her," Fancy said.

"Tell the nearest peasant to do it," Theron mumbled.

"King for an hour. Commoner after that?" Fancy teased.

"After my nap I'll be anyone you want," he said.

Tina thought the Jacuzzi was wonderful once she got past the noise of the jets. She had two rubber toys in her tote bag, and she stayed in the tub until her toes and fingertips were wrinkled. By the time Fancy had dressed her in a new pair of soft knit pajamas and combed out her tangled hair, her eyes were heavy. She picked up her old doll and new bear, and Fancy tucked her into bed.

She pulled Fancy down to her in a hug and said, "I'm the princess."

"Yes, you are," Fancy answered. She gathered up her things and went back to the bathroom. She ran a tub of water, got in, and turned on the jets. She rolled up a towel and leaned her head back on it and shut her eyes. She wished Maria would have called the child Echo instead of Tina. When she had children, she intended to name every one of them something unique and wonderful. And she planned to have at least six. She'd always begged Santa for a brother or sister when she was little, but he never came through. Her kids would definitely have others to stand beside them when the going got tough. The wandering thoughts eased into dreams, and she dozed. When she awoke, the water was barely lukewarm.

She jumped and covered herself with her hands when the door opened slightly. "Who is it? I'm in the tub."

"Are you all right in there? I just woke up, and it's been two hours," Theron asked.

"I'm fine. I'll get out and get dressed, and you can help me with my hair."

"Call me when you're ready."

She dried hurriedly and put on her pajamas. It hurt when she pulled the top over her head, and she moaned. Theron was immediately at the door, only this time he didn't stop. He plowed right inside.

"Are you all right? Feeling faint? Do you need to sit down? You've got to get your head checked again when we get home, Fancy." Worry was etched into his face.

"It hurt when I jerked my shirt on. The doctor said there were no internal problems, and my insurance would probably balk at paying for another scan."

He took her arm and backed her up two steps. "Sit down, and let me check the bandage."

He heaved a sigh of relief when he found it intact and no bleeding. "It looks all right. You do need a hair washing. It's pretty greasy," he said.

"How romantic!"

"Do you want me to be romantic?" he asked.

"No, sir! I just want my hair washed," she lied, feeling a blush rush up her neck.

"Then why did you say that?" he persisted.

"Even a good friend doesn't tell a lady that her hair is greasy," she improvised.

He looked at her for a moment, but she wouldn't meet his gaze. "Your good friends should always be honest. Kate or Sophie wouldn't tell you if your hair was greasy?"

She had to agree with a nod. "Kate would. Sophie would tiptoe around it and ask if I needed to buy shampoo."

"I'm more like Kate. Your hair is a fright. Let's get it washed and put back up in horse tails," he said.

She carefully removed one of the elastics. "Get your terminology right. They are pigtails."

"You want to do this bent over the tub or the sink?" he asked.

"The tub," she said, leaning over to adjust the water to the right temperature and dropping to her knees, bending her head to one side over the edge of the tub. Theron took the plastic wrapper off a glass and began the job of very gently pouring water through one side of her hair, holding one hand at the edge of the bandage to keep it dry.

Not one of the men Fancy dated had ever washed her hair. His fingers were magic, working the shampoo into her hair and rinsing it. He used a towel on each side, being careful not to touch the wound as he dried it. The sparks that danced around the room left no doubt that Fancy Lynn Sawyer wanted more than a friendship with Theron Warren.

His breath caught in his chest. It would be so easy to kiss her slender neck, to run the back of his hand down her jawline, to get lost in those big blue eyes. His mind ran in circles, but finally he admitted that he'd fallen for Fancy Lynn Sawyer. Now what did he do about it?

By the time they'd finished with the second side of her hair, Tina had joined them. She held on to her doll with one arm and the bear with the other. "Go outside and play?"

Theron took her by the hand and led her to the window, where he pulled open the drapes. "Still raining, ladybug. Want to watch cartoons?"

"I'm Cinderella, Daddy," she said seriously.

He bit back a grin. "Then do you want to watch cartoons, princess?"

She had come a long way in a few days. He was no longer "New Daddy." The *New* had gone by the wayside.

"Yes, yes, yes." She smiled.

He flipped through channels until he came to one she liked. She laid her toys down on a bed, crawled up into the middle of it, and sat cross-legged to watch the show. Theron went back to the bathroom door to see what was taking Fancy so long.

She had the blow dryer from the wall working on the pigtails. Once they were dry, she brushed them out again, and they hung in huge curls to her shoulders.

"Mighty cute hairdo." He brushed past her and went to sit on the edge of the tub. "What were you thinking about anyway? Your mind was off in la-la land."

She scrambled for something to say that wouldn't incriminate her. Theron Warren would fall backward into the tub with acute cardiac arrest if she opened her mouth and blurted out that she'd been envisioning what their children would look like.

"I *was* off in neverland. I forgot to put my phone on the new charger, so it'll be another hour before I can call my mother. I know she's worried. We usually talk at least once a day."

"At thirty you're still Momma's little girl?"

"Don't make fun of me. She's all the family I have other than Kate and Sophie."

He grabbed his chest. "I'm so hurt. We've lived together for practically a week now, and you didn't include me?"

"We've lived together for a few days, and the jury is still out on what you are in my life," she told him.

"What's your momma going to think about your living with me?" he joked.

"What's yours going to think?"

"Who's going to tell her?"

"I'll tell your momma," Tina said from the doorway.

Fancy hugged her. "You smell good." She lifted a section of her own hair up to her nose and took a deep breath. "Me too."

"My two girls both smell wonderful. But I don't. So if you will scoot out, I'd like to take advantage of this big tub," Theron said.

It wasn't until Fancy and Tina were on the bed channel surfing for something to watch that she realized what Theron had said.

My two girls.

It was only because they'd been thrown together for days, she concluded. When they were back in Albany, things would get back to normal.

Tina pointed toward the television. "Doggies."

"It's a rerun of *Homeward Bound*. You'll like it." Fancy laid the remote control on the bedside table and stretched out on her stomach, elbows on the bed, head in hands, to watch the movie with Tina. The child looked at her for a few minutes and then lay down the exact same way.

"What's this?" Theron asked when he came out of the bathroom.

"Shh," they both said at the same time.

Fancy regarded him out of the corner of her eye. He had a towel around his neck. Water droplets still clung to his dark hair. His dark green T-shirt matched his eyes perfectly. He sat on the edge of the bed and dried his hair with a few rough tumbles, then combed it with his fingertips. He pulled his legs up and rolled up the hems of his green and burgundy plaid flannel pajama pants. He was so handsome that it took her breath away, and whatever that shaving lotion was, it smelled like heaven. How could she ever have thought he looked like a boy? There was nothing boyish about him. He was definitely all man.

Pillows propped behind him against the headboard, he turned his attention to the television. Something about cats and dogs, but at least they were real creatures and not something computer generated. He laughed at the big dog sniffing through a suitcase and tearing up a shirt. Fancy would have a cussing fit if a dog did that.

"What is this movie?" he asked.

"It's called *Homeward Bound*. You've never seen it?" Fancy whispered.

He shook his head.

"Keep watching. It's one of my favorites."

He laughed at all the right places, held Tina when she worried that the cat was truly drowned, and almost clapped with her when it survived after all. But mostly he watched Fancy. Even in childish pigtails she was gorgeous.

Tina sighed as the credits rolled. "I want a cat like that one."

"We don't have one exactly like that, but there's lots of yellow ones and gray ones," Theron assured her.

She changed the subject abruptly when her stomach growled. "I'm hungry."

"Guess that means we all get dressed, or else I go find some fast food and bring it back," Theron said.

"Chinese?" Fancy suggested. "But something less spicy for Tina. Maybe a hamburger or chicken nuggets."

"Chinese, it is," Theron said. "What do you like?"

"Anything but garlic chicken," Fancy said. "Get a couple of things, and we'll share."

He picked up his jeans on the way to the bathroom. Seconds later he was back out, putting on his shoes. "Chicken or hamburger, Tina?"

"Both. We can share."

"Good Lord, your influence on her is . . ." He stumbled for the right words.

"At least it's about sharing," Fancy said quickly. "That's a good trait, isn't it?"

"Don't get testy with me. I wasn't going to say anything derogatory."

"I don't want any . . . dogatory. That sounds yucky," Tina said.

Theron left with a grin on his face.

Chapter Fourteen

Tell me one more time that you are all right. Good grief, Fancy Lynn, I raise you for thirty years without a single stitch or accident, and . . . ," Gwen fussed.

Fancy held the phone out from her ear. "It's okay, Momma. The doctor even did a scan. Can you believe that? Must have been a really slow day at their hospital."

"Don't tease me or try to put me at ease. Do I need to fly to Texas to take care of you?" Gwen asked.

"No, Theron washed my hair today, and I'm sure I can get Kate or Sophie to help me when I get home."

"Tell me more about this Theron. Is he good-looking?"

"Very. He's thirty-one, and he's been married once, briefly, and he's got a little girl he didn't know he had until four days ago. Her name is Tina, and she's a sweetheart."

"How old?"

"Three."

"That's a wonderful age. Where are you all right now?"

"We're at a nice motel in Decatur, and Theron's gone to buy us supper. Tina and I just watched *Homeward Bound,* and now she's involved with her doll and new teddy bear. She's 'reading' them the new books we bought her."

"You're already attached to her. I can hear it in your voice. Be careful you don't get the man and the child all mixed up together," Gwen said.

"I love her. I tolerate him."

"Call me when you get home, and no hanky-panky in front of baby."

"Momma!"

Gwen laughed and hung up before she could say anything else. She called Kate next.

"Girl, where are you? We're thawing out. Are you at home? I'll come over this evening," Kate said.

"I'm in Decatur in a motel with Theron and Tina, his daughter. We'll be home tomorrow," Fancy said.

"You're in a motel? Oh, boy! But I've got a shift tomorrow. Can't come until Sunday, then," Kate said. "So, are you in love?"

"I am not. But I did have to go to the hospital for this bump on my head." She went on to give Kate a short version of the accident.

"He saved your life, and you're not in love? He could be your knight in shining whatever, you know. Don't slam the door in the face of opportunity."

"It's you who wants a shining whatever. I want a forever thing, remember?" Fancy said.

"Chinese and McDonald's!" Theron called from the doorway as he carried in two enormous bags of food.

"Gotta go. Food is here," Fancy said.

"Sounds like a forever thing just walked in," Kate said.

"Don't hold your breath. You never did look good in that shade of blue." Fancy flipped the phone shut.

Theron unloaded the food onto the table in front of the windows, and they watched the rain as they ate. "So your phone is up and running? Mind if I use it to call my folks?"

"Not a bit," she said. The sweet-and-sour chicken was scrumptious, the rice cooked just right, and the steamed vegetables were wonderful.

Tina pointed toward the rice. "What is that?"

"Try it," Fancy said.

She opened her mouth, and Fancy put a forkful in. Tina chewed and nodded at the same time. "More."

Fancy piled some onto one of the paper plates the restaurant had provided, and Tina ate every single grain.

"You know," Theron said thoughtfully, "Tina is the image of my sister when she was young, except for the coloring. Melissa has lighter hair, and her eyes are green. Still, I think I should have DNA testing done to be sure. I don't want Maria to have a leg to stand on if she ever comes back around with ideas of taking Tina away."

"You mean, so she can't say she's someone else's child?" Fancy asked.

"It's just a formality. But I want to be sure of my legal rights here."

"What's 'mality?" Tina piped up. "Can I have some of it too?"

"It's this stuff right here." Fancy put a piece of broccoli and a snow pea onto her plate.

She tucked in her chin and looked up from under her dark eyebrows and lashes. Finally, after she'd studied the two vegetables and watched Fancy eat the same thing, she gingerly picked up the broccoli and put it into her mouth. "It's yucky. I don't like 'mality."

"Then you won't have to eat any more of it, but you were brave to try it," Fancy said.

Tina went back to her hamburger and apple.

Fancy pointed to the cell phone on the nightstand. "Go ahead and make the call. Talk as long as you like. I've got lots of minutes on it."

Theron called his parents, and what Fancy got from the one-sided conversation was that he'd like to give Tina a few weeks to get settled before he sprang all the relatives on her. Then he phoned his ex-mother-in-law, and the conversation was so terse that Fancy got nothing from it. Most of the time he listened, interjecting an occasional "uh-huh," or "thank you for that."

When he finished, he laid the phone down and stretched out on the bed, staring at the ceiling. Fancy's sweet tooth kicked into overdrive when she saw Tina eating her chocolate-chip cookie, and she remembered the vending machine down the hallway.

She took Tina's hand in hers. "Let's go buy some candy bars now that we've eaten right. You got a favorite kind?" she asked Theron as she picked up her purse and rustled around in it for loose change.

"Snickers. Why are you looking at me like that?" he asked.

"No reason," she said. Snickers was her favorite also. She'd kept miniatures in her desk drawer at school.

They walked down the hallway hand in hand, and Fancy let Tina put the money into the vending machine. They bought three chocolate bars, a bag of gummy bears, two sodas, and a container of milk for Tina.

"Cute little girl, but she must look like her father," a lady said when they passed her on the way back to the room.

"Thank you," Fancy said. It didn't hurt to pretend. She'd never see the woman again. "She does look like her father's side of the family."

"She's a doll, no matter who she looks like." The lady unlocked the door across the hall and went inside.

"Who's that?" Tina whispered.

"Just a sweet little lady who's probably missing her grand-daughter," Fancy said as she knocked on their door.

Theron threw it open and returned to the bed. While Tina munched on the gummy bears and sipped her milk, Fancy ate a candy bar.

"It's worse than I thought but better than it could be," Theron said.

"What's that?"

"Tina, you want to watch some more cartoons?"

"Yes, yes, yes. About the dogs and cat?"

Fancy surfed a few minutes but couldn't find another channel playing anything about cats. She did find an old Scooby-Doo movie on the Disney Channel, though, and that excited Tina. She grabbed her doll and bear and crawled up onto the bed.

Theron took Fancy's hand and led her to the other bed. Both of them sat down on the side away from Tina. He laced his fingers in hers and held on tightly.

"Maria had a terrible time giving birth and wouldn't even hold the baby. Her mother says she never did bond with her and that three weeks after Echo—she calls her that instead of Tina—was born, Maria went back to work at two jobs. Kayla kept Echo, only she hated the name, so she's the one who started calling her Tina."

Fancy listened intently, shocked all over again at Tina's sad childhood. But she couldn't help noticing how perfectly her hand fit into Theron's and how, even in the midst of her sadness, it made her feel bonded to him.

"Kayla's place of work had a day-care center available," Theron finished, but he kept Fancy's hand in his.

"So what do you do now?"

"Hire a lawyer. Do a DNA test. Change her name to Warren. Raise her."

"You make a pretty tough job sound simple," Fancy said.

"Well, I've got a really big favor to ask of you," he said.

Fancy looked at him.

"Tina knows and likes you, and, well, you're not working right now. Could you please keep her for me for a few days until I can find a good day-care center for her? I could drop her off on my way to school and pick her up as soon as I can get away afterward," he said.

She continued to look at him while her mind said no. A clean break from the little girl would be infinitely easier than saying good-bye after getting even more attached to her.

Her mouth said, "Of course I will. She'll have to go to the beauty shop with me on the days I fix hair, but we'll be fine."

Chapter Fifteen

Joe Frank had built the house fifty years before with the best foundation, wood, and labor that money could buy. It had been constructed to stand for a lifetime, and with every board that went into the framework, he had looked forward to the sounds and laughter of children filling the place. But that had never happened—until Theron opened the door and led Tina into the massive great room.

He tried to see it through her eyes. Oak hardwood floors in the living and dining area, a long table with ten chairs around it reflected in the glossy finish. A huge window overlooked the backyard where Joe had planned to watch birds and deer with his wife and children. One wall of the living area featured a stone fireplace, the mantel decorated with only one picture: that of Joe and his new bride on their wedding day. An enormous rug in shades of mint green and burgundy stretched from the edge of the fireplace, under the leather sofa and oversized recliner, back to the bookcases at the other end of the room. The kitchen had never been updated. Oak cabinets, white double sink, white stove and refrigerator. But it had character, so the thought of replacing any of it had never entered Theron's mind.

"This is your new home," he said softly to Tina.

Her gaze moved from one place to the other, taking in everything. "*Who* lives here?" she whispered.

"You do and I do."

"Where's Fanny?"

He squatted down in front of her and laid a hand on her shoulder. "She lives in her own house in town. You are going to stay

with her during the day while I work. Tomorrow we will go to
church, and you'll see her there. The next day I have to go to work
at the school, and you will stay with Fancy. Would you like to see
your new room?" he asked.

He hoped for a "yes, yes, yes."

He barely got a nod.

He led her down the hallway to the bedroom right across the hall
from the one he'd chosen when he moved into the house. A brightly
colored quilt in pastel shades of pink, yellow, and mint green covered
the four-poster bed. A lamp sat on a white crocheted doily on the
nightstand. The matching dresser with a triple mirror stood waiting
for someone to finally use the drawers. The walls had been painted
bright yellow at one time, but they'd faded to a pale shade that brightened prettily when the sun filtered through the lace curtains on the
windows.

"We can put your toys in here and all your new things in the
closet," Theron said.

"It's so big," Tina said.

"What? The bed? Would you like a smaller one?"

She waved her hands around. "All of it."

"Yes, it is a big house."

Her face finally brightened. "Kids? Where are they?"

"There are no other kids, Tina. Just me and you. Are you hungry?"

She shook her head and took a deep breath. She removed her
hand from his and took a few steps forward, carefully touched the
quilt, and then laid her doll on the pillow.

"She likes it," she said.

"I'm glad." He had had no idea how she would react to the house.
The cabin had been small and the motel room not even that big.
She'd been raised in a trailer, from what he understood. When he
had opened the front door, he had seen some fear in her eyes, but
when she put the doll on the bed, he figured she'd managed to accept the place as it was.

"Why don't you get up there beside her, and I'll bring in your
things? We'll put them away, and then we'll go outside and check
on the cats and cattle."

"Kitties! Yes, yes, yes!" She clapped her hands.

Those words convinced him that they'd make it through the day and night. After that she'd start to feel more at home, and everything would be fine. She seemed remarkably resilient for such a little thing. She'd adjust to her surroundings, and he'd adjust to having a child. He hoped Uncle Joe had a lucid day or two so he could tell him that laughter now rang through the house.

Fancy had kissed Tina on the forehead before she got out of Theron's truck at Hattie's house. Then she had carried her duffel bag into the house and tossed it into her bedroom. She'd turned up the heat and thrown herself down on the sofa. She didn't even care if Hattie rose up from the ashes and gave her an evil glare about putting her muddy feet on the sofa. The "80s Ladies" ringtone suddenly turned her purse into a jukebox. Without getting up, she fished inside it and found her cell phone.

"Hello, Momma," she said.

"Are you home?"

"I'm at Granny's. It will never be home, but I've got my dirty shoes on the sofa," she said.

"Is her ghost glaring at you?" Gwen giggled.

Fancy looked up and then shuddered. "I don't see it," she whispered.

"Are you alone?"

"Unless Granny's ghost is hiding under the couch."

"No Greek god to set your heart racing or little girl to make your biological clock tick louder?"

"Theron is no Greek god, Momma. He's barely taller than me."

"Blond hair?"

"Brown."

"Blue eyes?"

"Green."

"Hmm. Certainly not the original man of your dreams, is he? How about your biological clock? Is it driving you crazy?"

"Don't you read the tabloids at the checkout counter? Movie stars have babies when they're in their forties now. I've got lots of time. Somehow I don't think you called to tease me, did you?"

"No, it just came out. Are you still planning on having lots of kids someday?"

"I'm going to have a dozen," Fancy said quickly.

"Tick-tock, tick-tock."

"I told you, forties."

"Your twelfth one at forty isn't so bad. Your first of twelve is pushing it," she teased. "Oh, and one more thing. Les has bought us a two-week cruise for Christmas. Leaving a week before Christmas and coming home the day after New Year's. Want to go with us?"

Tears welled up. A lump the size of a grapefruit formed in Fancy's throat.

"Are you going to answer me? Is your non-Greek god going to keep you in that godforsaken land of mosquitoes and mesquite trees?" Gwen asked.

"No, he's not, but I'm not going with you. For the first time in your married life you two are going on a vacation by yourselves— the honeymoon you never had because there was a sulky teenager in your lives. I'm staying right here and helping Sophie get through her last holidays with Aunt Maud. You go, and if you have one guilty feeling about leaving me behind, I'll . . ."

"You'll what?" Gwen asked.

"Cry. And then you'll feel guilty."

"Okay, then come home for a few days when we get back?"

Fancy's heart lay in shambles on the floor in front of the sofa. "With bells on. And I expect to see tons of pictures."

Gwen hung up, and Fancy looked around for a black cat. One seemed to be around every time something crazy-bad happened. She would have bet one had just walked across the porch. Just because she couldn't see it didn't mean it wasn't close by.

The house began to warm, so she sat up and removed her dirty shoes and jacket. She went to the bedroom and dumped everything in the duffel bag onto the floor, where she sorted it into two piles for laundry. She picked up the white things and carried them to the utility room and stuffed them into the washing machine.

Then there was nothing to do.

Bright sunshine continued to melt the last vestiges of ice. She put a CD in her player and turned up the volume. She didn't want to be reminded of the days she'd spent in the cabin with ice everywhere. Sara Evans sang about looking into those blue eyes and hearing nothing but lies while Fancy two-stepped with an invisible partner who was the same height and size as Theron Warren.

Sara sang a song called "Three Chords and the Truth."

The truth? What was it? Was her mother right even in her teasing?

"When did I fall for him?" she asked herself aloud; then she fell back onto the sofa again. "I can't have fallen for him."

But you did, and now what the devil are you going to do about it?

"Fall the other way," she said.

It don't work that way, girl.

"Then I'll just have to live with it and do the best I can. He's not interested in a wife or a forever thing, and I won't settle for anything less."

She dragged herself to the kitchen and made a peanut butter and jelly sandwich. She ate it standing up at the kitchen sink watching a cardinal searching for food in the backyard. The bright red bird brought on a vision of Tina's excitement at feeding the birds at the cabin.

Sara continued to sing in the background, and the lyrics to every song seemed to speak to Fancy. Finally she turned the music off and decided to have a long bath and a nap. She sank down into the tub of water and tried to let the warmth penetrate her bones, but she was so antsy that she quickly got out and wrapped a towel around herself. She padded barefoot on the cold floor to the bedroom, where she dragged out a pair of warm flannel pajamas that were at least a size too big. She should have cut the legs off and hemmed them when her secret Santa at school gave them to her two years before, but she'd lived in Florida, where she never wore flannel. She rolled up the hems of the pants and the sleeves of the top.

It was seven o'clock, but it was already dark out. She couldn't take a nap that late, or she'd be awake until the wee hours of the morning. She picked up a book and carried it to the living room. J.A. Jance could entertain her until bedtime.

She'd barely fallen asleep when the alarm went off. She forced her eyes open, expecting to see sun rays drifting in through the curtains, but it was still dark. She reached to hit the snooze button, only to find that it was three o'clock in the morning and not eight. She figured she must have been dreaming, so she put the pillow over her head and tried to go back to sleep. In five minutes the noise started again, and she realized it was her cell phone. She hustled out of bed and down the hall and barely answered it before it stopped sounding.

"Hello?" Her first thought was that something had happened to Aunt Maud.

Theron talked fast and furious. "I'm so sorry to call you at this horrible hour, but I didn't know what else to do. Tina's in the bathroom throwing up, and she's practically hysterical. I'm lost, and all she'll say is that she wants Fanny, she's had a bad dream, and in between sobs all she says is your name."

She pictured him wringing his hands and yanking at his hair.

"How do I get there?" she asked.

"Call me when you leave, and I'll talk you here, and thanks, Fancy. I don't know how to handle this. I'm going to be a terrible father."

"No, you're not, New Daddy." She picked up her jacket, slipped her arms into it without dropping the phone, and slung her purse over her shoulder. "I'm leaving right now. I'm walking out the door."

"Go south toward Moran. Five miles. There's a big ranch sign on the left about a quarter of a mile farther. Turn at the next section line road, take the first right, and follow it to the end of the lane. I'll turn on the porch light."

"Okay, I'm in the car and headed toward Main Street. Put Tina on the phone if she can talk, Theron."

She could hear the weeping as he neared the bathroom.

"Tina, it's Fancy. She wants to talk to you," Theron said softly.

"Fanny?" Tina whimpered into the phone a few moments later.

"Yes, it's Fanny, and I'm coming to see you. Do you want to tell me about the bad dream? Was it monsters?" Fancy asked.

"No. It was about you. The man was going to hurt you. He looked all mean, and you were fighting with him," she said.

"I'm fine, Tina. It was just a nightmare, and I'm on my way. Can you stop crying now?"

Snuffling took the place of sobs.

"She's nodding," Theron said in the background.

"Right now?" Tina asked her.

"Right now. Can your daddy take you to the living room and rock you until I get there? Is that okay?"

" 'kay," she said.

"Give Daddy the phone," Fancy told her.

"What do I do?" Theron asked.

"Pick her up and take her to the living room and rock her until I get there. She's agreed to that."

"Thank God," he said as Fancy heard him pick up Tina and walk to the living room. "I've been out of my mind for a couple of hours. I hated to call you."

"Why? Because it was the middle of the night? Or because you didn't want me to think you needed me?" she asked.

Silence filled the space.

"It's nice to be needed," she said.

More silence.

"Are you going to talk to me or not?" she asked.

"She's . . . she's finally falling asleep," he whispered. "I think you can go on back home now."

"I promised her I'd be there, and I'm on my way. If you don't want to admit that you need me, that's your business. But I don't make promises I don't intend to keep."

"You are smart-mouthed, aren't you?" he said softly.

"Honey, you don't know the half of it."

It was three twenty when she pulled up into the gravel circular driveway. The size of the sprawling white frame house before her was intimidating. The porch stretched the entire length of the front, and two lights beckoned her. She didn't have to knock; the door was unlocked, and she walked in.

Theron was sitting in a wooden rocker in front of the fireplace with Tina in his lap. She had her thumb in her mouth and was sound asleep.

"I told you we finally had it under control," he whispered as he looked up at her.

Fancy's hair was still in pigtails. She wore pajamas covered with pictures of apples, and they were a mile too big for her. She wore no makeup and oversized fuzzy slippers.

And Theron thought she looked beautiful.

His heart skipped a beat and then picked up a full, rolling head of steam.

"And I told you that I don't make promises I can't keep. How long have you been awake?" she asked.

"Three hours, I think. I don't know. It was horrible."

"Give her to me, and go to bed. Where does she sleep? We both have a Sunday school class to teach in a few hours. I'll sleep the rest of the night with her. We'll have 'pandy cakes' for breakfast, and you can cook them. Wake us up in time to get ready for church, and I'll need half an hour at my house. The preacher might not like me showing up like this."

She slipped her arms around Tina and again experienced the shock of electricity between her skin and Theron's when he transferred the child.

"Come on, baby girl. Let's go get some sleep," she crooned as she followed Theron down the hallway. She curled up beside Tina, and in minutes she was asleep. Not even one crazy dream interrupted their slumber.

Chapter Sixteen

The coffee table in Hattie's living room was, for today, Tina's "cabinet." Hattie's smaller pots and pans were scattered as the child played pretend cooking. Underneath the table was evidently the oven, because when she put something under there, she had to have a hot pad to get it out. She stirred excessively, baked only a few minutes, and tasted with slurps regularly. Her doll and bear listened intently to her prattle about macky cheese and chocolate cake and tasted them often from the couch.

Sophie, Kate, and Fancy sat around the kitchen table with hot chocolate and powdered-sugar donuts. Tina had eaten half a donut. Her chocolate was cooling until she could drink it without burning her mouth. She looked up periodically to make sure Fancy was still in her sights and kept playing.

"So, tell me how it is you've got that cute little thing today. I'm going to have a dozen who look just like her someday, you know. With my heritage it could happen. You want to give her to me so I'll have a head start?" Kate asked.

"I've got her because Theron has to catch up on schoolwork to get ready for tomorrow. She could have gone with him and played in the office, but that wouldn't be nearly as much fun as baking chocolate cakes in the oven under the coffee table. And, no, you cannot have her. If she's ever up for grabs again, I get first dibs," Fancy said.

"How could anyone just walk off and leave something that precious?" Sophie asked.

"I guess it's easy to leave something you didn't ever want in the first place. Look what Hattie did. She might as well have left Momma."

"Okay, now that we've established why we get to drool over a child today, start with Monday and tell us, play by play, what happened," Sophie said.

"In the beginning God created dirt," Fancy said.

Kate rolled her eyes.

Sophie giggled.

"And then he made man, and the devil put an ego on him, and Theron Warren was born," Fancy intoned. Then she went on to tell the story about the previous week in detail and how she'd gone to Theron's house in her pajamas on Saturday night and slept with Tina.

"This morning we got up, and, sure enough, he had pancakes and sausage ready. I fixed her hair and dressed her while he got ready for church. Don't those French braids look cute? Anyway, we drove into Albany together. He dropped me off here so I could get ready, and I met them at church. She clung to me like she was afraid I'd disappear again when I made it to the Sunday school room."

"After church?" Sophie asked.

"We ate at the Dairy Queen, and I brought her home with me. You all showed up five minutes later, and that's my story and I'm sticking to it."

Kate swept her black hair back over her shoulders. "We got the history lesson. I want the whole story now. Did he kiss you?"

Fancy blushed.

"Out with it," Sophie said. "We've been cheated out of the day-by-day because you didn't take your charger."

"Don't squirm. It makes you look guilty," Kate laughed.

"Okay, he kissed me."

Both Kate and Sophie nodded emphatically.

"And?" Kate asked.

"And I saw fireworks and heard bells, and it was a very fine kiss," Fancy said honestly.

"Where's it going?" Sophie asked.

"Probably nowhere. He's got Tina to worry about right now."

"Right," Kate said with a giggle.

"Okay, we've covered my week in two cups of hot chocolate. I'm making a pot of coffee to cut the sweet, and then it's your turn," Fancy said.

Sophie sighed. "After a red-hot week like that, mine is barely pale pink."

Kate riffled through the cabinets and found a bag of Oreos. "Well, mine sure ain't burgundy, but it was a pretty good one."

"Me first, then. I don't want to bring up the rear with a puff of wind against two tornadoes," Sophie said. "Aunt Maud made her will and left me her half of the ranch. The other half is left to my uncle's great-nephew. That was done back before he died and can't be changed."

"So what are you going to do when she's gone?" Fancy asked.

"I'll use my insurance money and buy him out. I hope he hates ranching and whatever his half is worth will put dollar signs into his eyes."

"Sounds like a good plan to me. Are you really going to run that ranch for the rest of your life?" Fancy said.

"I hated it as a child and a teenager, but it's my life now. So, yes, I am."

Kate ripped open the bag of cookies and scattered them all over the table. "Oops."

Tina heard the noise and came running, braids bouncing, red dress swishing against her legs. "I want one."

Kate handed her four.

She stared at them and looked at Fancy.

"It's all right. You can have them. See if your doll or the bear wants to help you eat them," Fancy said.

Tina smiled and took off to the living room. She put a cookie in each of the pots, and they instantly became "macky cheese" and "mean beans."

"What was that all about?" Sophie asked.

Fancy lowered her voice to barely a whisper.

Sophie and Kate leaned in to hear.

"She's been raised literally since birth in a day-care center, so rules have to be followed. She sits at the table and puts down her fork between bites. After lunch she goes directly to her pallet or wherever for her nap. No hassles or begging."

"The perfect child. How horrible," Kate said.

"Did she have a nap today?"

"Soon as we ate lunch and got here. She curled up on the sofa. Slept thirty minutes and had just gotten up when y'all arrived."

"Wow," Sophie said. "I fought my momma tooth, nail, hair, and eyeball not to take naps after I was three."

Fancy nodded and changed the subject. "Now tell us about your week, Kate."

"I won the betting pot at the police station."

"And what were you betting on?" Sophie asked.

"Wrong question."

"How much was it?" Fancy asked.

"Bingo. Right question. Two hundred dollars to do with whatsoever I please. I can't make up my mind if I'm going to blow it all on massages or buy a new pair of boots."

"Now what were you betting on?" Sophie repeated the question.

"Had to be football. You can't bet with Kate when it comes to football. Cowboys against who?" Fancy asked.

"Wrong again."

"Okay, I'll play. It was how long it would take a fly to find the donut in the wastebasket," Sophie said.

Kate shook her head and blushed.

"It's got something to do with Hart Ducaine. Nothing or no one else in the world can make Kate's face hot enough to ignite," Fancy said.

"Right on the money, all two hundred dollars."

"So what was the bet?"

"He was at the pro-bull-riding in Nevada. We had a bet going whether he'd get the buckle or not. All those young fellers want it so bad, and Hart's already got two. So the bet wasn't who got it but whether he would get it."

"How'd you vote?" Sophie asked.

"For him. Two things that man can do: ride a bull and kiss. I knew he'd win if he rode, and he did. I got the pot."

Fancy giggled. "You weren't even sixteen when you knew him, and he was barely eighteen. How many other boyfriends have you had since then?" Fancy asked.

"I don't kiss and tell." Kate laughed.

"How about you, Sophie?" Fancy pressed on.

"One in my whole life, and I married him."

"Good Lord! We've got to find you a boyfriend. But you'll hardly have anything to compare him to," Kate said.

"I'll find my own boyfriends, thank you. Mercy, it's five o'clock. I'll barely make it home in time to help Aunt Maud do the chores," Sophie said.

"Aunt Maud should leave that to the foreman. What's she thinkin'? Doin' chores in the middle of the winter in her condition," Fancy said.

Sophie busied herself getting into her coat and the boots she'd taken off at the door. "You want to tell her that?"

"No, I do not!" Fancy gave her a hug and waved good-bye.

"Me too." Kate slipped her feet into boots. "I've got a shift starting in a couple of hours. Give me a hug."

Tina reached up her arms and said, "I want a hug too."

Kate dropped down onto her knees and gave the child a fierce hug. "I get one and Sophie doesn't?"

Tina hugged Sophie next. "Fanny gives hugs, and so does Tina."

Kate stood up and blew kisses before she closed the door. "You'd better watch what you do. I think you've got a follower here."

Fancy had barely finished cleaning the kitchen—washing mugs, putting the rest of the cookies back into the torn bag, wiping the table—when Theron poked his head in the front door without knocking.

"You want to go home?" he asked Tina.

"No, I do not!" she said in the same tone Fancy had used.

Theron stepped inside. "What did you say?"

"She's just repeating something I said earlier," Fancy said from the kitchen door.

"Well, let's clean up your mess and get on home. I've got chores to do," he said.

Fancy dropped down onto her knees. "Here, sweetheart, I'll help you collect the pots and pans. Remember, I'll see you in the morning, now. Daddy will bring you to me, and you get to spend the whole day and meet my beauty-shop ladies. They're going to love you."

Tina picked up her doll and bear and headed to the nearest corner. She dropped both toys, put her hands over her ears, and leaned her face into the wall.

"Tina, we have to go," Theron said.

Her shoulders shook as she began to sob.

"What do I do?" he whispered.

Fancy went to the corner and sat down beside Tina. She put her arms around the child and hugged her close. "You get to come back tomorrow."

Tina shook her head.

"What do you want me to do?" Fancy asked.

"Go home with me and Daddy."

Fancy looked at Theron.

"Tina, Fanny has a house here that she has to take care of, and we have the ranch. She can't live with us," Theron said softly.

"Why not?" Tears rolled down her tiny cheeks and dropped onto her new dress.

"You got a problem with my coming over?" Fancy asked. Theron had bags under his eyes, and his shoulders drooped. If he didn't get a full night's sleep before school on Monday after the past traumatic week, he'd collapse.

Theron shook his head.

"I'll pack a bag. We'll come in tomorrow morning in time for the ladies' beauty-shop appointments. She can sleep as long as she wants that way," Fancy said.

"I can't ask you to do this," Theron said.

"No, but you can prevent me from doing it. Are you going to do that?"

He shook his head. "After four hours of sleep last night and school tomorrow, I would be beholden to you. Maybe after a week she'll be adjusted, and I can get her into a good day-care situation."

"Tina, I want you to go home with Daddy now. I'm going to get my pajamas and toothbrush and drive out to the ranch right behind you," Fancy said.

She pulled her thumb from her mouth with a loud pop. "Promise?"

"I promise. You won't even have time to miss me. Daddy can go do his chores with the cows, and we'll start supper. You can help me."

Tina bent down to get her doll and bear and went straight to Theron. She slipped her hand into his and looked up at him. "Let's go, Daddy."

"It's going to be a long twenty years," he muttered.

"Want to change your mind?" Fancy asked.

"No. Thank you for this," he said as they went out the door.

Fancy packed a bag with two pairs of jeans, a couple of T-shirts, pajamas, and her toiletries. She picked up her purse and locked the front door, leaving Tina's mess in the living room.

It's only for a week. It's for Tina. But it's also for me. If a body eats nothing but chocolate every day for a month, they'll hate chocolate. The more time I spend with Theron Warren, the more I'm going to know that my feelings are nothing more than the result of the moment.

She kept telling herself that the whole way out to the ranch, but somehow she couldn't really convince herself, and it all went out the window when she saw Tina's nose pressed to the storm door and Theron's face above that. She parked the car, got out, opened the back door, and pulled out her duffel bag.

It feels good to be needed and wanted, she thought.

Tina fairly danced into the living room. "You're here! You did it. Let's cook."

Theron shook his head. "She's been in front of the door ever since we got here."

"Go on and get your chores done. Need help with that before we start supper?" Fancy asked.

"I can do them. It'll take the better part of an hour. If you're hungry, go ahead without me." He headed through the kitchen and out the back door.

The rumble of an old work truck with a bad muffler drifted through the house.

"Okay, Tina, let's me and you have a little talk. I'm going to stay with you, but I'm going to have my own room," Fancy said.

Tina nodded. "Okay. Can we cook now?"

Fancy hugged her tightly. "Let's go see what we can find."

Pickings were slim in the refrigerator. A can of biscuits. A frozen pizza. A six-pack of Coke and one of Dr. Pepper. Two withered carrots and a stalk of celery that a bunny rabbit would run from.

She checked the freezer in the utility room. It was loaded. White butcher paper wrapped up hamburger, steaks, roasts, ribs, bacon, and sausage. Potatoes and onions were in a wooden box beside the freezer. She removed a package of steak and a roast, a package of frozen corn and one of carrots.

"Thank goodness for the defrost button on the microwave. Can you bring me some potatoes, Tina?"

"Yes, I can," she said.

Fancy smiled.

In minutes she had steaks thawed and marinating in a sauce she'd made from what she could find. Worcestershire sauce, half a handful of brown sugar, a little juice she poured from a can of pineapple slices she found in the pantry, a pinch of garlic powder, and salt and pepper.

Tina carried two potatoes at a time. When she had six, Fancy told her that would be enough and pulled a chair up to the cabinet beside the sink. She peeled the skins while Tina looked out the window, keeping up a steady chatter about the birds in the trees and the cats in the yard.

At the mention of cats Fancy peeked out. Sure enough, they were lying on the swing, lounging at the base of a huge pecan tree, and meandering across the yard toward the garage.

"Did you name the cats?" Fancy asked.

"Yes. 'Vester is over there on Daddy's truck. And that one is Sunshine," she said, pointing out an orange cat.

"You don't have a Tweety to go with 'Vester?" Fancy asked when she finally understood that Vester was a shortened form of Sylvester, the black and white cat on cartoons.

"No Tweety. 'Vester would chase him and try to eat him. The yellow one is Sunshine, like Care Bears. The gray one is Grumpy, like Care Bears."

"So you've named four of them," Fancy said.

Tina held up her fist.

"'Vester." She popped up her forefinger.

"Sunshine." Another finger.

"Grumpy." Another one.

"One. Two. Three."

"Okay, three of them. That's pretty good. You can count?"

"One. Two. Three. Four. Five." Tina showed her one finger for each number.

"How about ABC's?"

Tina took off on the song, only missing *T* and running *L, M, N,* and *O* all together to sound like *el minnow,* but it impressed Fancy, and she made a mental note to have Tina sing and count for Theron. With her intelligence, Tina could be taught to read long before she started school.

Theron looked even worse when he trudged in the back door. He removed his heavy buff-colored coat, kicked a pair of rubber boots off his feet, and stuck his nose in the air. The aroma evidently sparked up his spirit, and he smiled.

"Is that fried onions?"

"Taters," Tina said from her perch on the chair.

Theron raised an eyebrow. "You fried potatoes?"

"You don't like them?" Fancy answered his question with one of her own.

"Love 'em. I don't care if that's all there is for supper. I'm starving," he said.

"Not all. Catch me," Tina said, and she bailed off the chair into his arms.

It took a major portion of his strength to keep standing under the unexpected force, but he managed, and he grinned at his daughter's excitement.

"Wash up. I should have dinner on the table by the time you get done," Fancy said.

He set Tina on the floor and washed his hands at the kitchen sink. His overalls were dirty from the knees up where his rubber boots stopped. His thermal knit shirt had frayed cuffs, and at least two strands of hay were stuck in the back of his hair.

Fancy thought he was totally handsome.

He sat down at the head of the table and could scarcely believe his eyes. "Would you say grace, Fancy?"

She made it very short for fear that he would go to sleep and fall face forward into his plate.

She passed a platter to him. "I hope you like your steak medium rare."

He forked a T-Bone and laid it in the middle of his plate. "Yup. Well done is a waste of good Angus."

She made sure the rest of the food was within reaching distance, picked up Tina's plate, and carefully cut a portion of steak into bite-sized pieces for her. Then she added fried potatoes and green beans.

Tina blew on the first bite of potatoes and then eased them into her mouth. "Mmm," she said as she chewed.

"Like those as well as mean beans?" Fancy asked.

Tina nodded.

"This is too good for words," Theron said. "What did you do to it?"

"Grilled it in a cast-iron skillet."

"What's the marinade?"

"That's a family secret, and if I told you I'd have to . . ." She paused and thought for a minute. Tina was listening to every word. ". . . commit justifiable homicide, and I'm too tired."

He smiled, and her heart melted.

"Thank you for doing this."

"Don't get too full. Tina and I made a little pan of brownies for dessert. I found a gallon of rocky road ice cream in the freezer. Thought brownies would be a good base for it."

"Are you up for sale?" he asked.

"Honey, you couldn't afford me," she answered.

"What's your price?"

"Like I said, you can't afford me, so there's no use naming one."

"What's a price?" Tina asked.

"It's the cost of something. When you go to the store and pick out a toy, we pay what it costs at the checkout counter," Theron explained. "That's the price."

"Buy Fanny! You can have my bear. Take it back and buy Fanny," she said.

Theron laughed. "It's not that simple, but we've got her for a few days. At least until I can make some arrangements."

They shared cleanup detail after supper, but Fancy insisted that she get Tina ready for bed and read her a book. "If you don't sit down, Theron, you are going to fall down. You need to take all next week off and catch up. You look like warmed-over sin on Sunday morning."

"Thank you again," he said.

"What's sin?" Tina asked.

"That, little girl, is something we'll talk about much later, like when you are in school." Fancy took her hand and led her down the hall toward the bathroom. Once Tina was bathed and in bed, she ended up reading her three books before the child finally fell asleep. Then she took a shower and donned her pajamas. She wasn't a bit surprised to find Theron snoring in his recliner in front of the dark fireplace.

She poked his shoulder. "Hey, Mr. Warren, it's time for a shower and bed. You're going to have a kink in your neck."

He grumbled as he awoke. "I could have slept right there until tomorrow morning."

"I don't think the school board would like you showing up in overalls and that shirt, though. Get on out of here. And don't wake us up."

"You sleeping with Tina?"

"No, she needs to learn to sleep alone. I told her if she had a bad dream, she could get into bed with me," Fancy said.

"Good night, Fancy, and I really do appreciate all of this." He gazed at her for a moment, then headed down the hall toward the bathroom.

She heard the shower running, footsteps in the hallway, the door to his bedroom creaking but not shutting all the way, and a sigh when he crawled into bed. She sat down in his recliner, still warm from his body heat, and tried to find her way out of the maze of crazy thoughts she'd had that day. Every single time she thought she'd found the answer, she ran into a dead end. Finally she turned off the lights and went to bed.

Only to dream about Theron. They were sitting on the front porch in two rockers. Longhorn cattle grazed in the pasture surrounding the yard fence. The trees were shades of yellow and orange, so it had to be fall. A truck kicked up dust as it came down the lane.

Theron looked at her and said, "There's the first of them. Is the turkey almost ready?"

She awoke before she could answer his question, and it was a very long time before she went back to sleep.

Chapter Seventeen

Monday morning brought sunshine and sixty-degree weather. Fancy's first thought when she and Tina went out to get into the car was that at least the schoolchildren would be able to play outside. The first day back after a holiday was always rough on the teachers. If the kids couldn't go out and run off the pent-up energy, it made for a very long day. She drove five miles under the speed limit and kept a wary eye out for black cats when she passed the courthouse.

They went through the house and left Tina's bag with extra clothing on the sofa. Hattie wouldn't like even that much clutter, but Fancy only gave it a second's consideration. It was her house now, not her grandmother's. At least until it sold, and hopefully that would be soon, because every day she spent with Tina stole away another portion of her heart.

She went through the door into the utility room and turned on the heat in the beauty shop, just enough to take the chill off. If it got too hot, the ladies would begin to "dew up," as Tandy said with a giggle when she talked about sweating under the hair dryer. Tina stood in the doorway and took in yet another strange place.

"Did you ever go with Kay-Kay to the beauty shop?" Fancy asked.

Tina shook her head and looked at the big metal things in the corner. They didn't appear to be something that Fanny was afraid of, so she took a step farther inside the room.

"How about with your momma?" Surely someone as self-centered as Maria would want to keep her hair cut perfectly.

"No," Tina whispered.

"Well, then, come on in here, and I'll show you what we do. First we'll wash the ladies' hair right here. They sit in this chair that goes back and put their head right here, like this." Fancy sat down and slung her head backward. Now why in the devil didn't she think of this place before? It would be the perfect way to wash her hair without getting the bandages wet. Leander would probably be more than glad to help her with it.

She hopped out of the chair and went to the styling chair. Tina followed her cautiously, staying away from the two big things on the other wall. Fancy picked her up and set her in the chair and took a clean brush from the roller rack.

"Watch me in the mirror. I'm going to put your hair in pigtails this morning. First we part it down the middle and put a clamp on this side, and then—shazam!—we make a pigtail."

Tina stared at the little girl wearing a brand-new pink jogging suit in the mirror. She held a doll and a bear in her lap, and when Tina blinked, she did too.

"Who's it?" she asked Fancy.

"That's you. Aren't you beautiful?" Fancy laughed.

"And that's Fanny!" Tina giggled.

"You've seen yourself in a mirror before, haven't you?"

Tina's face went serious. "Too big."

"The mirror is too big?" Fancy mused aloud. Then she remembered when she was a child. She'd always been short, and even with a bathroom stool to help her brush her teeth, for years all she could see in the medicine-cabinet mirror were her eyes and the top of her head.

"Up higher?" Tina whispered.

Fancy used the foot pump to raise the chair. "There you are right now. See what pretty pigtails you have?"

Tina tilted her head to one side and then the other, smiled, and frowned but didn't take her eyes from the mirror. She held up the doll and the bear both so they could see themselves too.

"Fanny has pigtails too."

"Yes, I do. Just like you."

Tina shook her head. "No. Fanny's pi'tails are brown."

"That's right, and yours are black. We're different, but we're alike because we're both short, and that makes the mirror too 'big.' Now let's look at the dryers before the ladies get here. They're over here." Fancy swirled the chair around and brought it down to the lowest level.

Tina took one look at the big metal contraptions and grabbed Fancy's hand, squeezing tightly. Since Fancy had been raised from a tiny baby in the beauty shop, she couldn't understand at first why, of all things, Tina would be afraid of the dryers.

"They won't hurt you," she said.

Tina held back and whispered, "Monsters."

"Hmm. They do sort of look like monster heads, don't they? But they aren't. They just dry wet hair. Let me show you." Fancy flipped the dial and sat down in a chair, pulling Tina up into her lap. She adjusted the dryer over her head. The heat made her scalp prickle, especially around the bandage. She threw the dryer back, and it automatically went off.

"Hot," Tina said. "Loud."

"It makes a lot of noise and gets hot, but that's all it can do. It can't eat you up."

Tandy and Leander arrived at the same time. Tandy's short, slightly blue hair was definitely in need of a shampoo and style. Leander's blond hair didn't need anything, but she headed straight for the hooks at the back of the shop and put on a snap-front duster over her jeans and long-sleeved blouse.

"We got company?" Tandy followed Leander.

"This is Tina. And, Tina, this is Miss Tandy and Miss Leander."

"Looks like her father only prettier," Tandy said.

"She's his, all right. Look at the shape of her face," Leander said.

"How'd you two know?"

"Kate called Tandy, and she called the rest of us. We've been dying to see her, but we didn't want to make a big to-do for fear we'd scare the bejesus out of her," Tandy said with a laugh.

Viv carried a pan of brownies when she pushed the door open. "I thought we'd eat in today. Mary's bringing tamales, and Myrle is supposed to bring a salad."

Tandy stooped down and looked at Tina. The little girl returned her stare without fear. "Can you and Fancy make sweet tea?"

"I can put the sugar in it," she said seriously.

"Good, that'll be your job after a while when it's lunchtime. Do you like tamales?"

"Tamales and macky cheese," Tina said.

"Well, we don't have macky cheese today, but we do have salad."

"That's yucky."

"How about brownies?" Tandy asked.

"I have brown crayons in the box. And lellow and red and brue."

Tandy sat down on the floor and roared. "This is going to be a fun morning. I can feel it in my bones. Where is Pansy?"

"Right here. I wouldn't miss today for one of Miss Maud's prize Angus bulls. So where is she?" Pansy shed her black leather jacket and kicked off her muddy boots at the door. She wore snug-fitting jeans and a tee, and her dyed black hair definitely needed the roots done that day.

"She's right here, and we're discussing brownies. Go get your hair washed, and Fancy can get at those roots. They look horrid," Tandy said.

"Well, darlin', you need to have Fancy put something on your hair that doesn't turn it blue. You're too young to go around looking like an old woman. Let her make it the color of her hair. That's what color it used to be."

"What do you think, Tina? Should I make my hair the color of Fancy's?" Tandy asked.

Tina reached out and touched Tandy's short hair. "No pigtails."

"No, but Fancy is fixing to tell us all about those pigtails of hers."

"Yes. Like Fanny's," Tina said.

"So you are first today, Pansy?" Fancy started the water, holding the spray over her hand until the water warmed.

"Yes, and if Tandy is going blond, then I'm doing something different too. Strip it. Take as much color as you can off."

"I've never done that," Fancy said.

"It's just hair. If you ruin it, I'll buy a wig until it grows back. I want one of those short dos. Light brown with blond highlights until the gray grows out; then I'm going blond. That should shock everyone."

Tandy pulled Tina into her lap and asked, "What's his name?"

Tina held up the bear. "He's Smokey, and this is Dora." She introduced her two toys.

"I can tell what she watches on television. I was really talking to you, Pansy. What's his name?" Tandy asked again.

"I might just want a new style," she protested.

"Yes, and I'm the queen of Albany," Tandy said.

"Oh, all right! I might as well tell you. It's Thomas James."

"The lawyer. Where'd you meet him?"

"At Maud's sale. We've been out a couple of times."

"He's ten years younger than you," Mary said.

"So?"

Tandy giggled like a schoolgirl. "So can he dance?"

Fancy laughed with them as she washed Pansy's hair and followed her to the chair, glad that they were far more interested in Pansy's new beau than in quizzing her.

It lasted until she picked up the scissors to cut Pansy's hair.

"Okay, enough about us and our love lives. We want the whole story, including what happened to your head," Myrle said. "And, Tandy, you will share Tina with us today. It's been a long time since we've had a baby in our midst, and we all get a turn to hold her."

"She's almost three," Fancy said.

"Are you sure you didn't birth her? She's as tiny as you were at that age," Myrle said.

"I wish I had. She and I get along just fine," Fancy said.

"Talk. Begin with Monday after we all left, and bring us up to today," Tandy said.

"Little corn has big ears."

"Then don't say her name, but don't you dare leave out anything."

"It's not that big of a thing. I went to help Theron Warren because he'd just found out he had this daughter, and when he went to meet her, he wanted someone there who was good with little kids," she said.

"Monday night. Start there, and details. The long version, even if it lasts all day. I ain't going nowhere until I look as young as Thomas James," Pansy said.

Fancy told the story for the second time. The six older ladies pried even more information out of her than Kate and Sophie had. She finished the story up to and including the night before at the same time she turned Pansy around to see the new hairstyle. It was still a rich dark brown even after they applied stripper, but she had applied highlights according to the directions on the box she'd found in the storeroom. If all else failed, she might make a half-decent hairdresser someday.

Pansy hopped out of the chair. "It's lovely. See? We don't need a full-fledged beauty operator. We can all read instructions. Thomas is going to kiss me tonight for sure!"

"Speakin' of kissing, do you mean to tell us, Fancy, that a whole week you've been close to that good-lookin' hunk of man, and you didn't even kiss him?" Myrle asked Fancy.

"No, I didn't say that, but Little Corn is listening." She motioned to Tina, who was sitting on a footstool listening to every word.

"Well?" Myrle looked at Fancy.

"It was just one of those in-the-moment things. Remember what I told you about those ears," Fancy said.

"When Fanny got blood on her ears, I gave Daddy my hair things," Tina said.

"Yes, you did, sweetheart, and that helped so much. On his own he would have made me look awful," Fancy said.

Tina smiled brightly.

"She reminds me of you," Leander said. "She's an old soul."

"Oh, don't start that stuff," Myrle said. "I don't believe in astrology or any other New Age stuff. We make our own decisions and live with the consequences. We don't get reincarnated to get a second chance."

Fancy was glad they'd gone on to another subject and she was out of the spotlight. They argued about old souls versus new souls for a while, went on to the latest gossip about every man, woman, and child in Albany, and had lunch. Tina slept on a pallet as far away from the dryers as Fancy could get her, and Fancy finished the last touches of Tandy's hair, turning her into a light blond.

Tandy checked her reflection in the mirror and smiled. "You done good. I'm going to Abilene tomorrow. Want to make a list, and I'll go by the beauty supply? I've been doing it for Hattie for years. You're probably getting low on some things."

"Thank you. That would be great," Fancy said.

Chapter Eighteen

Tina only showed up in Fancy's bed twice during the next five days. On Monday, Wednesday, and Friday they went into town to the beauty shop. Tuesday they cleaned house for Theron and did laundry. Thursday they grocery shopped. The weather had been fairly nice on the beauty-shop days, so when the ladies were gone, she and Tina played at the city park for half an hour. On Tuesday and Thursday they'd played in the backyard, with Tina being careful not to go too near the yard fence because she still wasn't sure about the longhorn cattle on the other side.

Theron called the beauty-shop number on Friday afternoon and told her not to cook supper, that they were going to Abilene to eat out that evening as a thank-you to her for all she'd done that week.

"Where are we going?" she asked.

"My treat. Your choice."

"I'll be thinking about it, then," she said.

Dinner out would be a nice way to sever the ties between her and Tina. Surely by now Theron had found someone to keep her or else a day-care center. Fancy's job was within hours of being finished, but it didn't bring the freedom she'd figured it would. Tina—and Theron, if she were honest—was plowing deeper and deeper into her life, and she wasn't sure she could handle the pain of the upcoming separation.

Fancy chose a pair of jeans and a starched western-cut shirt from the closet. She'd wear her new boots, and her hair was coming down out of the pigtails even if it did irritate the wound. When Leander helped her wash her hair that afternoon, they'd changed the bandage, and she said it was scabbed over and drying up. So maybe the pigtails were finally and permanently a thing of the past. She'd just have to be very careful she didn't yank a brush through her hair.

She packed long, loopy earrings with a matching bangle bracelet and her makeup kit into a small bag, then carried her clothing to the car and came back for Tina.

"What's that?" Tina pointed to the shirt and jeans hanging on the hook in the Camaro's side window.

"We're going to a restaurant for dinner tonight with your daddy."

"Pizza?" she shouted.

"I don't think so, princess. I think something a little fancier than pizza," Fancy said. She drove toward Main Street, made a right turn, and then a left beside the courthouse.

She and Tina were dressed by the time Theron got home. They looked alike in their jeans and shirts, belts cinched around their waists, and boots. She'd swept her hair up to cover the bandage on the back of her head.

"So are my girls ready for a night out on the town? I thought if we had an early supper, we could go see that new Disney movie that's just coming out."

"I guess the days of R-rated and even PG-13 are over for you?" Fancy said.

"Only if there's a child with us," he said.

Us? Now, exactly what did that mean? That there was even the possibility that they'd have dinner and a movie without Tina? There'd be angels wearing bikinis and selling snow cones in Hades before that happened.

"What's a Dizzy?" Tina frowned.

"*Disney*," Fancy corrected, gently. "Like *The Little Mermaid* or *Cinderella*."

Tina continued to look puzzled.

"It'll be fun. You'll see," Fancy said.

Theron transferred the car seat back to the truck, belted Tina safely into it, and started around to open the door for Fancy, only to find her hopping into the truck without his help. He felt cheated. Even though it wasn't a formal date, he wanted it to be.

"So where's this wagon train going tonight?" he asked.

"To Cracker Barrel. I've got a yearning for dumplings, and I can't make them," she said.

A smile tickled the corners of Theron's mouth. He'd rehearsed his speech several times that day, but he didn't want to deliver it until after he'd taken Fancy to dinner.

"So what did the ladies talk about today?" he asked.

"Well, Pansy has a new beau. Tandy's hairstyle brought lots of compliments at her club meeting. Myrle's decided to go less red with highlights now so that maybe she can catch a square-dancin' hot dude—her words, not mine. Other than that it was the regular fare of who's cheating on whom, who got caught, and all that small-town stuff."

"What's that supposed to mean?"

"Just what I said. Small-town stuff. Grapevine gossip. You know what I'm talking about. Don't the teachers in your school gossip during recess and in the hallways?"

He shrugged. "Wouldn't know."

"Well, they sure do in the beauty shop. But I'm talking when I shouldn't be. What's said in the beauty shop stays in the beauty shop. It's a rule I cut my teeth on, and Granny really would rise from her ashes if she heard me repeating a word of beauty-shop talk. So let's talk about something else. Did you . . . find a sitter?" The words came out like bitter gall.

"I . . . well . . . I . . . ," he stammered.

"You didn't, did you?" She shot him a look. After another week with Tina, it would take the Navy SEALS to separate her from Fancy. Tonight was supposed to be the last one. She'd already allotted until dawn the next day to cry a river of tears.

Theron put on the right-turn blinker in Moran and took a small state road to the west. "About that sitter?"

"Yes?" Fancy folded her arms over her chest. Her heart almost stopped while she waited.

"I checked out the day care, and I can't do it. She's been in one her whole life, and I want her to have something more personal. One lady was recommended to me. She's fifty or so. Sweet old girl who keeps two kids, and one of hers moved away, so she's got room for another one. I went to her house. Her husband is a lot older. He sits in front of the television smoking cigarettes. And there were roaches in the kitchen."

Fancy shivered.

"I was going to wait until after we ate, but here's the deal. Leaving her with you makes her happy, so please say you'll work for me. I can pay you. You can move all your things to the ranch and live there, or we can keep things like they are. I think maybe we're at the point now where you could take Sunday off so you could have your friends thing. Think about it. Don't give me an answer right now. But please say you'll do this, even if it's just until you get the house sold and have to leave."

She stared straight ahead.

"Did you hear me?" he asked.

"You said to think about it. I'm thinking. You said I don't have to give you an answer right now, so I'm waiting until we have dinner."

"Fair enough."

She laid the pros and cons out in lists in her mind.

Pros:

1. She wouldn't have to cry all night.

2. She wouldn't have to worry about Tina breathing secondhand smoke.

3. She couldn't stand the idea of a roach touching Tina.

4. She would have every evening with Theron to get over her silly infatuation.

5. She could still keep her beauty-shop hours.

Cons:

She couldn't think of one, but while she was thinking she did add a dozen more items to the pros list. Other than dying from acute heartache when the job was finished, she couldn't think of a single reason why she shouldn't take him up on the offer.

He pushed a button, and George Strait began to sing about rolling on the river of love. In spite of her determination to think and not listen, she started wiggling her foot to the tempo. When she looked in the backseat, Tina was moving her shoulders and wiggling all over.

"You like that one?" Fancy asked.

"Like to dance," Tina said.

"When she's a little older, would you set her up with dance classes?" she asked Theron.

"Begging you to keep taking care of my daughter is my priority today. Dance classes never entered my mind. Isn't she a little young for that kind of thing?"

He caught I-20 at Baird. She thought about asking him to stop at Sophie's for a minute and running the idea of caretaking Tina by her, but she was starving and was sure Tina was also.

Serves him right to sit and wonder, she thought.

"You going to answer me?" he asked.

"About what? You said I had until after dinner."

"About how old she needs to be for dance lessons. Look at her."

A fast song by Whitney Duncan was playing on the country radio station, and Tina was bopping along to the music.

"Oh, that. I've had first-graders who are in their second year of dance already. Based on that, I suppose she's still a little too young, but you need to keep it in mind. She definitely likes music and moving to it."

"That could be because she's with us right now. If she was tossed in with a bunch of other kids, she might retreat to a corner," he said, a parent's worries etched into his fine features.

"It's just something to keep in mind for the future," Fancy said gently, touched at his concern for Tina.

"Then I will," he said firmly.

A deep-voiced singer started a song about the people in the black-and-white picture he was showing his grandson, and he kept saying that if it looked like they were scared to death, his grandson should have seen it in color. She thought of the black-and-white picture of Hattie and Orville. What would those shades of gray show if they'd been in color? Was Hattie a blushing bride? Was Orville's coloring high and proud?

Had someone asked Fancy to put her thoughts into words, she couldn't have done it, but in that moment she knew that she had to keep Tina as long as she could. She couldn't bear for the child to be raised by an indifferent sitter the way her momma had been raised by a once-happy but then embittered mother.

They pulled up into the Cracker Barrel parking lot, and Theron looked across at her, and as if reading her mind, he asked, "Had enough time to think?"

"I'm hungry. Is there macky cheese?" Tina asked.

"Yes, baby, there sure is," Fancy said.

Fancy's mind still said, "no, no, no." But her heart delivered a much different message. She nodded.

"And your answer is . . . ?"

"Yes, yes, yes, macky cheese." Tina wiggled against the seat belt.

"Yes, I'll do it," Fancy whispered.

Her heart leaped.

I will tell you "I told you so," her conscience chided.

"Thank you," he said quietly but with evident feeling. "You figure out a salary, and I'll pay it. You've made this whole thing a lot less traumatizing for her and a lot less hectic for me. I can't tell you how much I appreciate your doing this, Fancy."

"Let's go eat," she said.

They were seated right away. Tina sat in a booster chair beside Fancy and tried to see everything at once. Fancy didn't need a menu. Cracker Barrel meant chicken and dumplings, pinto beans, and fried okra. Afterward she would have an apple dumpling, and if Theron didn't want to share it, she'd take what she couldn't eat home for breakfast.

After they ordered, Theron looked across the table at Fancy and asked, "So, do you have a price in mind?"

"Honey, I've told you before, you can't afford me. But let's get this over with so you can enjoy your supper. One, I don't do windows. I want room and board and . . ."

"Okay." He nodded. "I expect we can have them cleaned if they get so dirty we can't see the birds through them. What else?"

"You have to take us out on Friday night. Our choice, and I want a cleaning woman twice a month to do deep cleaning so I have more time to cook and play with Tina."

"You got it."

"Okay, then that's settled. Let's eat."

She didn't really need the money and could not envision taking a paycheck for caring for Tina.

Theron studied her. "And the money?"

"I told you my price. Friday night supper even when there's a ball game on television. A cleaning woman and room and board, and remember, I eat a lot. Besides, what are you going to pay Tina to keep me company?"

She heard her name and looked up. "Tina stay with Fanny."

"Look, Fancy, I can pay you. I'm not broke. I'm trying to put everything I can toward the bank note, so if times get tough, I'll own the place, but I can certainly pay you."

"It's settled. Tina is going to take care of me, and I'll take care of her. Any more arguing, and I swear I'll change my mind," she said.

"Thank you is so little."

"Remember that when we fight."

He threw back his head and laughed raucously right there in the restaurant. Several people turned to look in their direction. Tina caught the infectious laughter and giggled. Fancy had no choice but to join them.

Chapter Nineteen

A blue norther hit Albany the week before Christmas. Pansy said it might be unexpected but it was unavoidable, since there wasn't anything but barbwire fences and mesquite trees to stop the blasted cold wind. On Friday night Tina had another bad dream, so Fancy awoke on Saturday morning with big brown eyes staring up at her from the pillow right next to her. The wind whistled through the trees, and the metal chimes hanging on the end of the porch tinkled out a melody.

"Mornin'," Tina said.

"Good mornin' to you, sweetheart. Bad dream?" Fancy asked.

She nodded.

"Want to talk about it?"

"Don't 'member now."

"Well, then, it's time to get up and have some breakfast. Your daddy will eat with us today. What do you want?"

Tina had come a long way in the three weeks since she'd come to Theron. She was slowly becoming more flexible in her schedule. Some mornings she actually slept past seven o'clock. This morning was one of them. When Fancy looked at the clock, she was surprised to see that it was eight thirty.

She heard the front door open and Theron stomping around. She sat up in bed and frowned. He never came in and out the front door when he did early-morning chores. He used the back door. If he'd tracked dirt and mud in on the hardwood floor, then he was getting a royal piece of her mind. Friday-night supper didn't pay for keeping the hardwood shining.

She bounded out of bed, found an old red plaid flannel robe that

Uncle Joe had left hanging on the back of the bathroom door, and started down the hallway, barefoot and with Tina right behind her. She stopped in her tracks when she got to the end of the hall.

Theron looked up and grinned from behind the branches of the biggest cedar tree she'd ever seen. He had already stuck a stand on the bottom and was fastening three screws that held it fast. While they watched, he set it upright. It was at least seven feet tall, with barely room between the top and the ceiling for an angel.

Tina clapped her hands and ran to touch the branches. "Is Santa coming to my new house?"

"Yes, he is," Theron said.

Hattie had never allowed a tree in the living room. When they moved to Florida, Gwen had bought the biggest artificial tree she could fit into her house and decorated the whole place every year. Les put on his Santa suit, and it was a merry old day.

"It smells heavenly," Fancy said.

"Nothing like the real thing, I always say."

"It's beautiful," Fancy declared.

Theron grinned again. "I hauled the decorations out of the attic. Uncle Joe insisted on a tree every year. His wife loved Christmas, and it was a way of bringing her memory back to him."

His heavy caramel-colored insulated jacket hung on the back of a dining room chair. Mud dotted the floor from the door to the fireplace, hardwood and area rugs alike. The knees of his overalls were so dirty, it would take at least two wash cycles to get them clean. And Fancy didn't care. She'd gladly clean up the mess and sweep up dried cedar needles every day for a real Christmas tree.

"Breakfast or decorations first?" she asked.

He hugged Tina to his side. "I made an early-morning run into town and picked up doughnuts. They're on the table. Coffee is perked. Milk in the fridge for a little girl with brown eyes."

He'd had a dream about Fancy the night before and awoke at four o'clock. He'd tossed and turned for an hour and finally arose. In the dream they were sitting around the tree on Christmas morning. Tina had finished opening a whole raft of presents and was jumping up and down when she found the red tricycle from Santa. It was then that he realized he hadn't bought a single thing for Fancy. He awoke with a sense of urgency to get her a present and couldn't go back to sleep.

So he'd gotten dressed and slipped out the back door. Somehow the tree hadn't looked nearly so big out there in the north pasture as it did in the living room. He'd chosen that particular one because it had a flat side that would fit well into the corner of the room. He'd cut it down with a chain saw and dragged it to his truck bed and then realized how hungry he was. It was only a couple of miles into town, and the doughnut shop was always open early for the early risers.

Tina skipped to the kitchen nook and pulled out her customary chair, the one with a big thick phone book on the seat. "Doughnuts!"

"You done good, Mr. Warren," Fancy said.

He offered her his arm. "Thank you, Miss Sawyer."

They marched into the kitchen, Theron in his dirty overalls, Fancy in Uncle Joe's robe, as if they were entering a ball at the Hyatt Regency in Dallas.

Theron opened the lid of the doughnut box. "What kind would you like?"

"Good grief!" Fancy exclaimed.

"I was hungry and couldn't decide, so I got an assortment. I bet Tina wants the chocolate with sprinkles," he said.

"No. The pink one," she said.

"I think we really may have a girly-girl here. I want that one." Fancy pointed to the maple cruller.

He poured two cups of coffee and a glass of milk. "No girly-girls on a ranch."

"Don't be so sure. Ranch girls can be feminine just like a city girl can be a tomboy," she argued.

He picked up a glazed doughnut. "So you'll have her taking ballet soon? What good is that going to do her?"

"Ballet teaches form and grace, which could keep her on the back of a bucking bull for eight seconds," Fancy pointed out.

"Why not just teach her bull-riding?" Theron said.

"Okay, let's ask Tina. What would you like, honey? Bull-riding or dancing?"

She wiggled her shoulders to imaginary music. "Dancing!"

Theron rolled his eyes and sighed. "Ballet or salsa?"

"She doesn't know the difference, but you can start with ballet and jazz," Fancy said.

"Maybe I'll start by putting her on a horse and teaching her to ride."

Fancy looked puzzled and seemed to have drifted off somewhere else.

"Penny for your thoughts. Are you picturing Tina on a pony in a tutu?" he asked.

"That sounds like a circus stunt," she said, laughing.

"What were you thinking about?"

"That here it is a week before Christmas, and I've not got my shopping done. I need to buy something for the girls and for Aunt Maud and . . ."

"Your folks?"

She nodded. "And it has to be mailed, so it will be there when they get home from the cruise they left on yesterday."

"They're not going to be home at Christmas?"

"It's the first year they don't have a kid in the house, even if I am thirty, so Les bought Momma a cruise. They offered to let me tag along, but I couldn't do it," she said softly.

He grabbed another doughnut and carried it with him toward the boxes cluttering the living room floor. "Well, we've got a tree to decorate. I'll start the lights while you girls finish breakfast."

Fancy literally sucked air when he pulled out antique big-bulb lights. "Where did those come from?"

Theron talked as he circled the tree, clipping the lights to the branches. "Uncle Joe had all this in the attic. I remember being here one time a couple of weeks after the holiday. We'd already taken our decorations down, but he still had his all up. Said it reminded him of the good days, and he always kept them up until the tree got so bare, he couldn't stand to look at it."

"Bless his heart." Fancy polished off the last of her cruller and went to open the other boxes of ornaments.

Tina sat at the table and watched them until she finished the last drop of milk; then she hopped down and skipped into the living room.

"I help," she said.

"Yes, you will. When your daddy gets the lights on, we'll put this garland around the tree. You can help with that," Fancy said.

Tina touched the red, green, and gold garland that had seen years of holidays. When Fancy pulled out a string of popcorn, she frowned. "What's that?"

Fancy held it gently, afraid it would fall apart in her hands.

"Now, that's a story. Aunt Molly didn't have much there in the beginning, so she popped corn and strung it to use on her tree. That's from their first year together. Uncle Joe was afraid it would disintegrate, so he patiently varnished every single bit of it, not once but twice. So basically it's the remains of popcorn inside a bubble of varnish. We'll be very careful with it, won't we, Tina?"

She held up gold tinsel. "Pretty!"

"The old and the new. If Joe is lucid, we could bring him home for the holiday. He would like seeing Tina in the house," he said.

"Who cares if he's lucid?" Fancy asked. "Bring him home for the day anyway. If he's going to have a good day, it will be here among his memories. If not, then who cares? He can still play with Tina."

"Wonderful idea." Theron finished one strand of lights and plugged in the second. Nothing lit up. He started replacing bulbs, one at a time, until he found the culprit, and the whole strand lit up.

Two hours later the tree looked finished, but something wasn't right. The lights were evenly spaced, the garland and the popcorn looped perfectly, the antique ornaments shining in every nook and cranny.

"We need the skirt. It's got to be in one of these boxes." Fancy searched through three before she found it folded neatly under several layers of tissue. When she pulled it out, she almost cried at the beauty of the thing.

"Why does that bring tears to your eyes?" Theron asked.

"It's a handmade quilt. Look at all these tiny stitches. And I bet every single piece of fabric has a story to tell. This might have been a piece of the dress Molly wore when she met Joe. That could have been a scrap from a baby blanket she made for someone she loved."

"Okay." He drew out the word to three syllables. "Put it around the tree, and I'll plug in the lights. We'll see how pretty it looks."

Fancy and Tina stood back and watched the tree come to life.

"Ooh, magic," Tina said.

"You had a Christmas tree at Kay-Kay's, didn't you?" Fancy asked.

She shook her head. "No, at school. Is Santa really coming here?"

"Yes, he is," Fancy said.

Tina's black curls bounced as she hopped around.

"What's on your agenda for the rest of the day?" Fancy asked Theron.

"I expect we'd best go to Abilene if there's going to be presents under the tree. Think the truck is big enough to haul it all home, or do we need to put on a stock trailer?" he teased.

"Depends on how big a fortune you're willing to spend."

"It's Christmas. Time to go crazy," he laughed.

"Tina," Fancy said, "you'd better get on back to your room, and we'll find something special for you to wear today. I want your picture taken with Santa Claus, and he's going to be at the mall today."

"Santa Claus!" Tina singsonged down the hallway toward her bedroom.

Theron took a step forward and wrapped his arms around Fancy. The kiss was a spur-of-the-moment meeting of lips in front of the tree they'd worked so hard on. When it ended and he stepped back, the only thought that crossed Fancy's mind was how Sophie and Kate were going to hum the wedding march when she told them on Sunday.

"So?" he asked.

"So what?"

"Are you going to wear that robe to shop in today?" he asked.

"Are you wearing those dirty overalls? If so, I'll fit right in with my present attire," she answered with a wicked gleam in her eyes.

"I suppose we'd better get dressed then, before Santa leaves the mall." He hummed a Christmas carol all the way down the hall.

Chapter Twenty

Tina had unwrapping presents down to an art by the middle of Christmas morning. On Friday the ladies had each brought her a small gift. On Christmas Eve she'd had presents from Sophie and Kate at the ranch. She tore into the presents under the tree with the gusto allotted to three-year-old children, but the thing that amazed her most was the pink tricycle with a basket on the front. Her doll and bear were already in the basket, and she kept stealing peeks at them as she opened her other presents.

Fancy had been dreading the holidays ever since her momma had told her she was going on a cruise, but instead it had been a great week. She held a present in her lap, wrapped poorly with tape stuck everywhere and three mismatched bows stuck on the top. It was the most beautiful thing she'd ever seen, next to Tina sitting in a pile of ripped wrapping paper.

"Open yours first," Theron said.

Fancy shook it. "What's in here, Tina?"

"It's little and red," Tina said.

Fancy cut her eyes at Theron. Surely he hadn't done something stupid like buy her something red and lacy.

If he did, what do you intend to do about it? Maybe it's a joke because of your boxer shorts and oversized tees, not to mention Uncle Joe's old robe you've fallen in love with.

Theron read her mind. "It's not that."

"You're the one who can't hide anything," she said.

He smiled. "Not today. The look on your face is priceless. I couldn't tell her what was in the box because she would have told you, but it is red, and it is little. Want to guess?"

She ripped the paper from the shoebox-sized present and held her breath as she opened the lid. It was filled with crumpled tissue paper. She removed it slowly. Halfway to the bottom she looked up. "Is there anything in here?"

Tina watched from the seat of her tricycle. "Daddy said it's little."

When she reached the bottom of the box she found a small red velvet box. An open gold heart necklace rested inside. She gasped and looked up at Theron for an explanation.

"Do you like it? Tina and I saw you admiring it at the Penney's store in the mall."

She couldn't tell him that she hadn't even seen it; she'd been looking at a tie tack for him.

"It's beautiful. I love it," she said.

"Let me put it on you. It doesn't really match the robe, but I don't suppose you'll be wearing that all day."

He brushed her hair back and draped the necklace around her neck. The warmth of his fingers set up a blush that found its way to her face. It was her thoughts that brought on the high color; she wanted to turn her face slightly and really lay one on him. A week had gone by, and every day Fancy had thought about their last kiss. It haunted her dreams and made her biological clock spin like a merry-go-round.

"See? Little and in a red box," Tina said.

"I'll think of you both whenever I wear it. Thank you."

"Now yours, Daddy."

Theron opened a gold tie tack in the shape of longhorns. "Oh, my!"

"You have a dozen, right? You can take it back," she said.

"I don't have a single one. Matter of fact, I only have three tie tacks period, and they're all plain silver. I'll wear it every day at school and on Sundays at church."

"Daddy put your heart on, Fanny. You put his horns on," Tina said.

"Fair enough," Fancy said.

Theron handed her the tie tack and raised an eyebrow. How could she put it on him without a tie? He wore baggy green flannel pajama pants and a dark green shirt.

Fancy scooted over to him and ran her hand holding the back of the tack under his shirt very slowly, barely touching the soft brown hair on his chest. The other hand slipped down the front side and chose a spot right where his tie would be if he'd been wearing one. She leaned forward and fastened it to his shirt.

At her tentative touch Theron's heart beat like he'd just run a marathon and won first place. He'd relived that last kiss a dozen times a day since it happened.

She stood up and quickly started cramming paper into a big black garbage bag. When she picked up the paper her gift from Theron and Tina had been wrapped in, she deftly slipped a small piece of it into her robe pocket.

He helped with the cleanup. The tie tack looked strange on his shirt, and the chain on the inside tickled his chest.

Their hands met during the cleanup, and he teased her palm with his thumb. She shivered involuntarily. "Payback time," he murmured.

She blushed but just kept working.

"Did you hear me?" he asked.

"Honey, if you want to play with the big dogs, bring it on. If not, get off the porch," Fancy boldly challenged him to cover up quivering at his touch.

"Is that flirting I hear?"

"It's . . . stating facts."

Theron took a deep breath. "I'm attracted to you, Fancy. But with my track record, I've got to steer clear of anything . . . permanent. So," he said softly, "do you want me on the porch or off it?"

"With such romantic talk, I'll kick you out into the yard with the rest of the dogs, and you can lick your pride along with your paws," she retorted. Then she got serious. "What are we doing here, Theron?"

"I think we're skirting the issue of how we feel by teasing. I've put my cards on the table. Are you bluffing or holding something better?" he asked right back.

"I keep my cards close to my chest, but we can settle this right now. I'm attracted to you too. But I'm too old to play games. I want a forever thing in my future or nothing."

"You proposing to me?" he asked.

"No, I'm not. Go get Uncle Joe. Here's hoping he's having a good day. I'd love for him to tell me the stories behind some of those ornaments."

"Changing the subject?"

"Protecting my hand. I've got a full house. What have you got?"

His eyes twinkled. He loved the bickering and the flirting, the underlying passion in her eyes. What he was going to do about it was much less clear.

Tina played with her new things, lining them up around and under the tree and pretending to open them again. Fancy made a cup of hot tea and sat at the kitchen table for a few minutes, trying to make sense of what had just happened. She sure hadn't planned on telling Theron that she was attracted to him, but it had come out, and now she had to face it.

The house phone rang, and she picked it up. "Warren residence."

"Fancy?" her mother's voice questioned.

"Merry Christmas, Momma!" Fancy said.

"And a Merry Christmas to you. We're on land, and I had to call. Everything all right there?"

"No, but there's not much you can do about it. Theron and I just . . . had words."

"An argument?"

"Of sorts."

"Want to talk about it?"

"We've laid our cards on the table."

"And who's winning?"

She sighed. "I think we're both losers, but I suppose I'll have to live with it."

"What'd he get you for Christmas?"

"An open heart necklace."

"Symbolism?"

"Just a gift he thought I was looking at. I didn't even see it."

"Don't shut the door on possibilities. You in love with that man?"

"Probably, but I can get over it." She hoped. "Anyway, what'd you get?"

"Les bought me a beautiful diamond ring."

"They don't make them like Les anymore."

"At least not in Albany, Texas. When you find that forever thing, I hope he's in Florida, not Texas. Gotta run. Les is here, and we're going to have dinner on the beach. Just had to hear your voice. I think my baby has grown up. This is our first Christmas ever without seeing each other."

"The jury is out on that grown-up thing," Fancy said.

She'd barely said good-bye and hung up when the phone rang again. It was the real estate agent who had Hattie's house up for sale. "I've got a wonderful Christmas present for you. We've got an offer on the house. Mary's granddaughter just finished beauty school and got married. She's offered just two thousand less than you were asking. Interested?"

"Yes, I am. I won't even bicker over that much. When does she want to move in?"

"Next week. It's a cash deal. Mary is giving her the money, and they're making an arrangement for repayment between them. Is that doable?"

"You bet it is."

"Then I can tell them they can be in the place by New Year's. She and her husband want to start off the year in their own home. She's very excited."

"So am I, and thank you. It is a wonderful present." She laid the phone back on the stand.

Surely it was an omen. She could give Theron two weeks to make arrangements for Tina and promise Sophie that she'd fly home for a month when Aunt Maud died. She was still making her painful plans and sipping tea when a blast of cold air preceded Theron and Joe into the house. Theron helped Joe out of his coat and led him into the living area to see the tree.

Tina stared at the older man with big eyes.

Fancy left her tea and went to the living room.

"Uncle Joe," Theron began, "this is my . . ."

"That's Melissa, only I don't remember her having dark hair and eyes like that. And that is . . ." He looked at Fancy for a long time. "How'd you get here?"

"This is Fancy Lynn Sawyer. She helps me with Tina. She's a schoolteacher, but she's taking a year off," Theron said.

Uncle Joe rubbed his square chin. He sat down in the recliner and took everything in. "You look like a girl I knew once. She worked at the bank. She ran off with a man."

"That would be my mother, Gwen," Fancy said. "I'm glad you're home for Christmas."

"This his home?" Tina whispered.

Fancy sat down on the sofa and pulled Tina into her lap. "Uncle Joe and his wife, Molly, lived here for a long time."

"That's Molly's tree and her popcorn," Joe said.

"Pretty, isn't it?" Theron said.

"We're havin' turkey," Tina said.

"I like turkey." Joe's brow wrinkled as he tried to remember what it was about Molly that he needed to remember.

"Want to play with my bear?" Tina offered it.

He took it and hugged it close to his chest. "Molly loved kids, but we never could have any."

"You can play with bear, and I'll play with my dolly. Want to see me ride my tricycle?"

That set off a new friendship. Uncle Joe couldn't remember enough to tell Fancy about the ornaments, but he laughed at Tina's antics, which made her show off even more. She rode her bike around in circles and crawled up into Joe's lap and "read" him several books. He didn't care if the words didn't exactly match the pictures. He just sat there and enjoyed the child.

They were sitting at the dinner table when he looked at Theron and asked, "Where's Molly? She in the kitchen? That woman never could sit down long enough to eat a whole meal."

"Molly is gone, Uncle Joe. Remember?" Theron said.

"I guess I don't want to remember that. Most days I just think she's right here with me, and we talk."

"What do you talk about?" Fancy asked.

"Whatever we want. I tell her about my day, what I can remember of it. She tells me what-all she's done in the kitchen and the house. This is good turkey."

"Thank you," Fancy said.

"I'm full now. I'd like to take a nap." He got up and shuffled down the hallway to his room.

They heard a shoe hit the floor and then another one, followed by a long sigh and the squeak of the bedsprings.

"Good night, sweetheart," they heard him say.

Tears brimmed over the edge of Fancy's eyes. "Don't you look at me. I can cry if I want to. That is so sweet. He can't remember who he is, but he still talks to his wife. *That,* Theron Warren, is a forever thing."

"They don't make that kind of love anymore. It got done in by cell phones, faster planes, computers, and new technology."

"No, it didn't. I don't believe that, and I never will."

Tina finished a piece of pumpkin pie and gathered up her two old toys. She skipped down the hall and into her room for her nap.

Fancy started the cleanup without saying a word.

Theron put away leftovers while she ran water into the sink to do dishes: Molly's best china with red roses in the center of every plate.

She turned at the same time he reached to put a small bowl in the cabinet. He dropped his arms, and they instinctively went around her waist. She laid her head on his chest and listened to the steady rhythm of his heart.

She looked up. "Theron, we . . ."

His mouth covered hers, and she kissed him back. She wanted it to go on forever. As if Theron understood her wish, he broke the kiss but only to start another one. Finally she took a step backward and nodded down the hallway.

"Can't nap," Tina said, rubbing her eyes. "Where's Joe?"

"Shh, he's still asleep."

Tina put her hand in Fancy's. "Let's wake him up."

"You play with your toys, and he'll wake up in a little while."

"Fancy, we need to talk," Theron said.

"No, we don't, Theron. Granny's house sold today. I'm going home to Florida in a couple of weeks. You're going to need to find a new nanny for Tina."

"What?" Theron looked stricken. A big rope seemed to tie itself firmly around his heart and squeeze the life from it. "When did this happen?"

"I got the call while you went after Uncle Joe."

Tina took off for the bathroom. When she returned, she said, "Uncle Joe fell out of bed."

"How do you know that?" Theron asked.

"Because I peeked in, and he's on the floor."

Their conversation stopped as they rushed to his room. Theron quickly dialed 911 and stayed on the phone with them until the paramedics pounded on the front door. They loaded Joe into the ambulance, with Theron and Fancy and Tina following in the truck.

"I'm so sorry. What happened?" Fancy asked.

"Doctor will fix him, like Fanny," Tina assured them.

But the doctor couldn't fix Joe. He had died instantly of a massive stroke when he slung his feet over the bed to stand up. He'd simply slumped to the floor. "Nothing anyone could have done," the emergency room doctor explained. "It would have happened no matter where he'd been at the time."

Theron nodded.

"Do you have a funeral home that you'd like us to contact?"

Too much had happened too fast. Theron stared at him as if he were speaking a foreign language. "I have no idea. I need to make a phone call before I can tell you."

He called his father, who had taken over the care of Joe's business, and learned that Joe was to have a graveside service only and be buried next to his beloved Molly.

"I'll take care of it from this end," his father said.

"Dad, I feel so terrible."

"Don't. He was in his home with memories of Molly all around him. If he'd been able to choose his end, he would have wanted it just like it happened. We'll be down there tomorrow. We'll plan to have the funeral the day after."

"Okay," Theron said, and he told the doctor which funeral home to call.

Fancy led Theron out of the waiting room, and Tina held his hand tightly.

"Where's Uncle Joe?" she asked on the way back to the ranch.

"He's gone to live with the angels," Fancy said.

"Like the one on the tree?"

"That's right. He's very happy now because he's with Molly," Fancy said around the lump in her throat.

"Molly is his Fanny?"

"That's right."

"Can we have turkey when we get home?" Tina asked.

Theron nodded at Tina and patted her head. "Thank you," he mouthed to Fancy.

"Welcome," she whispered.

They got through the rest of the day and the evening, but neither of them talked about anything that had happened. They read to Tina, then watched a Disney movie she'd gotten for Christmas. Anything to keep busy; anything to avoid what was in their hearts.

Fancy went to bed at the same time Tina did, but she couldn't sleep. The strong desire to slip across the hallway and hold Theron was so overpowering that she kicked the covers off and went to the living room. She plugged in the Christmas tree lights and thought about everything that had happened since the first time she'd met him.

She felt his presence rather than saw him when he joined her on the sofa. The skin on her neck began to prickle, and her insides went to mush. His hand inched across the middle cushion and covered hers. The comfort in his touch brought tears to her eyes.

"Dad told me that Joe couldn't have left this world in a better way. That he would have wanted it this way if he'd had a choice."

"I keep hearing his last words. He said, 'Good night, sweetheart.' He was talking to Molly. He was in the bed they'd shared, wasn't he?" Fancy asked.

Theron nodded and swallowed past the lump in his throat.

"I still want that, Theron. I can't settle for anything less."

Chapter Twenty-one

Fancy was in the kitchen when she heard the familiar squeak of the front door. She inhaled deeply, dried her hands, turned around to face Theron's family, and hoped like heck that nothing in her actions would reveal the depth of her feelings for their son. Theron had already made it from the recliner to the door before she did, and everyone was hugging. Tina peeped around the edge of a rocking chair, and Fancy hung back too.

His father was only slightly taller than Theron. Gray sprinkled the brushed-back hair at his temples, and his eyes were that same mossy green. He carried more weight than Theron, but then, he was older. Fancy tried to squint and see Theron at that age with another twenty-five pounds on him.

Theron had been right. His sister could have been Tina's mother. She was only an inch or two taller than Fancy's almost-five-feet; her hair was light brown, her eyes pale aqua. But her features were grown-up Tina.

His mother was the same height as his father. She wore her hair highlighted to cover the bits of gray showing up; her eyes were the same color as Melissa's, her features just slightly more rounded.

Theron had been right. Other than for legal purposes, he didn't need a DNA test at all. Tina fit into the family perfectly.

Theron finally pulled back from the little group. "Come and meet Tina and Fancy."

His mother and sister eyed her a moment before they smiled.

"This is my sister, Melissa; my mother, Elaine; and my dad, Robert, Fancy. Tina, this is Grammy, Poppa, and Aunt Lissa."

Fancy covered the floor quickly and shook hands with his father. "I'm so glad to meet you, sir."

"Same here." Robert smiled.

When she offered her hand to Elaine, Theron's mother bypassed it and gave her a hug.

"We are so thankful for the help you're giving Theron. I don't think he could have handled this situation without you," she said.

Melissa joined them for a three-way hug. "I'm seconding that."

Tina eased over to Theron and wrapped her arms around his legs. He picked her up, and she laid her head on his shoulder.

"Okay, son, let's look at her," Elaine said.

Theron whispered into her ear. "Tina, can you look up at these folks? They've wanted to meet you for a long time."

"They won't fall on the floor and go see the angels, will they?" she asked.

"No, I promise. We won't let them go away."

She raised her head and looked slowly from Robert to Elaine to Melissa.

"What is she talking about?" Elaine asked.

"Uncle Joe came to see us on Christmas Day, and she made friends with him. Then he went into the bedroom and . . . you know," Theron said.

"Oh, honey, we aren't going to do that." Elaine reached out her arms, and Tina went to her.

"While these ladies get settled in, let's go to the funeral home and take care of the arrangements," Robert said. "I called them last night, and there's no problem with a ten o'clock service tomorrow morning,"

"Bring in the suitcases and our garment bags before you go," Elaine said.

"I just put a cake in the oven. We have leftovers from dinner yesterday. Thought I'd make a turkey casserole for lunch," Fancy said.

Elaine led the way to the kitchen, Tina still on her hip. "We'll help."

Fancy wasn't sure she wanted two strange women in her kitchen, and it was taxing her patience to see Tina bonding so quickly and well with Elaine. Elaine shifted Tina to a chair beside the cabinet and rolled up her sleeves.

"I'll wash whatever you get dirty. Melissa will dry, unless you've got something you'd rather we do, like dust or vacuum," she said.

"I took care of all that earlier this week. Tina and I've got a routine going. It works well for us. We still go into town to do my grandmother's beauty-shop ladies' hair three days a week," Fancy said.

Melissa picked up a dish towel. "We are just dying to get to know you. When Theron calls, you and Tina are all he talks about. Six weeks ago it was just his job and the longhorns, but they've taken a backseat."

"And we're glad. He's been lonely a long time," Elaine said.

"And stubborn as a mule even longer," Melissa said with a laugh.

Fancy stood there, not certain what to say. They seemed to have hopes and expectations that Theron didn't share.

"Okay, dishes are done. Cake is nearly finished. I can smell it," Elaine said.

"Chocolate. I helped," Tina said.

"She talks clearly for her age. My boys were chatterboxes at that age, but I could only understand every third word," Melissa said.

"She really is a good talker," Fancy said, grateful for the change of subject.

Melissa hung up the dish towel. "Julie talked a little more clearly, but she was at least four before she talked really well. Julie is my daughter. She's twenty and pregnant. Terrance and Jody are my sons. Terrance is a senior. Jody is a freshman. It's nice to have a little one in the family again."

Elaine opened a cabinet door. "I'm going to pour three cups of coffee, and we're going to sit at the table. We want to hear all about how you met Theron."

Fancy sighed. She thought she'd told that story for the last time.

She took a cup from Elaine's hands and carried it to the table. "Didn't he tell you?"

"No. He just said you were fighting him for control of the Sunday school class," Melissa said.

"Well, that's the truth. He tried to throw me out the first time I went into the room to help. But then, he kind of had this preconceived wrong notion about me," she said.

Melissa's eyes twinkled. "I knew it, Momma. Didn't I tell you there was more?"

Elaine sipped her coffee and waited.

Fancy started at the beginning with the black cat and gave them the story up to the present, leaving out the kisses. In retrospect, telling it for the third time, it sounded like a romance novel. Only there sure wouldn't be a "and they lived happily ever after."

Tina interjected little bits here and there. She told them about the little red present. Fancy blushed as she pulled the necklace from under her T-shirt.

"Bless Uncle Joe's heart," Elaine said softly after gazing approvingly at the necklace.

"What makes you say that?" Fancy asked.

"For leaving the world at this time so we had a reason to come to Albany."

"That sounds awful, Momma."

"It's the truth. I've been dying to get down here and meet you and my granddaughter, but Theron said it would be best if we let her settle in until New Year's. Besides, Uncle Joe hasn't been happy since he left the ranch," Elaine said.

Fancy liked Theron's mother. She was forthright, honest, and spoke her mind.

"You'll come to New Year's for sure, won't you?" Melissa asked.

"What's that?" Tina wanted to know.

"It's our party of the year. Both our ranches join forces. Only time of the year when we get Daddy and Theron into fancy suits. It's a big thing in our part of the country. Theron has promised he'll come home for a few days and bring Tina. Are you coming too?"

"He hasn't invited me," Fancy said honestly.

"I'm inviting you right now. You've got a week to shop. I can see you in royal blue velvet," Melissa said. "I'd love to go shopping with you, but we've got to leave right after the funeral tomorrow. I'll tell Theron as soon as he gets back."

"But . . . ," Fancy started.

Elaine patted her hand. "Honey, sometimes menfolk aren't too good at expressing their thoughts, and Theron . . . well, he has a pretty high wall up around his heart."

"But . . . ," she started again. They were accepting her into their family entirely too easily. Something was surely wrong with them, or with Theron. Did he have a defect somewhere that she didn't know about?

"We'll expect you," Elaine said, then turned her attention to Tina. "Now let's go to that tree and see what all Tina got for Christmas. I see she's got her presents all fixed pretty. We'll have gifts at our house for you when you get there too."

Tina's eyes glittered.

"Poppa Robert bought her a Shetland pony," Melissa whispered behind her hand.

"Is it coming back here?" Fancy asked.

"No, it'll stay in Shamrock. Theron will have to buy one for here. My boys still have a pony at Grammy and Poppa's house, even though they're too big to ride it anymore."

Melissa saw the question in Fancy's eyes. "I was fourteen when Theron was born. He's been spoiled his whole life. I take part of the blame for it. Momma had several miscarriages between us, and she was in her late thirties when she had him. They've waited a long time for his children. You might as well let them spoil Tina like they did him and my kids."

"No wonder he likes to have his way," Fancy mused aloud.

"And once he sets his mind, a hurricane can't budge him. That's the Warren in him. We're all like that."

"So what's she like?" Theron's father asked on the way into Albany.

"She's adjusting very well. I think she'll be ready for a trip to Shamrock at New Year's."

"Your beautiful daughter will be fine. She'll adapt because she's loved. I bought her a pony and a saddle. Your mother bought the boots and fancy shirt. But I wasn't talking about Tina. I'm talking about Fancy. Where'd she get a name like that anyway?"

"Her mother was just sixteen and widowed when she was born. It's a long story."

"I've got time. We've got an hour before we have to be at the funeral home. Thought we'd have coffee at the Dairy Queen first," Robert said.

Theron stifled a moan. "Dad, I don't want to talk about Fancy."

"Well, you're going to. Right after we talk about Uncle Joe. So you might as well brace up and get ready for both."

A few minutes later he parked the black truck in front of the Dairy Queen and got out. He shook his pants legs down over his boots and settled his felt hat down on his head.

Theron did the same thing and dreaded going inside. He hoped his mother and sister were giving Fancy some kind of third degree. It damn sure wasn't fair that he had to answer questions if she was getting off scot-free.

Robert ordered two coffees and two Peanut Buster Parfaits at the counter. The server told him it would be a couple of minutes because they were brewing a new pot of coffee. She'd bring it out, so they should go ahead and have a seat.

Robert looked over the place and saw only a couple of men in a back corner. "Slow today, isn't it?"

"Everyone is still inside after the holiday," the waitress said.

"Well, son, you choose," Robert said.

Theron chose a booth as far away from the counter as possible.

Both men removed their hats and laid them on the seat beside them.

"You going to talk, or do I get to drag it out of you?" Robert asked.

"I'll talk, but let's talk about Uncle Joe first."

"Okay, that's a fair deal. He put me in charge of his finances when he sold you the ranch. He wanted to give you the property, but I wouldn't hear of it. You needed to know that you bought it with your own blood, sweat, and tears. Besides, you needed to work at the school and ranch both to get your mind off that deal with Maria. Without people around you, you'd have become an old hermit bad as Uncle Joe after Molly died. So I made the decision, and I'm still standin' by it. Didn't hurt you to do two jobs."

"Two jobs? I do three. I work as a relief police officer in the summer too. And Maria is not part of this. We don't need to rub salt into old wounds."

"Got 'em healed up yet?"

"I believe I do."

"Okay, you paid Joe with the bank note, and he put the money in with whatever else he'd accumulated through the years. I paid his nursing home, medical, pharmacy, and kept up his life insurance policy. He left a will and made sure it couldn't be contested, not that any of us would anyway. But your momma was his favorite niece, so that made you his next favorite in line, so to speak."

"Okay," Theron said.

"Bottom line is that I'm to turn it all over to you, son. You are the sole beneficiary of his estate. Plain and simple. Your momma doesn't need it. You do. He set up his funeral and paid for it before he went to the nursing home, back when he still had a few good days, so there's not much we need to do except talk to them about minor details. We'll go to the nursing home and get his favorite overalls and shirt for his burial. He was adamant about that. Molly wouldn't know him if he didn't meet her in his overalls."

Theron chuckled.

The waitress brought their coffee and sundaes and put them on the table.

Robert picked up the plastic spoon and dug in. "Don't you dare tell your momma I ate this. She's been tryin' to get me to lose a few pounds. She's scared to death I'll drop with a heart attack. I keep tellin' her that would be better than havin' what Joe had. Fancy ever fuss at you about your weight?" Robert asked.

Theron shook his head.

"She will. After forty-six years she will. Trust me."

"Dad, Fancy and I aren't married. There will never be any forty-six years for us."

"You shouldn't use that word, *never.* It's a bad omen. You ready to talk about Fancy now?"

Theron changed the subject. "Tell me about this account of Uncle Joe's."

"Won't work, son. I know your tactics. Knew them in high school and know them now. We *will* talk about Fancy. I hate to tell you about the account, because it'll be harder for you to talk with your tongue glued to the top of your mouth."

"What?"

"Life insurance: half a million, taken out years ago, so it's still good even though he had Alzheimer's and was in a diminished state in his later years. Bank balance: three million. Stock portfolio? Well, you know how that fluctuates with this recession, but he didn't invest in anything risky, so it's about three times what the bank balance is most days."

Theron was speechless.

"Told you it'd be difficult to talk in that condition. Eat your ice cream before it melts and you don't have anything but milk and peanuts. It'll sink in, and you'll be able to blink in a little while. I reckon this'll be your last year at the school. If I know you, by summertime you'll be a full-time rancher."

Theron put a spoonful of ice cream into his mouth. In a minute he would wake up and find Fancy in the kitchen making breakfast. He'd tell her about this crazy dream, and they'd have a big laugh over it. But when he did force his eyes to blink, his father was still sitting across from him with a silly grin on his face as he made his way down to the bottom of a peanut butter sundae.

Robert scraped the inside of the tall plastic glass and picked up the coffee mug. "Okay, now let's have at it. I want to know about this girl. How'd you meet her, and is it serious?"

Theron told the story in a monologue and ended with, "I like things just as they are. I want someone to live in the house and take care of Tina while I work. I can ranch and take care of my daughter on my own after school lets out in June."

"What're you intendin' on doin' when the time comes that she needs a mother to talk to her about girl things?"

Theron shuddered.

"And what is it that Fancy wants? Not that any woman wouldn't be proud to be your live-in cook and bottle washer," he said with a touch of sarcasm.

"She wants something she calls 'a forever thing.'"

Robert pursed his lips and nodded. "She say that right out loud?"

"She did, and she also said she's going back to Florida soon. Her grandmother's house here has sold."

"Looks to me like you don't have much time. What're you going to do with it?"

"Dad, you only met her for a few minutes. Fancy's beautiful, but she's also obstinate. Hard to live with. Argues with me all the time. Angels with halos and white fluffy wings couldn't live with her, and I'm no angel."

"That depends on whether you're talkin' to me or your momma." Robert laughed at his own joke. "I see new life in you, son. I ain't seen it in four years. Not since you married Maria and things went sour. It wasn't there last time I saw you. I figure Fancy put it there."

"Maybe Tina did," Theron argued.

"New granddaughter is beautiful. We're goin' to get along just fine, me and her. But what I see in your eyes wasn't put there by a child. It's what your momma puts in my eyes every time she walks in the door. Don't waste time, son. Now, let's go take care of Uncle Joe. He deserves it, since he's taken such good care of you."

Chapter Twenty-two

A handful of people stood around the grave while the preacher read the twenty-third Psalm and said a few final words about Joseph Theron Frank. The north wind whipped against the sides of the small tent set up for the service as if it had come to carry Uncle Joe on up to heaven to meet Molly.

Then it was over, and everyone left with their heads down against the cold, blustery winds that threatened to suck the air right out of their lungs. Theron's family gave Tina hugs and said they'd see them at the party the next week; then they headed north in their truck.

Fancy belted Tina into the car seat. She shivered, glad that she'd found the old black wool coat in the closet at her grandmother's house that morning. Without it she would have frozen in the cemetery. Theron started the engine of his truck and turned on the heater. In a few minutes the air inside was warm, and the tension in her muscles began to ease.

"Time to talk," he said.

"About what? That was the sweetest service. When I die, I want something that simple. Just a few old friends to tell me good-bye and then a good wind to carry me on up to my beloved."

"That's so like a female," he grumbled.

"Uncle Joe planned it, so it's not at all female. He was a romantic soul. Too bad you only got his name and not his heart," she snapped.

"What's female?" Tina asked.

"It's a girl. A girl is female like me and you. A male is a boy, like your daddy," Fancy explained.

Tina looked at her doll. "You are female. Bear is boy. He's a . . . what is it?"

"Bear is a boy, so he's a male," Fancy said patiently.

"Why are you so patient with her and so impatient with me?" Theron asked.

"Because you already know. Is that what you wanted to talk about?"

"No, I want to talk about Hattie's house. So, the deal is going down exactly when?"

"It's going down this afternoon. Mary's granddaughter is buying it because she wants the beauty shop. Mary is financing it for her, so it's a cash sale."

"How long are you staying after that?"

"Honey, I can be gone tomorrow if that's what you want."

"No! Fanny no go!" Tina whimpered.

"Now look what you did," Theron whispered angrily.

"What I did?" she questioned. "We'll talk later," she told him. "I'm not going anywhere right away, sweetie," she added, leaning down toward Tina. "We're going home and making lunch together."

"You mean we'll *argue* later," Theron whispered.

"Something like that."

The whimpering stopped, and Tina kept up a constant chatter, talking to her toys in the backseat.

Theron and Fancy kept their silence.

She wondered what had bitten him that morning. Ever since he and his father got back from making the funeral arrangements the day before, he'd acted strange, as if he wished she'd simply disappear off the face of the earth.

Tina went straight for the Christmas tree to play when they arrived back at the ranch. She set up two of her new stuffed animals and told them that they were "fee-tails" and not boys.

Theron poured a cup of coffee and sat down at the kitchen table. "You ready to speak to me?"

"I'm not, but I suppose we'd best get it over with. When will you have my replacement?" She took a Dr. Pepper from the refrigerator and joined him.

He raked his fingers through his hair. "I don't want you to leave. I want you to stay. I want to talk about hiring you at least until June. Please don't go right away."

"June?"

"Uncle Joe left me his entire estate," he explained eagerly. "I've always wanted to be a rancher. My dream was to own an operation like my folks, but they started small, and I knew I'd have to do the same. I wanted to do it on my own like Dad did. It was the beginning of my dream when Uncle Joe offered to let me buy him out at a fraction of the retail value. I knew I was getting a deal because I was family and named after him, but at least I was making the payments with my own money."

"What's that got to do with my staying until June?"

"Everything. He left me his whole estate. That means I can pay off the ranch and build a new house and make this a bunkhouse or build a bunkhouse and hire help when I need it. It means I can be a rancher, so I don't need to work at the school. So I need help until June, when school is out. And, dang it all, I've fallen in love with you, and I don't want you to leave."

"Oh?" She raised an eyebrow. He'd said the magic words, but he hadn't promised her a forever thing.

And she wasn't settling for anything less.

Chapter Twenty-three

The sky was blue. No clouds. A nice breeze and sixty-degree weather.

Fancy should have been playing with Tina at the park that afternoon, but instead Elaine Warren and Tina were waving good-bye to her from the ranch house porch. It was over and done. Theron's momma would look after Tina until June, and Fancy was going home to Florida. She'd drive to Hattiesburg that night and on to Panama City Beach the next day. Her mother had clean sheets on her bed and her little apartment aired out and ready. Her life would go back to normal.

Tina had accepted the new caretaker fairly well, especially since Theron's mother, Elaine, was there to help make the transition. Dessa Ortega, the housekeeper Theron had hired, must have reminded Tina of her maternal grandmother, because she'd been comfortable with her from the first. Fancy couldn't find a thing wrong with the woman except that *she'd* get to spend her days with Tina and Theron.

Fancy wiped at blinding tears with the back of one hand. It took every ounce of willpower in her body to keep driving and not turn the car around. She had wanted to stay, but without her forever thing, she couldn't stand to prolong her own misery. If she couldn't have the whole ball of wax, she didn't want enough to make a puny birthday candle.

She and Theron had managed to keep their distance after the New Year's party. Only once, and that had been the night before, had he broken the rules and kissed her again. But it had been on the forehead when he asked her once more to change her mind and stay.

She wanted to, but she couldn't, and she didn't want to go. Waving good-bye at that child on the porch was almost as difficult as watching Theron get into his truck that morning and go to work. She hadn't slept well, and she couldn't bear to have breakfast with him that last day. They'd said their good-byes the night before, and he'd held her close without kissing her. But that morning she'd tipped one single slat in the miniblinds and watched him leave, taking her heart and soul with him.

Now a shell of a body was driving south to catch I-20 all the way to Mississippi. From there she'd drive on 49 until she reached 10, and that would lead her home. But that was a misnomer; *home* was on a ranch between Albany and Moran, Texas, where Theron and Tina lived. Where her friends, Sophie and Kate, came to visit often.

She flipped open her phone and called Kate.

Kate answered the phone with questions. "Was it terrible? Did you cry?"

"Yes. Not there, but I am now," she said.

"He didn't beg?"

"No."

"Wait till he's speeding through my town. I'm going to make him pay."

"It's not his fault, Kate. It's mine. We've been upfront and honest with each other since day one. I shouldn't have fallen for him, but I did. Not one time did he ever really lead me on. It was just so hard to leave Tina on that porch. I'm on my way toward Mississippi now. I just needed to hear your voice. Please bring Sophie to Florida in the spring."

"You know as well as I do that she's not budging an inch from Aunt Maud until it's over."

"Bring Maud too. The warm weather and salt air might do her a world of good," Fancy said.

"Yeah, right. Don't hold your breath until that happens, darlin'. You going to be all right?"

"Yeah, I'm going to be fine," Fancy lied. "I'll call you later in the day."

"If you don't, I will. Keep the cell phone charged, and be careful."

"Will do." Fancy snapped it shut and tossed it over onto the seat beside her. She inhaled deeply and caught a faint whiff of almonds. That brought on a fresh batch of tears.

At noon she stopped in Mesquite, Texas, at a Dairy Queen, and she was still crying. She ordered sweet tea and drove on. By midafternoon she was starving, so she pulled into a McDonald's and ordered one of their fruit-and-yogurt parfaits.

At Cracker Barrel in Shreveport she had pancakes and bacon. She ordered an apple dumpling to go. Every time she stopped for gas, she fought the urge to turn the car around and go back to Albany. She had called the house four times during the course of the day. Each time Elaine told her that Tina was playing, Dessa was cleaning or cooking, and things were fine.

It began to rain just outside Jackson, so she pulled into a Holiday Inn and checked in for the night. The room reminded her of the one she'd shared with Theron and Tina in Decatur. She tried not to notice, but the memories wouldn't be put aside, so she stretched out on the bed and let them wash over her like a flood. She had the phone in her hand and had dialed before she realized what she was doing.

"Hello," Theron answered.

"I'm in Jackson, Mississippi. It's raining and cold, and I was tired, so I didn't make it to Hattiesburg," she said.

"Okay," he said slowly.

If only she'd keep talking. He loved that sweet southern twang with just a hint of huskiness. He missed her. He wanted her to come home. But it was her decision to leave. He'd given her the promise of the moon and all the stars. He couldn't give her the sun, though, and that's what she wanted.

"How is Tina?" she asked.

"Dessa's first day was fine. She and Tina are bonding very well. She made homemade tortillas and let Tina help. She did ask for you when Dessa went home. She asked when you and the girls were coming back. I guess she thinks you've gone for the day with Sophie and Kate."

Fancy's heart fell. "Tell her I love her."

"I will do that," Theron said past a baseball-sized lump in his throat.

"I'll call when I get home tomorrow," she said.

"I'd appreciate it. I'm sure she'll be fine. She's had to adapt to lots of changes, as you well know," he said.

"Good night, then," she said, and she waited until he said the same and the connection was broken.

But I'm not so sure I'll *be fine. As a matter of fact, I'm sure I won't. I'll have to adapt too, but I damn sure don't have to like it.*

Five days later she was sitting on the beach in Florida watching the sunrise, a bag of saltines and a glass of sweet tea beside her. The pink sky promised another beautiful day. She wore a loose T-shirt over a pair of jean shorts. The water lapped up to touch her toes. It was cool enough that she wouldn't want to swim in it but not so cold that it chilled her toes. A faint breeze stirred the sea oats and the fronds of the palms.

An older couple walked hand in hand down the beach. Had Molly Frank lived, it could have been her and Joe on a fiftieth-anniversary honeymoon.

A black cat darted out from the sea oats. It slithered, body close to the sand, then pounced toward a sea gull, but the bird flew away at the last minute. The silly cat looked up at the sky as if the breeze would push the bird back down to its paws.

"Doesn't work that way," she said.

Good grief, she'd started talking to herself and to black cats. She had to get control or she'd be ready for a straitjacket by the end of the week.

She dug her cell phone out of her pocket and dialed the number at the ranch house again. No answer. Since yesterday afternoon all she'd gotten was the answering machine. Surely nothing catastrophic had happened to Tina, or Theron would have called. Maybe they had gone to Shamrock for the weekend, but that didn't sound like Theron. They'd moved on; they didn't need her.

She sighed and shut her eyes against the bright rising sun.

"Fanny! Fanny!" a small voice called out behind her.

She opened her eyes but didn't turn around. She'd dreamed that Tina was calling for her the night before too. It had felt real then too, but when she got out of bed to go check on Tina, she realized she wasn't at the ranch anymore. She was in her tiny apartment on the beach with only one bedroom.

"Fanny!" The voice came again.

It had to be someone else. Perhaps it was a little girl from the Sugar Sands motel behind her; coincidence that she knew someone with the same name.

When Tina threw herself into Fancy's arms and knocked her backward into the sand, Fancy still had trouble believing the child was really there in Florida. "What are you doing here?" she asked.

"I wanted you, and Daddy wanted you, and he said we could get on an airplane and go get you. So we did."

She looked up to see Theron in his jeans and cowboy boots staring down at her, a wary smile on his face. "Hello. I guess you don't live far from here?"

"Just down the beach a little way. This is my normal morning walk or run. Y'all stayin' at the Sugar Sands? You should have called. You could have stayed in Momma's house, or I would have stayed there and given you my apartment," she babbled, in shock that he and Tina were really there.

He sat down beside her. "Glad to be home?"

How did she answer that honestly? *Home* was no longer Florida. It was where the heart was, and hers had been left somewhere between Albany and Moran on a ranch with a man, a little girl, a herd of longhorn cattle, and half a dozen cats. She merely nodded, hoping it wouldn't be laid up as a major sin when she faced the judgment day.

Tina gave her a squeezing hug. "Where'd all that water come from anyway?"

Fancy was glad to be back on solid ground and answering questions. "It's the ocean. It's always been there."

"Can I play in this dirt? It's clean dirt," Tina said hopefully.

"Yes, you can. You can dig holes in it and fill them up with water or make castles. Where's your doll and bear?" Fancy asked.

"They had to stay home. Can I dig with my hands?"

"You sure can. Don't go too far. Not past those blue chairs. You might find some seashells," Fancy said.

"Can I take my shoes off?"

"And roll up your britches' legs. Here, I'll help you," Theron said.

After that Tina ran off down the beach.

The waves lapped against the sand; gulls fussed as they flew overhead; Tina giggled. Noise everywhere, but the silence between them was deafening.

"So?" he finally said.

"What?" she answered.

"I can't do it. I'm miserable, and I can't live without you."

"Know just how you feel," she said honestly.

"I practiced a thousand speeches on the flight. I couldn't sleep last night for revising them in my head. Now they're all gone, and I'm as tongue-tied as a high school sophomore on his first date."

She waited.

"You're not making this a bit easier."

"My turn is coming around here in a few minutes," she guessed.

"Well, I hope it makes *your* hands sweat and *your* heart hurt," he said.

"You are a real gentleman."

"I love you, Fancy Lynn Sawyer. Living with you isn't easy, but living without you is pure torture. I hate coming home to find you not there. I miss your sass, brass, and your smile. I miss kissing you. I dream about you."

He paused again.

She waited.

"Albany is a long way from Florida. I can't give you a beach. All I've got is longhorns and a ranch."

"Are you proposing or—"

"I love you," he said, cutting her off. "I'm not sure I can give you a forever thing all at once. But I can wake up every morning and give you that day, and maybe by the time we get to the end of our lives, it will make up one of those forever things you talk about. I just know that I don't want to live another day without you, so please say you will marry us. Please say you'll come back to Texas with us tomorrow. I bought an extra plane ticket."

"Kiss me," she barely managed to say.

"Is that a yes?"

"Yes, darlin', it is a yes, yes, yes!"

Chapter Twenty-four

The wedding took place in the Shackelford County Courthouse, which seemed very fitting to Fancy. It was a simple affair with only Theron's parents, Gwen and Les, Sophie and Kate, and the bride and groom. Theron wore his Sunday suit, and Fancy wore a plain white dress, cowboy boots, and a new white Stetson with a pouf of illusion at the back.

The reception was a different matter. It was held at the ranch in the sale barn, and Gwen, along with help from Sophie, Kate, Aunt Maud, and all the beauty-shop ladies, had transformed it into a lavish wedding hall. Tables were covered in white lace and piled high with enough food to feed half the state of Texas. A band played on a newly erected stage in a corner that Les had supervised the building of that week. The walls were draped with yards and yards of white illusion and baby blue chiffon that reminded Fancy of clouds on a summer day. The four-foot wedding cake decorated with lilies and daisies stood on a table beside a Champagne fountain.

"I'm not sure if it's a wedding or a high school prom," Fancy whispered when she and Theron walked through the archway trimmed in flowers, lights, and illusion.

"It's partly for your mother too, you know. She didn't get the white dress or fancy reception, so you're both supposed to shut up and enjoy this."

Fancy's heart welled with love and gratitude at his thoughtfulness.

"By the way, have I told you today that I think you're gorgeous?"

"You'd *better* tell me I look good when you just issued an order like 'shut up and enjoy this,' " she said, laughing.

217

He grinned. "Kiss me, and let's make them all proud."

She didn't hesitate to do so.

"Don't they make the cutest couple?" Kate said.

"I said that from the beginning," Sophie answered.

"And they'll make the best parents." Gwen hugged them both.

"Ain't it the truth? They're already so good together with Tina. I can't wait for them to have a few more of their own. Reckon it will be soon, or will they wait a couple of years? None of us girls is getting a bit younger," Kate said.

Theron held out his hand after the kiss. "Shall we dance, Mrs. Warren?"

"How long do we have to stay?"

He led her to the middle of the floor and signaled the band. "Until your momma says we can leave. I wish I could take you to some faraway island on a honeymoon."

The singers sang "Real Love," an old eighties song by Dolly Parton and Kenny Rogers. It talked about having real love, not infatuation; real love, not an imitation. When the song ended, he kissed her again, and she motioned the band. They went right into "Mama, He's Crazy," by the Judds.

Halfway through the song, Gwen tapped her daughter on the shoulder, and Les took Theron's place with Fancy.

"Do you think she hung the moon and stars like the Judds are singing?" Gwen asked Theron.

"And the sun," he said seriously.

"And are you crazy over her like it says?"

"Yes, ma'am. Don't tell her, though. I'd never win an argument again."

Gwen threw back her head and laughed. "You're going to fit in real well. Now go finish this dance with your bride while I find my new granddaughter. It's kind of nice to get one already potty-trained."

"What did you say to Momma? She was laughing so hard," Fancy asked when she was back in his arms.

Theron laughed. "What is said between a son-in-law and his mother-in-law on the wedding day does not fall under the wedding vows that say I have to share everything with you forevermore."

"I'll get it out of Momma," Fancy threatened.

"That's your job, but I'm not telling. Now, Mrs. Warren, about that honeymoon. We'll take it in the summer after I'm finished at the school."

She raised an eyebrow. "Changing the subject?"

"No, stating a fact."

"I don't want a honeymoon this summer or anytime. I want to be a wife, not a bride."

"Hey, can a girl cut in?" Kate tapped her on the shoulder.

Kate had taken no more than two dance steps when someone tapped Theron on the shoulder. "Mind if I cut in?" a deep Texas voice asked.

Kate looked up into the chiseled face of Jethro Hart Ducaine, and her heart all but stopped as Theron stepped back and went to look for Fancy.

Kate's heart set up a race that she feared would pop the buttons off the red satin dress she wore. "What are you doing here?"

"I'm a friend of Theron Warren's. I was invited. What are you doing here?"

"Fancy is one of my best friends."

"Small world. What's your name?"

She wished for a gun so she could shoot him graveyard dead. She'd do the time just to get to do the deed. "My name is Kate Miller. You don't remember me?"

"You grew up!"

The dance ended, and Kate stepped back. "Here's hoping you did too, Hart."

She turned her back and walked away from him, her hands shaking and her nerves raw. She grabbed a flute of Champagne and downed it in one gulp and reached for another before the hum in her ears stopped and she realized Gwen had the microphone.

"We want to welcome everyone with a toast. Raise your glasses high, and if you haven't got Champagne, waiters will be carrying trays among you. Grab one while I make this toast. When I left Albany for the first time years ago and then again a few weeks ago, I said I'd never set foot in Shackelford County again. Looks like my words came back around to bite me, because I definitely will be visiting here often. Raise 'em high, everyone. To Theron and Fancy. May they have a happy life that doesn't end with their last breath but goes right on through eternity."

Later that night, after Tina was sleeping soundly in her room, they turned out the lights, and Theron led his new bride down the hallway to their bedroom. Rose petals were strewn from the doorway to the bed, and candlelight flickered from the dresser, the chest of drawers, the windowsills, and every other place he had found a place to put one of the votives.

He picked her up at the door, carried her over the threshold, and kicked the door shut with his boot heel. "Welcome home, Fancy Lynn Warren."

"Is that Uncle Joe's old bed frame?"

"It is," he said.

"That's the most romantic thing you've done yet." She buried her face in his chest.

He laid her gently on the bed. "Let's do what Joe and Molly started and couldn't finish. Let's fill up this house with lots of children and love."

"Don't forget to lock the door," she said.